BISHOP TAKES KING

BISHOP TAKES KING

MARVEL

Los Angeles   New York

© 2023 MARVEL

All rights reserved. Published by Marvel Press, an imprint of Buena Vista Books, Inc.
No part of this book may be reproduced or transmitted in any form or by any means,
electronic or mechanical, including photocopying, recording, or by any information
storage and retrieval system, without written permission from the publisher. For
information address Marvel Press, 77 West 66th Street, New York, New York 10023.

First Edition, October 2023
10 9 8 7 6 5 4 3 2 1
FAC-004510-23222
Printed in the United States of America

This book is set in MrsEaves
Designed by Emily Fisher

Library of Congress Cataloging-in-Publication Number: 2023936510
ISBN 978-1-368-07899-3
Reinforced binding

Visit www.DisneyBooks.com
and www.Marvel.com

Logo Applies to Text Stock Only

To my cat, Paprika.

⎯⎯⎯⎯⎯⎯⎯

This was our last book together.
Thank you for keeping my feet warm.

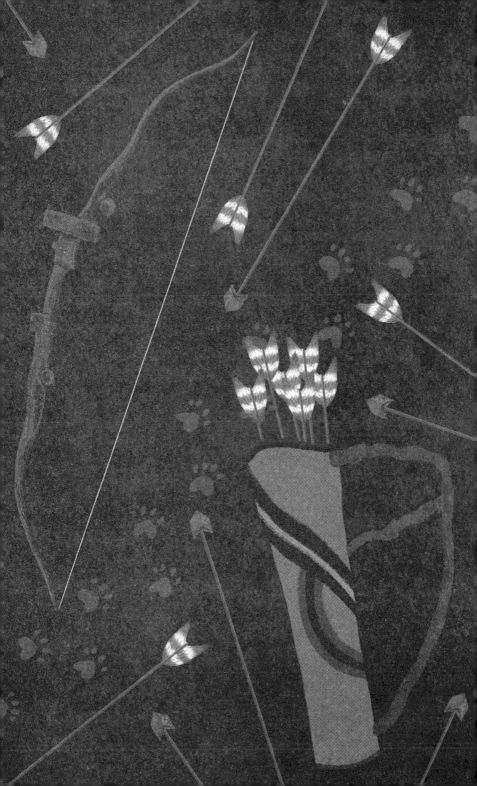

Transcript

[Katherine Elizabeth Bishop's Statement Regarding the Events at the New York Public Library Stephen A. Schwarzman Building on August 2]
Recorded by Misty Knight

KNIGHT: Let's start from the beginning, shall we, Miss Bishop?

BISHOP: I don't see why I'm being detained. This is a bit much, don't you think?

KNIGHT: You're just here to answer a few questions—

BISHOP: [HANDCUFFS CLINK ON THE TABLE] Handcuffed? [SIGH] Okay—hear me out: I'm the world's best archer. I'm not being cocky. Well, maybe I am—but just let me explain. I can hit a bull's-eye across a crowded room while hanging upside down with all the blood rushing to my head while a dozen guys in suits bear down on me ready to turn my hide to grass. Not just any guys in suits, though. Kingpin's guys. The worst kind of guys. Mostly. Anyway, there I was: me and Albright's grandson—

KNIGHT: What is his name?

BISHOP: I'm getting to that. Anyway, there I was, running on thirty minutes of sleep over two days. Hanging upside down in the New York Public Library's Astor Hall. Probably about to die. Did I have my bow? Not a chance. An arrow? I wish. But . . . I had a hair tie and a bobby pin.

KNIGHT: [SILENCE]

BISHOP: [SILENCE]

KNIGHT: Anything else, Miss Bishop?

BISHOP: And a heart full of dreams.

THE ONE AND ONLY HAWKEYE

THREE DAYS EARLIER . . .

Kate Bishop lounged back on the steps of the New York City Public Library, legs crossed and Aviators on. There was nothing quite like New York City in the summer. Sweltering, smelling like trash, and much too crowded.

Home.

Lazing on the steps of the library terrace, because she had some time to kill, she watched a group of kids climb one of the two stone lions guarding the building. The kids belonged to a tourist group crowding the steps below her, and not a single one of them seemed to notice that a squirrelly little hellion had climbed his way onto Patience the lion's head with a pretzel from a nearby food stall in hand.

And honestly, Kate was impressed.

Beside her on the steps, a golden retriever with a missing left eye whined nervously as one of the kids' friends climbed up after him.

"They're fine, Lucky," she said soothingly, and fed him the leftover pizza crust from lunch. She'd ordered it from a food truck, which was a gamble anyway, but it was all the money she could scrape together after blowing her entire month's savings on her sister's birthday gift. Honestly, the whole morning would've been a bust if she hadn't found what she was looking for. America was *supposed* to meet her here so they could go shopping for Susan's gift together, but duty had called America away, so Kate had to deal with Saks Fifth Avenue on her own, which was a special kind of hell. When they didn't have the gift she was looking for, she visited every single small boutique in Midtown until she'd found it, and now she'd gotten subpar pizza from a guy in a greasy T-shirt, and her feet hurt.

If it wasn't for wanting to get her sister a present, she'd be lounging in the rooftop pool at Avengers Tower (there was a pool there—she knew there was, even though she'd never seen it), soaking in the rays. Instead, she was watching a middle-aged man with his polo shirt tucked into his jorts shout the kids down from Patience—*finally*.

"See?" she said to the dog. "Told you they'd be okay. You should listen to me more often. I'm *mostly* right."

Lucky snorted in reply.

She glared.

Kate and Lucky had been a team for . . . well, for a very long time. Technically, Lucky had been Clint's dog before he was hers, but trusting Clint with a pet? Absolutely not. Besides, she and this one-eyed pizza-loving dog were a good team, and they'd *been* a good team for a lot longer than she'd been teammates with *anyone*. Longer than her stint in the Young Avengers, longer than her team-up with Clint, longer than her own West Coast Avengers lineup. Super-hero teams came and went, but woman's best friend? Lucky was forever.

Suddenly a car horn blared. Tires squealed.

Kate tensed and glanced toward the sound.

A young man had been pushed into the road, a taxi inches from his face. Instinctively, Kate jumped to her feet—was he okay?

The young man quickly jumped to life, and patted himself down—as if to make sure he was still alive. Relieved, he felt for something on his chest—and realized it wasn't there. He looked around, disoriented, until he caught sight of what he was looking for. He jabbed a finger after a man darting away. "Stop him!" he cried. "Someone, stop him! That's a *collector's edition!*"

Well, that certainly wasn't something you heard every day.

A man in jeans and a T-shirt, a duffel bag under his arm, was sprinting off like a quarterback with a football, dodging between tourists like he was auditioning for the next season of *American Ninja Warrior.*

Kate pulled down her Aviators to get a better look at the scene.

It only took a half a second for her to deduce exactly what'd gone down: the man leaving the scene had snatched the young man's duffel, pushed him out into oncoming traffic on Fifth Avenue, and was currently making a rather clean getaway.

The young man, seeing no one jumping to help him, did the last thing she expected—he took off running after the guy himself.

Huh.

Not that he'd be able to catch up. The thief was *well* on his way to the next borough by now.

Beside her, Lucky stood, tail wagging. He looked at Kate expectantly. And she returned the look.

"We just ate lunch," she told the golden retriever. "I'll get a cramp if I run now."

Lucky *harrumphed.*

"Seriously? We're in *Manhattan*," she reasoned, putting her hands on her hips. "There's at *least* a dozen super heroes flying around."

The dog blinked. Judgmentally.

"I don't even have my costume on," she added as a last-ditch effort to persuade her sidekick, motioning to her purple T-shirt dress and bike shorts and—worst of all—*Converse* sneakers without any arch support. Definitely not the kind of clothes you want to chase after some perp in.

Lucky turned away from her.

Which was enough to make Kate feel guilty. *"Fine,"* she sighed, and unzipped her bag. She took out her collapsible compound bow, and with a flick of her wrist it popped out to its full length. She'd tossed a few arrows into the duffel, too, this morning, though she hadn't thought to pack any *fun* ones today—it was supposed to be a shopping trip, not a super-hero trip.

That was okay. It wasn't about the *kind* of arrows, it was all in how you used them.

On the other side of the street, the thief bobbed and weaved through tourists, the young man close behind, gaining on him with his long and reedy legs.

Kate pulled her duffel over her shoulder as she hurried across the stone steps, nocking her arrow. Lucky was close on her heels. She jumped up onto the pedestal holding the other stone lion—Fortitude—and then climbed up onto its back.

The kid who had gotten in trouble earlier pointed at her. "Look, *she's* doing it!" he lamented.

She pulled back her arrow, the fletching flush with her cheek. Her anchor point. She lined up her sight. And the crowd on the tourist-filled sidewalk parted like the curtains on the opening night of a Broadway musical. Just for a split second. Long enough for her to find her mark.

Breathe in.

Breathe out.

She let her arrow fly.

It darted across the street, over the taxis and courier bikes, and struck right through the collar of the thief's shirt—

And pinned him to the boarded-up building behind him that had probably once been a Starbucks, but was currently under renovation because—she was sure—some Machiavellian kind of villain had trashed it. Either way, it came in handy to Kate now, because her arrow stuck fast in the graffitied plywood, right under INHUMAN RIGHTS MATTER.

He tried to pull himself free, but he wasn't going anywhere anytime soon.

Leisurely, she hopped down off the lion. The kid

who had pointed to her stared with an open mouth. She pulled down her shades, winked at him, and was off across Fifth Avenue to the criminal in question. Lucky made it to him before she did, hunkering down on his haunches and baring his teeth as the man struggled to rip the arrow out of his collar.

She nocked another arrow as she crossed Fifth Avenue, taxi horns blaring, and stepped up onto the sidewalk. "Lucky, fetch."

Lucky darted toward the guy, grabbed the strap of the duffel bag slung around the thief's shoulder, and with a forceful tug pulled it off him and dragged it toward her.

"Good boy," she said, scrubbing him under the chin.

The young man finally pushed his way through the crowd to them, gasping for breath. He put his hands on his knees. *"Thank you,"* he wheezed. "I thought I'd never—oh gosh, I can't catch my breath—catch him."

"All in a day's work," she replied, lowering her bow and dumping her duffel bag on the ground beside his. She took out her cell phone and popped an emergency text to the police. "Okay, my guy," she told the thief. He was a short, stocky white guy. Blond hair. Pinched face. "You picked the wrong street corner today."

"I didn't do nothing," he spat in reply.

"Sure, and I'm the queen of England," she dead-panned, taking a zip tie out of her bag and securing the guy's hands behind him. Then she glanced behind her to the young man, who had finally caught his breath and was standing up straight. He was a good six inches taller than Kate, lean and gangly, like he was stretched a bit too far. He looked like he'd just come from a work meeting: his pressed work shirt was crumpled, his charcoal-colored trousers barely covered his ankles, and his black loafers were scuffed from the fall. Sweat plastered his dark ringlet curls to his forehead. She eyed him. "You all right there?"

"Fine, fine, though I can't thank you enough," he replied, and gave her a dazzling smile. "My hero."

"No pr . . ." The sound dropped from her mouth. She closed her mouth. Opened it again. Stared. Not that she made a habit of staring at strangers a lot—she *didn't*—

But this guy—well, he—

On first glance, he looked like any other person on the street, but when she looked at him again—*really* looked at him—he was, quite frankly, gorgeous. Like, model or Paris runway or Rick O'Connell from *The Mummy* sort of hot. Kate thought herself to be a connoisseur of abs and good looks (she appreciated them like some people appreciated a good wine), but *this* sort of pretty had Kate wishing she'd washed her hair this morning and hadn't stained the front of her dress with pizza grease . . . and did she stink? She wasn't sure, but she really hoped she didn't and *man* she should've worn mascara at least—

"Kate," she blurted. "My name's Kate Bishop."

That smile grew wider. "Milo," he replied, and he held out a leather-gloved hand. Which was peculiar; it *was* summer, but maybe it was just part of his vibe.

She took his hand, because she didn't quite trust her mouth right now. They shook, and he raked his free hand through his hair again, the curls looping around his gloved fingers in snarls. His skin was a pale olive-toned color and kissed with freckles, his eyes the color of summer grass.

Thank *god* Lucky snapped her back to her senses when he put his wet nose in her hand.

"Oh! And this," she added, motioning to the dog, "is Lucky the Pizza Dog."

"Is that the entire title?" he asked, tongue-in-cheek.

"He's very particular about his pizza."

"A cheesy dog?"

"The cheesiest," she replied, and he laughed. He had a nice laugh—the kind that she would *absolutely* want to date. Take out for a night on the town. Maybe go dancing with . . . She *was* single at the moment, after all, and she didn't have any plans on a Tuesday. Absently, she grabbed his duffel from the ground and handed it back to him. "Do you usually get robbed in broad daylight, or is this just an unlucky day for you?"

"I think I was pretty lucky that you were around," he replied smoothly, taking the duffel and looping it over his shoulder.

"Wow, are you this charming to everyone?"

"Just to pretty archers," he replied, his mouth twitching into a grin.

"God," the thief groaned, "stop flirting. Can you take me to the police station already?"

She shot a glare at him and Milo chuckled. "I should be going," he said, and hesitantly took one last look at the thief as he gave him a wide berth on the sidewalk, and waved goodbye to Kate and Lucky.

She said after him, "Don't you want to give a statement?"

"I'm a bit late to a family thing. You can do it for me," he said. "It was nice meeting you, Kate Bishop, Lucky," he added, nodding to the dog, and walked down the street and around the corner.

Lucky whined at her heels.

She sighed. "Yeah, I should've gotten his number."

"You don't understand what you just did, Kate Bishop," the man muttered, shaking his head.

She gave him a peculiar look. "I think I definitely do." She picked up her duffel bag and looped it over her head. Then she finally pulled the thief off the plyboard and pushed him in the direction of the nearest police station, Lucky trotting at her heels.

CHAPTER TWO

AMERICA

"**H**ellooooo," Kate called through the apartment buzzer. "Your best friend who you bailed on this morning has come to accept your apology."

There was a crackle as she waited for a verbal response. Instead, the door buzzed and let her in. Lucky slipped in first and made his way up the steps as she followed close behind.

America Chavez—once a Young Avenger, briefly a West Coast Avenger, but always and forever a dimension-hole-kicking badass with a penchant for stylish jackets and high-top sneakers—lived in a one-bedroom apartment on the fourth floor of an unassuming four-story walk-up in Washington Heights, close to where her parents used to live. It was a newer building, definitely an upgrade from her last one. The stairs, for one, didn't smell like mold, as Kate's apartment did. Lucky planted himself on America's welcome mat and pawed at the door.

"No wonder her thighs are ridiculous," Kate muttered, finally pulling herself up the last flight of steps to the top, and knocked on the door.

"It's open!"

The second she turned the doorknob, Lucky nosed his way in, and the door flung wide. He took a running leap onto the couch, where America caught him with a laugh and scrubbed him behind the ears.

"Oh, who's a good dog? You're a good dog," she told him, and yes, yes he was. And he knew it.

"No no, don't ask how *I* am, just pet the dog," Kate muttered, dumping her duffel bag and bow by the convention of shoes by the door and closing it behind her. The apartment was small, but the windows on the two outward-facing walls were gloriously large and looked out onto the city. The afternoon light streamed in through the gauzy curtains, catching against the stained-glass wind chimes, spewing colors into the apartment like a kaleidoscope. It was just the kind of apartment Kate expected America to have— warm and cozy, with hues of reds and purples, the couch a loud yellow. The AC unit in the closest window hummed loudly, though even as it did, summer in the city had crept its way into the apartment and hung on everything like a sticky second skin.

America eyed her after giving Lucky all of the kisses. "Oh, I guess hi to you, too."

"Don't sound so enthused." Then Kate eyed her friend on the couch. "Wow, you look . . ."

It was clear that America hadn't moved in a while. There was a melted ice pack, a bottle of aspirin, and a drained glass of water on the coffee table. "Say another word and I will portal you to a dimension full of lobsters," America warned.

"Lovely," Kate said. "You look *lovely*." Then she plopped down on the couch beside her best friend. "Absolutely lovely."

"And *you* are damp."

"I know," she groaned, picking at her T-shirt dress and the splotches of sweat on it. "I had to chase a guy down Fifth Avenue at *noon*. And then I had to walk him down to the police station on Thirty-Fifth Street, and you know what a cluster *that* was. Apparently Daredevil or Jessica or someone busted some maggia joint, so it took forever to get my guy into the system."

America inclined her head. "I thought you were shopping for your sister's present?"

"I was, tragically."

"At Saks?"

"No, a little boutique shop over in Koreatown." Lucky rested his head on Kate's leg, and she absently rubbed him behind the ears. "How was your mission with Billy and Teddy?"

America gave her a tragic look. "Awful."

"Did it end up being . . . ?"

"A sentient cockroach bent on turning humans into mind-slaves dedicated to the All-Mother Roach Queen?" she deadpanned. "Yes, yes it was."

"Wow. That's . . ."

"I don't want to talk about it." She gave a shiver. "It was *so* gross. I would've rather braved Saks."

"I would've rather taken the cockroach."

They sat in silence for a moment, listening to the AC hum loud and tired, until Kate said, "You know what else is gross?"

"The fact that you're sitting, sweaty, on the couch right beside me?" America asked.

"Pfff, that's a perk." She rested her head on her friend's shoulder and closed her eyes. "The guy whose purse—well, duffel bag—I saved today was *so* hot. Like, tongue-tied hot."

America wrinkled her nose. "That *is* gross."

"And he actually flirted with me."

"Good flirting, or cringe-y flirting?"

"It wasn't half-bad, and the grossest part?"

"I'm scared to ask."

Kate sighed dejectedly. "I didn't even get his number."

"Probably for the best." America rested her head atop Kate's and closed her eyes, and Lucky crawled up onto the couch and sank down on the other side of America, and they sat there for a while in the quiet.

Then one of their cell phones buzzed. Once. Then again.

America sighed. "It's mine," she mumbled, and dug her phone out of her back pocket with a wince. She groaned as she read the text.

"Work?" Kate asked.

"Isn't it always?"

"Tell them you're busy tonight—let's go out. Have a girls' night."

America snorted. "Oh-kay, yeah. Do you want to be roped into *Roach Queen 2: Electric Boogaloo*?"

Kate scrunched her nose. "On second thought . . ."

"Exactly. Lemme go see what they want."

"Fine, fine, can I take a shower here?" Kate asked, and when her friend gave her a confused look, she relented. "My apartment doesn't have hot water right now."

"You're kidding—*again*?" America asked, and when Kate was about to argue that it didn't happen *that* often (it did), her friend said, "You really need to find a better apartment."

Kate thought about her studio, which had hot water every other day, an infestation of pigeons on the roof, and a landlord who refused to turn on the furnace until halfway through winter. "The rent is *so* cheap, though."

"And why move anywhere else when you can just take showers at my place? Fine, go, you know where the towels are," America added, and they both got to their feet. Taking this opportunity to claim the couch for himself, Lucky stretched out on the cushions the second they stood, impossible to move. "While you're in the shower I'll go put in an order for Wok It to Me? It's only four, but I'm starved."

"*Please*, I could eat a bear I'm so hungry."

"Perfect, I'll run to get that—the usual?"

Kate nodded. "You're the best."

"You know it." America grabbed her apartment keys from the dish on the counter, slipped on her high-tops, and pulled out her phone to call someone as she left out the door.

Kate grabbed a towel from the hall closet and went into the bathroom. From the window in there, she glanced down to see America exit the building and take a left, twirling her hair around her finger agitatedly as she went. The Roach Queen fiasco must have *really* not gone well.

Her phone buzzed; she expected maybe one of her friends on the West Coast, but when she checked the caller ID—she groaned. Always at the worst times. "Hey, old man. What do you want?"

"Wow, tell me how you *really* feel, Katie," Clint Barton remarked dryly.

She rolled her eyes. "Aren't you in Florida or something?"

"Reconnaissance. You know, secret stuff."

"Uh-huh." She turned on the shower and sat on the side of the tub as she waited for the water to get hot. "Found a good retirement home yet?"

"Ha-*ha*." Then, quieter, "Actually yes. They have a pool and serve margaritas by the *pitcher*."

"Do they serve them with those little umbrellas?"

He scoffed. "Of *course* they do."

"You called just to gloat, didn't you?"

"And what if I did?"

Kate rolled her eyes. "Then you're doing a terrible job. Sounds like the worst time."

"You should take a vacation someday, Katie. You might actually enjoy it."

"When I can stop super villains and save kittens from trees? Hard pass," she said as the water began to get hot. "So, why did you *really* call?" she added as her phone beeped, and she glanced at the notification. Low battery.

"Can't I call and check up on my dog sometimes?"

She stood and went to fetch her phone charger from her duffel bag. "Sure, say hello to Lucky," and she held the phone out as Clint shouted something inaudible and returned the phone to her ear. "He was a very good boy as we hunted for a present for my sister that she'll have to open in front of all her rich friends at her birthday and absolutely *despise* me for."

"Wow, that's specific."

"I try to be," she replied, and unzipped her duffel. Except when she reached in for her charger that she *knew* she had packed under her arrows, it wasn't there. Neither were her arrows, actually. Her phone slid off her shoulder onto the tile floor as she pulled the duffel wide. Her heart dropped into her toes.

Clint was saying, "You know, maybe after this reconnaissance I *will* take a vacation—"

"Hey, Clint?" She tried to keep the worry out of her voice. "I'll call you back. Remember, sun's out, guns out."

"Never a tan line in sight. See ya, kid."

"Don't die," she replied, and hung up.

And she stared down into a duffel bag that held

none of her things—not her arrows or her rappel hooks or her favorite snacks or her charger or her toothbrush or her costume *or*, most tragically, her sister's birthday gift.

Trying not to panic—she *couldn't* panic—she reached into the bag and pulled out a leather-bound book among some papers that had spilled across the bottom, along with some gum wrappers, a wallet, and keys with a fun Ms. Marvel key chain. There was strange writing on the book in gold foil, and when she opened it, the words were all in the same jagged writing.

"Oh," she realized with mounting dread. "Oh *no*."

CHAPTER THREE

NOT IT

This wasn't her bag—like, of *course* it wasn't—and she knew exactly whose it was.

"Oh no," she murmured again, dropping the book back into the bag. "No no no *no*."

She hadn't even gotten Milo's *phone number*!

The arrows she could live without, the clothes, even her toothbrush—but it'd taken her half a year to track down her sister's gift. And now it was gone.

Cursing, she dug through the bag again for Milo's wallet and flipped it open. The knot in her chest unwound a little. Milo Smith. (Smith? *Really?*) With an address in Brooklyn. If she caught the A Downtown to the F into Brooklyn, exchanged bags . . . she could get hers back in a few hours. Not ideal, but it's not like she had a choice.

She turned off the water in the bathroom before shoving everything back into the duffel bag and pulling her compound bow over her shoulder. Lucky looked over at her, half hanging off the couch, upside down. He didn't make a move to go anywhere.

"Oh, don't worry, I don't need you for this," she told him.

He stayed, happily, and watched her go.

> Gotta go run an errand in Brooklyn. Watch Lucky for me? **KB**

> **AC** What the heck's in Brooklyn?

> My bag—long story. I'll tell you when I get back. **KB**

Then she put her phone into her back pocket as she descended into the subway. After squeezing into a crowded car on the A train, she changed to the F at Washington Square and found a few open seats between a woman reading on her Kindle and a tourist melting in their seat from the excessive heat. She sat down, dropping her bow and the duffel onto the seat beside her, and checked her watch. Of all the careless things to do, she *had* to get their bags mixed up.

She should've noticed the difference in weight from the beginning, and wanted to kick herself for being so charmed by Milo she didn't even *think* to look. Never mind the fact that their bags looked *way* too similar, but now that Kate squinted, his was a *lot* nicer than hers, since hers had been a freebie at one of the influencer parties she'd been invited to. (There had been free food, so of course she'd been there.)

Her phone vibrated as the train surfaced from underneath the harbor and into Brooklyn. She glanced at it.

It was from her sister.

> **SB** I'm donating some of Mom's old books to the Schwarzman collection at the NYPL. Hope you didn't want anything.

> All of them? **KB**

> **SB** Why would I just donate half of them?

> Right. No, I'm fine. **KB**

SB Good.

The train bumped and jostled along the tracks. The woman reading left a few stops in, replaced by a young teenager listening to music on her chunky headphones. As the train grew crowded, Kate took her bow from the seat beside her and placed it in her lap. Unfortunately for her, the one arrow she had left after the duffel mix-up had to be submitted to the police as evidence when she turned in the thief. The cell reception was spotty, or else Kate would have taken out her phone to play *Chess Unlimited.* She'd gotten a little addicted to it on a stakeout a few weeks ago, when she and Clint had to hunker down for a few hours above a warehouse in Gowanus. She and her sister used to play each other when they were younger. Suze usually won because Kate was always more invested in making the most dramatic moves possible.

"You'll never *win* that way," her older sister once complained. "Why do you play like that?"

"Because it's fun," Kate had replied, "and dramatic. The loyal knight dying in service of the queen! The king taking revenge!"

"Chess doesn't tell a *story*."

"It can."

And Suze would always roll her eyes and make one or two smart moves and declare, "Checkmate. See, if you spent more time on strategy, you'd win."

But that was always so boring, and on the stakeout Kate found herself making the exact same wrong moves, just for the drama of it. A bishop in service to her lover on the other square, never able to meet on the same color. Two pawns sacrificing themselves in a last-ditch effort to save the king. It was all more exciting than any of the theories that Susan had painstakingly tried to teach her.

It was one of the many, *many* ways they were different.

She checked this *Milo Smith's* ID again. She'd have to get off at the Carroll Gardens stop. There was a good ice cream shop in the area—a nice cold mint chocolate chip sounded *amazing* right about now. As she dropped his wallet back into his duffel, the book caught her eye. She had to admit, she was a bit intrigued by this *collector's edition* of whatever it was, especially the strange writing. And it wasn't like a small peep would hurt anything, so she settled back in her seat and took out the book.

The Immovable Castle by E. L. Albright.

Surprising even herself, Kate knew this book. She used to read it as a kid, though this one looked nothing like the paperback that used to sit on her shelf in her childhood bedroom, the spine broken and pages dog-eared.

Another thing Susan loathed.

Inside the book, that strange angular language stared back at her. She didn't recognize it at all—and it wasn't Kree or Asgardian, either. But it *did* look familiar in a way she couldn't put her finger on. What language had the book been translated into? And why?

She skimmed her fingertips over the strange words.

Her mom used to read this series to her, the memories vague and soft, like looking through a blurry, rose-tinted film. There she was, six and a half and lying in bed, covers pulled up to her nose, daring to listen as her mother read to her, and even though the words in this edition were strange and foreign, the story was there.

" 'And then the wizard said, even as the Blight curled across his skin, each pox a roiling, terrible eye, "I may not be powerful, and I may be a coward, but I never leave my family behind," ' " her mother read, licking her thumb to turn the page. Everyone said Kate and her sister looked like her—silky dark hair and soft pink lips—but she looked tired then, pulled in every direction at once. Like living was prickly, and she'd caught herself on every barb along the way. " 'The eyes on him, the rippling inky Blight that floated on his skin, replied, "Then the Nowhere Lord will have a nice feast." ' "

"No! The Nowhere Lord can't," little Kate had said in a small voice, pulling up the covers. "Not the eyes. I hate those eyes."

Her mother comforted her. "Oh, darling. They can't hurt you. They aren't real. They're just imaginary. When he dreams, they'll go away."

Kate had wished, for years after, that dreaming things away worked in real life. Then she could've dreamed away her mom's murder. She could have dreamed away her dad's new wife. She could have closed her eyes and vanished everything terrible, everything wrong, and maybe her family would still be together.

She wanted to hold that kid who pulled her covers up over her head when her mom turned out the lights to leave, and she wanted to tell her that someday she'd be made of witty comebacks and razor blades, and she would be the one protecting people.

"Mom, I think she's going to the bookstore, too!"

Kate glanced up—and gave a start. A kid—eight, maybe nine—was leaning *way* too close to her, looking at the book in her lap with wide wonder-filled eyes. He had messy dark hair and brown skin, wearing too-large glasses and a shirt that read CAMP HALF-BLOOD. Two of his friends leaned in with him.

"Is that Unword?" one of them asked, her voice timid and soft. She was a gangly white girl with dirty-blond hair.

"I think so," the other, a stocky Black girl, confirmed.

"What? What? Lemme see," complained a fourth, and the friends parted to reveal a South Asian boy using a wheelchair. He fixed his glasses. "Where?"

Kate quickly pressed the book to her chest, staring at the gaggle of kids who'd surrounded her.

"Rajiv, Evie, Murella, *Martin*, please leave the nice lady alone," said a tired-looking mother, coming over to wrangle the horde of children away from Kate. She looked like the boy in the orange CAMP HALF-BLOOD T-shirt, her dark hair cut short, bags under her eyes. "I'm sure she's very busy. Go on, sit down over there. Hang on to the rail—Murella, you can't read and stand at the same time."

The Black girl raised her chin. "I bet I can."

"You probably can," the woman admitted, "but I'd rather you not just in case the train comes to a quick stop." Then she turned back to Kate with an apologetic smile. "Sorry, they're just *very* excited."

Kate didn't mind. In fact—

"Did you say Unword? You recognize this?" she asked suddenly, flipping the book to show them properly. "You know what this is?"

The kids all looked at her like she'd just smeared mud over her face and called herself a chicken. The South Asian boy said, "Yeah, of course? It's just from the best book series ever."

"Hardly anyone knows about it," said the last kid in the group, a blond white boy who looked identical to the white girl. He scrunched his nose.

His sister agreed, "It's *old*."

"The Immovable Castle series," Kate replied, and the kids' eyes widened. She added, "My mom used to read it to me when I was little. But so this is . . . *Unword*?" She'd heard that word before, the forgotten flare of a memory coming back, like the door in a wonderland you forgot. "It's the magic language in the series, isn't it? The original books had secret messages written in the margins with it."

The black-haired boy looked at his mom and said, "See? I knew she was going to the event, too."

Kate shook her head. "What event?"

The mother said patiently, "The event with E. L. Albright."

"He *never* does events," said Murella, and if she was excited, the deadpan of her voice didn't allow it to show. "So this is once-in-a-lifetime. I'm going to ask him if the wizard ever really found his way home."

"Obviously not, he succumbs to the madness of the

Blight," their friend said, pulling his glasses cleaners out of the bag attached to the back of his wheelchair.

"No he doesn't, Rajiv."

"Yeah huh."

"Nuh-uh—"

The mother interrupted them, still patient, telling Kate, "He's putting on an event at Books Are Magical in Brooklyn. You should come, if you haven't got anything else to do. We have an extra ticket, since Rajiv's sister couldn't make it."

"Thank you, but this book isn't mine. I'm returning it."

The woman nodded, and as the train came to a stop at Bergen Street, she and the horde of kids disembarked into the crowded station. Kate put the book back into the bag, and got off at the next stop—Carroll Street—and quickly made her way to the address on Milo's ID. It was one of the brownstones on Second Street, though when she got to the door she highly suspected she'd been duped.

An elderly woman came to the door, brown spots across her skin and pink rollers in her hair, and said in no uncertain terms that no one named *Milo* lived there.

"Well, did someone named Milo ever?"

"I've been here for forty-seven years!" the old

woman crowed proudly. "No one's going to run me out of my apartment! Not you, not those real estate sharks, not anyone!"

"Oh, I wasn't—I'm not—"

"I'll be here until I die!" she went on. "You can pry my carcass from the floor and—"

Kate thought it was a good idea to leave as quickly as she could, because people were beginning to look out their windows and doors to see all the commotion. She had quickly angled her head down and started back the way she came when a neighbor poked their head out and asked, "Milo, you said?"

"Yes," she replied, suddenly hopeful. "Do you know him?"

"No, sorry, but someone else's been by recently asking for him, too."

Kate inclined her head. "Who?"

He gave a shrug. "Dunno. Some guys. They looked rough. Sorry I can't help."

"No, that's perfect. Thanks," she added, and waved goodbye. If she wasn't the only one looking for Milo, that wasn't a great sign.

She returned to the subway station, biting her thumbnail as she thought. Okay, plan A didn't work, and she really didn't have plan B. . . .

If his ID was fake, then there was a pretty good chance that his last name wasn't *Smith*, either (though she could've guessed that *without* a fake address; she'd only met one Smith and he was a nice guy from Philly), and that just begged even more questions—why would he need a fake ID?

At least she had one more option left to try, thanks to those kids on the subway.

She pulled out her phone—which was on 13 percent battery—and texted America.

> Hey, looks like I'll be back later than I thought. **KB**

AC Everything OK?

> Yeah! **KB**

She hoped, putting the bookstore's name into Google. It was just a few blocks north, so she'd walk it.

AC My BS senses are tingling, Kate.

Everything's fine. **KB**

AC Text me if anything goes wrong?

Everything'll be fine. **KB**

AC You keep using that phrase.

AC I don't think it means what you think it means.

☺ I'll see you in a few! **KB**

AC Kate.

AC KATE.

AC Don't ignore me, Kate.

She'd tell America everything later, after she'd mustered up the courage to admit her very, very stupid blunder. She put her phone in her pocket and picked up her pace to Books Are Magical.

CHAPTER FOUR

BOOKS ARE, (NOT) MAGICAL

The bookstore was easy enough to find, but just her luck, all the tickets were sold out. Of course they were—the kids *had* said this was a special event. E. L. Albright never did in-person events. Instead, she decided to stand outside like a creep and hope Milo showed up.

She *really* wanted her arrows back and her toothbrush—but especially her sister's birthday gift.

The bookstore was a charming brick building with ivy crawling up the brickwork and a mural on the side that read, SOME IMAGINATION! with rainbows swirling from it, all sparkling with wild things and happy monsters and elves from distant lands. A group of teens took a picture in front of it for their socials, all holding up a different book in the Immovable Castle series.

There were six books in total, if Kate remembered correctly. *The Immovable Castle*, *The Immovable Castle Moves a Spell*, *The Immovable Castle Alone*, *The Trials of the Immovable Castle*, *The Immovable Castle at the End of Time*, and *The Immovable Castle Dreams of Death*. In the first chapter, orphan Maisey falls asleep and wakes up on a sandy, ethereal shore, and throughout the next books she travels worlds in an impossible, immovable castle that has stood through eons and countless wars, protected by a wizard who was more cowardly than courageous and fairy-tale beings from far-off stories. In the Immovable Castle series, the worst thing that could happen was waking up.

And finding the real nightmare was the one she'd left before the first book began.

Kate never got to the ending of the last book, though, so she wasn't sure how it ended. Her mom passed before they could read it together, and after she died, Kate used to wish she lived in a world like the one in *Immovable Castle*, too. Where when the worst thing happened—the thing that twisted your gut and made you feel hollow and alone—you could simply dream, and find yourself in a new story.

She used to go to sleep hoping that she'd wake up and everything would be back to the way it was before.

As the girls tried to figure out how to all be in the

picture while also *taking* a picture, Kate offered to take it for them, and as she was handing back the phone, she heard a familiar voice from the front of the bookstore.

"Oh, it's the lady again."

Lady? She wasn't *that* old. She turned toward the familiar deadpan voice, and the Black girl she'd met on the subway hurried over to her. What was her name— *Murella?*

"So you decided to come!"

Kate nodded. "I guess I did. I'm still looking for that friend of mine. Besides, I thought about it and I really can't pass up meeting *the* E. L. Albright."

Murella looked at her, as if trying to gauge whether she was making fun of them or not, but then decided that she *wasn't*, and dug into her pocket. She took out a ticket. "Here. Mrs. Strolle gave it to me for safe-keeping."

Kate took the ticket stub. It was one of those cheap hot-pink tickets you got at raffles. "Thanks. Really."

"Wanna come actually meet the crew?"

She hesitated. "I was just going to look around for my friend. . . . I think he might be here."

"Maybe he's inside?" Murella suggested, and Kate found herself following the girl into the bookstore. "We're all part of a summer-camp thing in Central Park," she went on, unasked, in that steady deadpan that unnerved Kate a little. "My friends and I are learning tabletop tennis from *the* Ms. Marvel. It's pretty cool. I try not to let it show."

"You do a great job."

"Thanks."

Murella led her to where a bookseller took their tickets, made a small tear in the top, and handed them back. Kate followed the girl over to the familiar group of kids, the mother sitting in one of the plastic chairs, reading an Emily Henry novel she must've just bought, since the receipt was still visible inside.

The kids in question looked about as excited to see her again as she was in literally every Avengers meeting ever—which was, to be blunt, not excited at all. The last time she saw Captain America, he had given her one of those *I'm disappointed in you* looks and she felt it in her *bones*. But when the white gangly girl eyed her and asked, "Aren't you a little old to be reading kids' books?" Kate found that she'd immediately die for them.

Or commit a class-one felony. Either way, she'd do it.

No questions asked.

Murella waved her hand around at the group: Rajiv, the South Asian boy with shaggy black hair and super-hero stickers stuck to every inch of his wheelchair, the other white kid with dirty-blond hair who looked like the one who just roasted her—twins, Evelyn and Irving, and then the Hispanic boy with brown skin, messy dark hair and wide eyes behind round glasses, Martin, who first saw her on the subway.

"Oh, hey! You came!" he said brightly. "Evelyn said you probably didn't read. Most adults don't."

His mother, sitting a little bit away in her chair reading her romance book, coughed into her hand, though it sounded suspiciously like a laugh.

Kate grinned. "I mean, some of us do."

Evelyn and Irving narrowed their eyes. "What was the last book you read?" Evelyn asked.

"Don't lie," Irving added.

The mother gave her a nervous look because Kate . . . didn't answer right away. Did warranty pamphlets count? Briefs about her next mission and bad guys? Directions? She opened her mouth. Then closed it again. Frowned. Finally, she said, "A really spicy alien romance."

"Spicy?" Martin asked.

Murella told him, "It means it has a lot of—"

"Oh-kay, stop harassing the nice lady," the mother interrupted quickly, snapping her book closed, before the conversation went down a rabbit hole neither of them was equipped to handle. She gave Kate a pointed look, but Kate just shrugged.

She didn't really have *time* to read much anymore, what between her private-eye business and saving the world and moving back to New York from LA. Relocating across the country was hard work.

The kids all sank back, clearly no longer interested in Kate—were they ever really interested? Or just ready to devour her?—and she suddenly felt like she'd failed an essential test. She didn't know *why* she wanted these kids to like her, or to think she was cool (because she *was* cool, she was freaking Hawkeye!) but she made a split-second decision that she would probably regret later.

She reached into her bag that was not her bag and pulled out the strange book. "I'm actually here to give this back to a friend. I was wondering if you'd seen him? Tall, dark hair, really cute? Green eyes, dressed in a button-down and trousers, probably a size-twelve shoe."

When she took out the book, their faces lit up instantly. "That's the book written in Unword," Rajiv said.

"Yeah, and I'd like it give it back to my friend."

Evelyn frowned. "If he's your friend, shouldn't you have his number?"

"It's really sus you don't," her brother agreed.

"Very sus," Martin echoed.

"Super."

"Yeah."

Kate's shoulder slumped.

Murella pointed at the book. "Can I see it?"

"Erm, well, it's not exactly *mine*, so I don't think . . ."

They all looked up at her with big puppy-dog eyes and she caved. "Just for a minute," she said, and handed the book to Murella. Murella's friends lurched to swarm around her like piranhas, and they all began muttering over the pages, all written in Unword. Though some letters, they commented, looked weird.

Meanwhile, Kate scanned the bookstore. She hadn't been to an event at one in . . . it had to be years. Not since she was a tween, at least. From what she remembered, the author waited in the back room until it was time, then they came out, read a few passages, and took questions, then did a signing, and by the look of the crowd, he'd be here awhile. There was a stack of new editions at the front of the store—reprints with colorful covers—which she supposed was the reason for the event to begin with.

She admitted that the timing for the event, and Milo, and this book written in Unword, could all be some fancy coincidence—but she doubted it was. He was probably planning on coming to this event today, if that strange book was in his bag, so she was rather certain she'd find him here.

The crowd, however, felt a little overwhelming. Maybe she *should* have brought Lucky along for this one.

Who knew that a series, whose last book came out ten years ago, was still so popular with kids? A lot of them had brought their parents, but quite a few of them came alone, dressed as characters from the series—the wizard, Maisey and her friends, the Nowhere Lord— and a few of the costumes looked better than some of the *super-hero* costumes she'd seen. Some of the kids had pristine books clutched under their arms, others' were well-worn with broken spines and stained edges, all of them loved differently. There were probably more kids in the aisles that she couldn't see. The kids' section was in the far corner, spewing rainbows across the walls that morphed into a stony-looking fiction section, then nonfiction, and then stationery and jewelry and stickers.

The middle of the bookstore had been cleared out, tables pushed to the sides to make room for a few dozen chairs. Trying to find Milo in this chaos was like trying to find a bee in a wildflower patch.

Until, of course, it wasn't.

Suddenly a terrible, high-pitched scream pierced

the steady noise of the crowd. The kind of scream that curdled blood. Kate stood ramrod straight, because the scream came from the back storeroom. The next she knew, a bookseller stumbled out of the door at the far end of the store, white as sheets and in hysterics.

"Someone call 911!" the bookseller screamed, gasping for breath. "Please! *Please!*"

One of her coworkers grabbed her by the shoulders. "What happened?" he asked. "What's wrong?"

Kate had a bad feeling about this already.

The entire bookstore had dropped into pin-drop silence as the hysterical bookseller said, barely above a whisper, "He's dead—Mr. Albright is *dead*."

CHAPTER FIVE

THE PLOT, THICKENS

"I'll go see what happened," Kate said before all hell broke loose, and asked the mother to call the police. Her face was pinched, as if she was trying to keep it together for the kids, who—for the most part—were reacting accordingly.

"*Dead?*" Evelyn whispered, tears brimming in her eyes. Her brother hugged her tightly.

Irving said, "No, it's not true."

"He can't die, he has to sign my book," Martin said, to which Murella sighed.

Rajiv patted him on the shoulder comfortingly. "Sorry, bro . . ."

"Stay together, okay?" she told the kids, taking the book back and shoving it into her bag.

They gave her a strange look. "What're you going to do?"

To which she smiled at them—as comfortingly as she could—and said, "I'm Hawkeye—the better one."

The kids stared, openmouthed.

She pursed her lips into a thin line and left toward the storeroom, pausing by two booksellers trying to calm the one who'd found Albright, and after Kate gave her some quick pointers on how to breathe—concentrate on things around her, count them—she hurried into the storeroom. The police would be there soon, since she could already hear the sirens, but she figured she'd take a look at things first.

Kate was used to going into places where she wasn't supposed to, but the back room of a bookstore was a first. It was . . . cluttered, to say the least. There were piles of books *everywhere*, the lone desk barely visible beneath the piles of paperbacks and paper orders and shipments of bookmarks and nerdy socks and key chains. Kate made sure not to disturb any of it as she slid into the room and stepped over a pile of coloring books on the floor.

And there, at the bookstore manager's desk, sat the body of Albright in a bright green tweed suit.

He looked old, because he was—but Kate was

surprised by just *how* old he looked. His hair was neat and silver, pale like his age-spotted white skin, and it matched his thick mustache. He had dark, baggy circles under his eyes. Tired and worn, less like a recluse and more like someone who had stayed up all night for thirty years dreading something that went bump in the night.

And it seemed, by the telephone cord wrapped around his neck, the monster finally got him.

In his lap was a piece of paper.

She took a tissue from the desk and picked up the letter on the man's body. She wasn't sure what she expected—a murder note? Magazine clippings pasted into a cryptic riddle? Instead, in long looping cursive was *My dear Milo*, and below this was etched a series of strange sigils. They looked like some cross between runes and hieroglyphs, and the longer she looked the more they seemed to shimmer. Like a mirage over hot pavement.

For a split second, she couldn't look away, her gaze glued to the dancing sigils.

A searing pain sliced through her head—

She winced, reeling away. It felt like an ice pick had been driven through her skull. Her vision doubled in pain as the letter dropped from her fingers onto the floor. Her brain felt like it had Pop Rocks in it.

Faintly, the emergency exit door clicked closed, and she forced herself to act. Compartmentalized the pain, like she was trained to. Whoever went out the back might've been the killer—or at least someone who knew something. In her experience, very rarely did innocent people run from the scene of a crime.

"Shake it off," she told herself, and hurried after the perp, hopping over stacks of books and boxes still waiting to be received. The exit door let out into the alley at the back of the store. Night had settled, hiding most of the alley's grime and trash that sat against the wall of the buildings on either side, the exit to the street at the far end.

And there was a figure running toward it.

She trained her blurry vision on the figure.

"Hey—hey you! Stop!" she ordered.

The figure stopped at the mouth of the alley and turned back to her. A streetlight shone down on him, throwing large shadows across his face. But it was him—the boy from earlier. Dark curly hair and sharp green eyes and leather gloves.

Milo.

"*You*?" she asked.

He seemed just as surprised to see her. "I swear this isn't what it looks—"

Suddenly an SUV squealed to a stop behind him on the curb, and the back door flung wide. Two men jumped out, threw a bag over his head, and hauled him into the backseat.

"Are you *kidding* me?" she shouted, and pushed herself into a full-on sprint toward the alley's exit. "Hey—hey stop! Let him go!"

The men didn't even glance at her as they piled into the SUV before it tore away from the curb. Of *course* this would happen when she didn't have her arrows! Of *course* she'd have to chase someone down, then have that person kidnapped while she was arrow-less. Of *course* she would.

She broke out of the mouth of the alley, grabbing her pull-off earring. The back was magnetic, a gift from her team on the West Coast, because it also happened to be a tracking chip. She threw it at the getaway car as it sped away, and it clamped onto the metallic bumper. The SUV took a right at the stoplight, tires squealing, and disappeared from sight.

Kate, lungs burning, that weird headache still throbbing between her temples, slumped over, her hands on her knees. "Nothing's ever easy, is it?" she gasped, taking a moment to catch her breath. She pulled out her phone, opened up the tracking app, and watched as the SUV made its way back into Manhattan.

She texted Clint—because if he *was* doing reconnaissance, he always forgot to put his phone on vibrate—

> Going to get some supplies from your apartment. I need some arrows. **KB**

CHAPTER SIX

KING OF CRIME

Fisk Towers.

Why did it have to be Fisk Towers.

Kate massaged the bridge of her nose. The head-ache from earlier hadn't abated, and—worse yet—it had started to make her brain a little foggy, but she chalked it up to stress and a long day. And since it was nearing midnight, it *absolutely* had been a long day. She'd picked up a snack at Clint's, because she hadn't had dinner yet, and she felt bad for how the evening had turned out, especially since she'd been looking forward to vegging on the couch with America and watching some crappy reality TV.

Fisk Towers hadn't changed much since she'd last scoped it out. Two entrances, one on West Thirty-Eighth

Street and the other on Fifth Avenue. There was, obviously, an armed guard at both. Most of the windows in the building were dark since it was near midnight, save for a few on the thirteenth floor. Of *course* it had to be the thirteenth floor. And she had a sinking suspicion that the elevators in the main lobby didn't even have that one as an option. What better place to hide a secret than in a superstition?

All she had wanted was to exchange her bag with Milo's to get her sister's birthday present back (and her arrows). That's *all* she wanted. And now she was saving a maybe-murderer from an actual-murderer.

"Whatever you've stepped in, Milo, I don't envy you," she muttered, situating the quiver on her hip. She *would* have changed into her costume, except it was in the duffel bag Milo had, so she had to make do with what she'd had on—knee-length T-shirt dress with bike shorts underneath, Converses without arch support and all—which wasn't exactly fighting material. She'd kicked butt in worse, though, and she'd borrowed a few of Clint's spare tools and stuffed them in Milo's bag. A quiver with a dozen arrows, a belt pouch for different arrowheads (some of them special ones that she decided to not tell Clint she took until *after* she used them, including a grappling arrow that hooked to her belt, a couple sonic-boom arrows, and a net arrow), and a few odds and ends. Staves. Metal cord. Zip ties. Binoculars. A lighter.

Oh, and a pair of Clint's safety glasses, since again, hers were in her duffel bag. They were yellow and garish and clashed *so* badly with her purple T-shirt dress . . . but she wasn't here to be stylish or impress the crime lords.

She'd leave that for daytime hours.

She was perched on a building opposite Fisk Towers, an older one with too many pigeons roosting on the rooftop for her to really feel comfortable being there for long. One landed on her head and cooed until she shooed it away.

Rats of the city, all of them.

She put the binoculars in the pouch at her belt and muttered to herself, staring up at the thirteenth floor, "Okay, Kate, you can do this."

She didn't feel like dealing with the guards at the entrances—and there were too many tourists *still* loitering around who would cause a scene if she just walked up and roundhouse-kicked one into oblivion. Then inside, she was sure there would be a front desk with *another* security guard—no, her best bet was to avoid as many guards as possible for as long as possible. So, she took out one of the arrows, attached the grappling arrowhead to it, and aimed for the thirteenth floor.

And fired.

Another sharp spike stabbed through her head and she winced. The arrow went off target—and smacked into the fourteenth-floor window instead. *What . . . just happened?* Her vision spun, but she shook it off. No time to figure it out—she was sure there were security cameras on the outside of the building as well as the inside. So she pulled her bow across her shoulder and let the grapple engine on her belt pick her up. She ascended quickly to the top, and then anchoring herself, she flipped upside down to reach the thirteenth floor and took out the sonic arrowhead. She embedded it into the window. It went off with a shriek—shattering the window—and she swung into one of the dark rooms on the thirteen floor.

She unhooked the rope from her belt and quickly nocked another arrow onto her bow, but the room was dark and quiet. It was also surprisingly . . . normal? Not in an office building sort of way, but the kind of normal she expected from a penthouse apartment on Fifth Avenue. There was a fainting couch by the far wall and a gallery of portraits above it, all of the same woman. Fisk's dead wife. The carpet was plush, an ivory-colored baby grand piano in the corner.

What sounded like a gramophone played Tchaikovsky's

Symphony No. 6 in B Minor, the notes murmuring faintly through the walls.

Quietly, she snuck over to the door and opened it a crack. It led to a long hallway that matched the study she'd fallen into, and on the other side a housemaid was dusting off a bust of—unsurprisingly—Wilson Fisk himself. At first glance, the maid seemed normal enough, but on closer inspection her hands were shaking. She was terrified.

And even fainter, underneath the waltz, was the sound of—screaming?

Well, *that* wasn't good.

It seemed to be coming from one of the rooms on the right.

The maid disappeared down the hall, and Kate snuck out of the room, quickly shooting the security camera in the top left corner. Then the one at the right. Neither of her shots hit dead-on. What the heck was *happening*? It couldn't be nerves—could it? Low blood sugar? An off night? Bad luck? Her headache was slowly subsiding, at least.

She pressed her ear against each door until she found the right one—

And without another moment's hesitation, she let herself inside. The room was full, from the floor to the ceiling, with white shelves stacked with books on each wall, next to busts of ancient authors and esteemed poet laureates. There was a chess match set up on a corner table, black pieces surrounding a lone white bishop. She knew from Susan that a lone bishop cannot force a checkmate. Never could, never will.

And, disrupting the library, in the middle of the room, was Milo tied in a velvet chair, blood leaking from a cut on his forehead and a busted lip. And beside him, curling and re-curling a length of rope, was a tall white man with a cowboy hat over messy brown hair, a leather jacket, and wide-cut jeans with cowboy boots, spurs at the heel.

He turned around as soon as the door clicked closed. He narrowed his eyes. "Well, well, what lovely company we've got here," he greeted in a Texan twang.

"And who're you?" Kate asked, drawing her bowstring taut. Aimed right at his face.

He tipped his hat to her. "Friends call me Montana."

"And how about your enemies?"

He grinned. "Also Montana."

She resisted the urge to roll her eyes. "Okay, *Monty*, I'm going to tell you how this goes. You're going to untie the guy and then get down on your knees and put your hands behind your head, capische?"

"And if I don't?"

"I don't think I'm a poor shot," she replied. *The last three shots notwithstanding*, she thought. They were flukes. "I've got a lot of references if you need to see them."

The man's grin only widened. There was a glimmer in his eyes as he shook his head, hands up behind it. "No, miss, I believe you."

"Then get along, little doggie, and untie him."

The man didn't move. In fact, he seemed to relax a little and lean against the back of the chair. She began to order him to untie Milo again when a deep voice interrupted from behind her.

"I think not, Kate Bishop."

She hadn't even heard the man sneak up, and that was quite a feat because he towered over her, as large as he was wide, a gigantic white man in a pristine white suit, holding his cane between his hands. He was bald, his eyes deep and set into his face, smirking as if he knew—without a doubt—he was the smartest guy in the room.

Involuntarily, Kate took a step back.

She'd heard about Wilson Fisk plenty of times before, but seeing Kingpin in the flesh was somehow different than anything she could've prepared for. He inhabited the space with the sort of presence that sucked the air right out of the room.

He lifted up a bag that looked very, very similar to

the one she currently wore cross-body. Her bag. The one with her bow and arrow and costume and her sister's gift inside. "I believe this is yours," he said, and then grinned as he added, *"Hawkeye."*

Crap.

The next thing she knew, Montana had flicked a knife out of his pocket and pressed it against Milo's throat. Kate made a move to stop him, until Montana pressed firmer—drawing a line of blood from the terrified young man's neck—and she froze in her footsteps.

She gritted her teeth. "This is low, Kingpin," she growled. "What do you want?"

"Easy. An exchange," Wilson Fisk replied. "Tonight has been a bit of a mess already, so I'd prefer to make the rest of the evening a bit easier. There's a book in that bag you have, I hope. I need it. And I'll give you your bag back in return."

Which was . . . technically what she'd been wanting to accomplish in the first place. This seemed too easy. She narrowed her eyes. "That's it?"

"That's it, Katie."

A muscle in her jaw twitched. No one could call her Katie except Clint and—*maybe*—her own sister. Definitely not this nefarious tycoon in white.

Behind her, Milo struggled against his restraints. "Don't! Don't do it. Don't—"

"If you don't, you know what's going to happen," Kingpin went on.

Oh, she knew. The same thing that always happened. The same unimaginative death threat. This was a corner she'd been backed into so often, she basically should set up camp there. She unzipped the duffel bag.

Milo fought against his restraints, making the knife wound deeper as he did. "Don't! Don't. You don't understand!"

"It's just a book," she snapped in reply. "Definitely not worth your life. Besides, you already look like you've been used as a punching bag." She glared at Montana as she said it, but the cowboy just shrugged.

"He wouldn't cooperate" was Monty's excuse.

Milo spat, "And I never *will*—"

Which was the wrong thing to say, because Montana sent his fist across Milo's cheek, and knocked him out cold. He hung limp in his restraints.

She winced. That was going to leave more than a bruise. She took out the leather-bound book in question and held it up. Kingpin grabbed for it, but she held it back. "*And* you'll let us go?"

"I'm a gentleman, Katie."

"Yeah, well, you didn't specify that part when you said you wanted this book, so I'm just covering my bases."

"I wouldn't expect anything less from you."

Still, this felt too easy. Though it wasn't like she had much of a choice. So, she offered the book to Kingpin, who took it and flipped through it, nodding at the strange symbols written inside.

"Good," he rumbled. "It's authentic. I keep my word." And he handed Kate's duffel back to her, and she instantly noticed that it was so much lighter—*too* light. The surprise on her face must have shown, because Fisk laughed. "Do you *really* think I'd give you back your arrows? Katie, you should know me better."

She tore open her bag and checked inside. Then she checked it again. Costume, check. Grappling hooks, snacks, police scanner—all there. Everything was there except her arrows— "And the white box?"

He clicked his tongue on the roof of his mouth. "Sorry, I don't recall."

She gritted her teeth and pulled the bag over her shoulder.

Behind her, Montana cut the ropes on Milo, and she pulled the young man's arm over her shoulder and heaved him to his feet. He hung against her like dead-weight as she lugged him out of the library. Wilson stepped aside to let her go.

"The elevator is to your right," he said. "I'll let you

leave this time—but, Katie? If I catch you breaking into one of my buildings again, I won't be so lenient."

"Then don't give me a reason to come back," she snapped, and dragged Milo out of the room and down the hall, the sound of Kingpin's laugh following them long after they'd slipped into the elevator and made it onto Park Avenue.

Only when they were out on the street and to the corner did she slump him against a streetlight and wipe the sweat off her brow. It was near one a.m., and the streets were finally—mercifully—devoid of people. Trash was piled against the curbside, waiting to be picked up, and the nightlife of the city, the rats and roaches, scurried across the sidewalks, looking for leftover crumbs from the daytime. She still felt the gazes of Kingpin's men pinned to her back, which made her wary. She didn't know where to take Milo—if anywhere. *Especially* if he killed Albright . . .

Kate hailed a taxi and told the driver to take them to the only place she knew to go.

Home.

CHAPTER SEVEN

NIGHTMARE SCENARIO

Home was a pigeon-infested building on the Lower East Side, above a pizza joint that served greasy Supremes with a side of money laundering (it was an open case she was actively working on—it had ties to the Tracksuit Maggia, she could *feel* it), and she'd never felt so relieved to see the dilapidated building. The taxi pulled up to the curb, and the driver put it in park.

"Cash or card?" he asked.

Kate dug into the duffel across her body, and then, realizing it was Milo's, grabbed the other one and found her wallet under her costume. "How much again? Thirty-two eighty-five? Do you take change?"

The taxi driver turned around in his seat and gave her a deadpan look as she began to count quarters past thirty.

"I think I have a dime, too . . ." she muttered. Beside her, Milo (still unconscious) moaned, his cheek smooshed against the window.

"Thirty-two is fine," the cabdriver said, taking pity on Kate as she rooted for a dime in her wallet.

"I must have at *least* two nickels. . . ."

Movement on the sidewalk caught her eye. She glanced—almost instinctively—across the street. There was a man leaning against a closed storefront, cap pulled low over his brow, hands in his pockets. To the untrained eye, he might've looked like any college Chad loitering, but he stood too guarded, his shoulders too straight.

That wasn't a normal kind of person.

Kingpin's men again? she wondered, because he *had* let them go *way* too easily. She'd been suspicious since she dragged Milo out of the building, and sadly her hunch was confirmed.

Then she looked up to her apartment. There weren't any lights on in her windows, which was quite odd because there *should* have been. She closed her wallet and sank back in the seat slowly. A curtain by an open window into her kitchen fluttered. A window that should have been closed. Well, this certainly was a pain.

"Hi, I'm sorry—I gave you the wrong address, silly

me. My new apartment's in . . ." Where could she go? *Think.* "Washington Heights."

The driver gave her a baffled look. It was quite a ways from here.

She gave a self-conscious laugh. "I shouldn't have had that last drink! Sorry, sorry, I'll pay."

He mumbled something under his breath and put his car in drive again. The meter ticked up slowly, and Kate dug out her credit card—the one that she'd wrapped in duct tape so she wouldn't be tempted to use it, and began to rip into it with her teeth.

If this wasn't an emergency, she wasn't sure what was.

When America opened her apartment door, Kate quickly said, "It's better than it looks."

"He looks pretty bad, Kate!" America replied, aghast, and yeah, Milo probably *did* look pretty bad. He hung, still unconscious, from her shoulder. He didn't have *a real* ID with him, and she wasn't sure what his standing was with hospitals. In her experience, people who had fake IDs didn't want people to find them, and that begged the question—who *was* this guy hanging unconscious from her arm?

America helped Kate drag him into the apartment, where Lucky quickly bounded off the couch and began to snarl at the new guy. "Hey, hey, stop! Bad dog!" Kate pointed at him. "Now go sit over there. I'm tired and I'm not in the mood."

She'd just spent over seventy bucks on a cab ride at two a.m. This really, *really* wasn't her day.

Lucky whimpered, tucked his tail between his legs, and with one last lip curl at Milo, went over into the corner and lay down on a dog bed America always had out for him. When they'd gotten Milo situated on the couch, America went to find her first-aid kit in the bathroom, and Kate went to the freezer for some frozen peas. Frozen peas helped everything. And soon they had Milo patched up, Band-Aid on the cut on his forehead, frozen peas icing his jaw, and he groaned. Tried to sit up.

Kate gently pushed him back. "You're safe here. It's okay." She sat on the edge of the couch beside him and checked his eyes with a mini flashlight. He winced against the brightness, but she didn't see signs of a concussion, which was fantastic. "Just get to sleep tonight, okay?"

"My book—what about my . . ." he mumbled.

"Everything's fine," she lied, and there was enough

of a soothing note in her voice for him to believe her, because he nodded, clutching the peas to his swollen cheek, and drifted back to sleep.

America darted her eyes toward the hallway, stood, and marched over to it. Kate gave a sigh, pushed herself to her feet, and followed. She was tired, and hungry, and just about done with today.

"The *hell*, Kate?" America whispered. "What *happened* tonight? Tell. Me. Everything."

"Honestly? I don't know." She massaged the bridge of her nose. "So, when I stopped that crime earlier today? I accidentally switched my bag with this guy's, Milo, and when I went to return his to him, I ran into some trouble."

America gave her long look. "I hope you're going to elaborate."

She sighed, and told her about the fake ID, the ornate collector's edition, and the murder—

"I'm sorry, the *what*?"

"I know. It's a lot. Then I heard someone leave the bookstore, and I followed them down a back alley, and it was this guy."

"So *he* killed the author?"

"I don't know. I haven't gotten to ask him, because Kingpin's men kidnapped him. So, I had to pay a visit to Fisk Tower, and after trading him for that ornate collector's edition, I took him back to *my* place, but there was some guy staking it out across the street, and the kitchen window was open. I didn't leave it open. So, here I am. With, um, Mr. Maybe-A-Murderer."

"That," her best friend said, scrunching her nose, "is a *lot* to process."

"I know. I'm tired."

"What does Kingpin want with a *book*? Does it have nuclear codes? The city's finances? Future lottery numbers?"

Kate shrugged. "Heck if I know."

"Okay," America muttered, more to herself than to Kate, "we'll figure this out in the morning."

"We'll be out of your hair tomorrow—I'm really sorry—"

"Kate, it's fine." Then she looked at Milo on the couch. "Though, I'm not sure where *you're* sleeping tonight."

Oh. Kate looked over at Milo on the only couch in the apartment, and then to the chair in the corner of the living room, by one of the two large windows. "Well . . . I've slept in worse, I guess."

"I'll get you a pillow." Her friend sighed and left for the hall closet. "And some pajamas."

Kate was more than thankful as she went to brush her teeth and splash some water on her face. She didn't like bringing America into this—whatever *this* was—but she couldn't think of anywhere else to go where Milo would be quite as safe. Also: If Milo turned out to be a problem, Kate liked the idea of America being close enough to portal him straight into a jail cell. Lucky followed Kate into the bathroom, as if he was afraid she'd disappear again, and watched her get changed for bed. America gave her an extra shirt and pajama bottoms, and put a pillow and a thin blanket on the chair in the living room.

"If you need anything, just shout," America said, wishing her good night as she slipped into her bedroom and closed the door.

Kate finished up in the bathroom. Every bone in her body was tired, and that strange, foggy throb in the back of her head finally lifted the moment her head hit the pillow, and she curled up in the plush chair, and she was fast asleep.

Except, when she dreamed, it was a nightmare.

She *knew* it was a nightmare but that didn't help. Her fingers wouldn't grip her arrow. Her aim was shaky. She didn't know where she was, but the setting didn't matter. It was blurry to her, shifting from one scene to another, from a fight-club ring to a super-villain base to an outdoor movie venue. There was black sludge everywhere. It sank into everything, devouring it.

"Kate!" America cried, a tongue wrapped around her middle. She clawed across the floor, trying to fight against the pull, as the tongue dragged her back into the mouth of a monster. The inky-black sludge parted into a mouth set with rows and rows of jagged white teeth as the tongue pulled her in.

Everything—everyone—it devoured molded into its horrible form. She watched her friends morph into the monster, their eyes and smile and laughs, all misplaced and floating in its gargantuan mass.

"Kate!" America cried again, reaching out to her, and she reached back. Their fingers almost touching. So close—so—

The tongue tightened around her best friend's middle, and with a ferocious yank pulled her into its teeth and snapped its mouth closed.

"NO!" Kate screamed, and desperately squeezed her eyes shut. "This isn't real. It's not real. It's not real—"

"I propose a trade," the creature said with Kingpin's voice.

Kate opened her eyes, and Clint Barton broke the surface of the sludge, like he was trying to fight through an undercurrent of miasma. Fear coated his face like slime. "Katie," he gasped. "Katie, *run! Run!*"

"No, no, no," she whispered, grabbing for her bow. Her fumbling fingers nocked the arrow like she'd done a thousand times before, but it felt foreign for the first time. *This is wrong—*

She couldn't *nock* it. Why couldn't she nock a simple arrow?!

"If you don't, you know what's going to happen."

She finally nocked one and drew it back, but it still felt wrong. The fletching scraped against her cheek. Blood poured out of the gash, black and sticky like—

Like *sludge.*

Strange runes bubbled to the surface of the creature, searing across the surface like hot brands. The same three symbols, over and over. She didn't recognize them at first—

Until she did.

From the letter found on Albright's body.

"This isn't real," she whispered, screwing her eyes tightly closed. "This isn't real. This isn't *real.*"

The inky sludge crept along her skin. It stuck to her like glue. She tried to pull it away, climb out of it, and as she did she found that the inky tar left bruised splotches on her skin that sharpened, then opened—like eyes.

One eye, then two, then three, crawling up the inside of her arm.

And she screamed. She screamed and clawed at the eyes, tore them out in large chunks, her skin coming off with them. Kept tearing, kept scraping, but they kept returning, over and over, blue eyes and green eyes and brown eyes and familiar ones, and if they'd had mouths they'd be grinning, smiling, relishing her panic.

Her fingers dug down to the bone and then—

"KATE!"

She came to with a gasp. Her heart slammed in her chest. Her mind buzzed—and that sharp, acidic taste of vomit itched at the back of her throat. Slowly, she came to her senses and her vision focused. America's dark curly hair poured down between them, and she realized that America was on top of her, pinning her down, hands to either side of her head. She was on the cool floor, morning light streaming in through the window. Her throat felt raw, her eyes stung. And America looked horrified.

"Kate?" she whispered, and then in relief, "You were having a nightmare. You kept screaming."

"I did?"

"Yeah." America finally let go and climbed off her. She pulled herself into a cross-legged sitting position, glancing at Kate's arms—and then away. "Are you okay?"

Kate sat up and looked down at her arms. Scratch marks were carved down them, red like welts, except for one bruiselike blotch on the inside of her arm that looked like— She quickly turned her arm over and hid it under the blanket. The back of her head throbbed from where she—presumably—fell off the chair and hit it on the ground. "I'm fine. It was just . . . a really bad dream."

America didn't seem convinced. "I've never heard you scream like that before," she whispered.

"I'm fine," Kate repeated, though the taste of vomit in her throat had her thinking otherwise. The bruise she hid moved—she could feel it.

"Nightmares rarely kill you," said a third voice from the couch. Kate quickly glanced up, and in the morning light she saw Milo standing a few feet away, a bruise on his cheek, but looking no worse for the wear.

Swallowing down her fear, she smiled at him. "Glad you're awake."

"Yes, well, I think I'd like to leave, if it's all the same to you," he said shortly. His hair was messy, sticking up at odd angles because he'd slept on it wrong. "Where's my book?"

She opened her mouth. Closed it again. Oh, *right*. She'd have to deal with this today.

"You said you had my book last night," he went on.

She glanced away. "I didn't, actually. I said everything was fine."

He clenched his jaw. "You lied."

"I didn't *lie*. Technically."

His green eyes turned instantly sharp. "Then who *does* have it?" he began to ask before he stopped himself, as if remembering last night. "Kingpin." He whirled around on his heels and went to put his shoes back on. "Of *course* it is. Of *course* you gave it to him."

"You were going to die if I didn't give it to him," she argued, pushing herself to her feet. America watched them silently. "You *could* thank me."

"Thank you?" he scoffed, turning back to her as he slipped into his shoes. "Oh yes, *thank* you—for absolutely nothing."

Lucky was lounging in a sunbeam in the kitchen— by the brightness of the morning, it had to be just past seven. Way too early for any of this. When Milo went to snatch his bag from the side of the couch where Kate left it, Lucky bared his teeth. Milo bared his own back.

"You're welcome," Kate replied sarcastically, rubbing the sleep out of her eyes. "And stop antagonizing my dog."

"He antagonized me first," Milo snapped back. "That book is one of the single most important manuscripts in the *world*. One of six, mind you. And now Kingpin has two of them. Mine and *The Immovable Castle at the End of Time*. Though, I didn't know that until last night."

She rolled her eyes. "So what, he has two rare, expensive books?"

Milo looked like he just might explode. "You're *kidding*—"

America interrupted, "Is that why you killed him?"

He waved her off. "Kingpin's still alive."

"No," Kate said, chancing a look at her friend, who had never been very subtle. "We mean the author. E. L. Albright."

He froze. "What?" His mouth tugged into a frown, his eyes unfocused. "Oh. Right. I saw him in the chair but I thought that maybe . . ."

"So you *didn't* kill him?"

He turned his face away. "No. Why would I?"

"You were there. You ran away from the scene of the crime."

"By that logic, so did you," he replied, and pulled

his gloved hands through his hair exasperatedly, a habit that seemed to calm him whenever he did. "And then you gave Kingpin my book."

She sighed. "Look, this isn't my fault. If you had your *real* last name on your ID, I'd have found you sooner."

He looked back at her, and to her surprise there were tears in his eyes. "My real last name, Kate Bishop?" he asked, his voice curling with irony. "My *real* last name is *Albright*."

CHAPTER EIGHT

A TINY BIT OF TROUBLE

"Oh."

Really, what else could she say?

Milo pushed his fingers through his greasy curls again, and that grounded him a little. Enough to ask where his bag was. The two girls pointed at it silently. "Thanks," he muttered, then grabbed it and started for the door.

Kate said, "Wait—where are you going?"

"To the police station. Unless there's somewhere else I go to pick up my grandfather's dead body?"

America and Kate exchanged a look, before Kate said, "No, that's the place. Be sure to give them a statement, too."

"And don't think about skipping town," America added. "It never works out well."

"Sure, thanks for the tip." Then he looped the bag over his shoulder and unlocked the door. He paused on his way out and said, a little reluctantly, "Thank you. For saving me."

And he was out the door before Kate could even mutter a *You're welcome*. She rubbed the back of her neck with a sigh, and when America gave her a look—the kind that told her she really shouldn't bring strangers into her home in the middle of the night—she shrugged and excused herself to the bathroom.

"Are you sure you're okay?" America called through the door to her.

"I'm fine," Kate called back, trying to keep her voice level as she looked at the bruise on her arm. She could've sworn, a second ago, it looked like an eye. She was just tired. Seeing things.

"You sure? Because you just let a maybe-murderer walk out my apartment," her best friend replied matter-of-factly.

"I realize."

"Do you think he's telling the truth?"

"I don't know."

"Okay. Well, I'm going for a run." There was a pause, and then, "Misty Knight called me last night, looking for you."

Misty Knight? Kate had heard that name quite

a few times before. Mostly from Clint. She splashed some cold water on her face, trying to wake up. "Isn't she with the FBI these days?"

"I dunno. She was just asking for you. I wrote down her number on the counter. Give her a call?"

Kate sighed. If it had anything to do with the murder, one of the kids probably told Misty that Kate was at the bookstore last night. Great. "Sure, thanks."

"All right . . . if you're sure you're okay—"

"I'm *fine*, America."

Even though her friend didn't believe her, she let the matter drop. "All right. I'll bring back some breakfast sandwiches after my run?"

"Nah, I think I'll head out, too, after I take a shower," Kate replied. "If that's okay?"

"Oh yeah, you aren't going anywhere. You're staying here for a few nights until things calm down with Kingpin."

Kate opened her mouth to object, but her friend put up a hand.

"I'm not taking no for an answer." Then America grabbed her earphones from the coffee table and slipped them on as she left the apartment.

Once she was gone, Lucky gave Kate a disapproving look.

"Oh, don't give me that," she said, annoyed. "I *am* fine."

She hoped.

Turning, she closed herself into the bathroom and put the water on as hot as it could go, so she could try to scrub away as much of last night as she could.

———

Kate picked up a late breakfast from the bagel shop at the corner—everything bagel with lox, heavy on the cream cheese—and decided it was time to call Misty Knight. The day was sweltering already, the kiosks selling today's newspapers all announcing it might be the hottest day of the summer.

The call rang three times before a voice answered, "Hello, this is Misty Knight."

"Hi, Misty," she began, pulling Lucky away from a fire hydrant. "This is Kate Bishop—you know, Hawkeye? The good one? I heard you were looking for me."

"Kate, it's a pleasure to finally chat with you. Clint has told me a lot."

"Oh, boy, I'm sorry."

"It's mostly good things, don't worry," the woman said with a laugh. "I work in the Aberrant Crimes

Division of the FBI. We investigate super-power-related crimes. I'm looking into the death of E. L. Albright. I was wondering if you had a few minutes to answer some questions? A few kids at the bookstore last night told me you were there."

Kate stopped in a green area and sat down in the shade on a park bench, trying to play it cool, but she wrapped Lucky's leash around her hand a little too tightly. Her mind was racing. If Misty was on the Aberrant Crimes Division, then that meant they thought that Albright's death was not only a murder, but one committed by a super-powered person. Not for the first time did she think about the note she'd read, the splitting headache that felt like a pickax to the center of her skull. "Ah—sure," she said finally, her knees pumping up and down. "Yeah, I was there. What do you need?"

"Did you see anything suspicious last night before you left? Reports said you left abruptly through the door of the storeroom where Mr. Albright was found. Witnesses said you were looking for someone?"

Jeez, how much did those kids *tell* Misty? Thinking back on them, she felt her surprise quickly morph into exhaustion. They probably told her everything. Kate rubbed her face with her free hand. "Actually, yes."

She told Misty about Milo, the thief she apprehended earlier that day, the bag switching, and finding him in the alleyway right before Kingpin's men kidnapped him.

That surprised Misty. *"Kingpin?"*

"He was after the rare book that Milo had. Anyway, he has it now, and Milo's safe, but he seems to think that Kingpin is collecting the rare editions. There are six in total, I think." She slumped back on her park bench. "Do you know anything about them? They're bound like old books and the insides are—"

"Translated into a fictional language. Yes, I'm aware."

Kate sat up a little straighter. "So you know about them?"

"Sadly," Misty replied. "This Milo person—is he still with you?"

"No, he left this morning."

"Maybe for the best."

Kate cursed under her breath. She *knew* there was something fishy with him. "Is he a suspect? Do I need to track him down again?"

"No, no. The less people involved, the better. Everyone who has been involved with those books has died—including the investigator who was on the case initially for the NYPD, after Kingpin stole the first book. Which is why the case has been handed over to me."

Suspicion curled in her belly. "So do you think Albright was murdered by the same person?"

"Unsure. While we don't have an autopsy report yet, initially it looks like he was strangled. All of the other deaths have been reported as natural causes."

"Seriously?"

"Yes."

"But you don't think they are," Kate guessed.

Misty chuckled. "That's what we're here to find out. You haven't had any strange things happen, have you? Anything out of the ordinary?"

Kate waved her away, even though Misty couldn't see it. "No, no. Nothing."

"Good. Thank you for your time, Miss Bishop, and please don't involve yourself further in this. I'll take it from here. And if you see that boy again—what was his name, Milo? Tell him to call me." Then Misty hung up, and Kate rested her head back.

Every bone in her body was *still* tired, and that headache from yesterday hadn't gone away. In fact, she was sure the nightmare had made it worse.

Lucky wiggled his way up between her legs and bit into her bagel with lox, and she yelped in surprise and shooed him away, though they ended up eating the rest of it together as she formulated a plan. She'd googled Milo with his full name and the closest she'd gotten was a Punderdome award championship three years ago—but if Kingpin was looking for the other four books, she had a good feeling that she'd find Milo wherever those books were, too.

So she shoved the rest of the bagel into her mouth and decided to go ask the only people she could *possibly* think of who could know anything about where to find ultra-rare editions of a children's book series, and those people were in the last place she ever wanted to go:

Central Park.

Transcript (cont'd)

[Katherine Elizabeth Bishop's Statement Regarding the Events at the New York Public Library Stephen A. Schwarzman Building on August 2]
Recorded by Misty Knight

KNIGHT: Wait—so your informants were *children*?

BISHOP: What's wrong with kids?

KNIGHT: Nothing, it's just—the contents of what was in *those books—*

BISHOP: We haven't even gotten there yet. This is way, way, way before any of that happens. And they're not really *informants*, they're just really nerdy. And trust me, they're the kinds of kids who can take care of themselves. I still have psychological damage from dealing with them. . . .

CHAPTER NINE

HOW FLETCHING

It was easy enough to find the summer camp in the park. All Kate had to do was follow the sound of children screaming playfully. She went up to the shaded booth where the kids checked in and asked where to find the Ping-Pong class. The sunburned man pointed in the direction of the tennis courts and said that she wouldn't be able to miss the tabletops there.

"The greatest sport known to man!" he said, giving her a paddle.

"I prefer archery myself, actually." She took the paddle and thanked him before heading for the tabletop-tennis area, which was near the tennis courts. A small group of kids crowded around the corner of one, in the only bit of shade on the entire court. She recognized them instantly, and they were all arguing over—*video games*?

"I'm telling you, the new Spider-Man is *amazing*," Rajiv was saying. "It should win game of the year."

The twins rolled their eyes. "The Avengers game is way cooler," said the sister, Evelyn.

Her brother, Irving, scrunched his nose. "No way, the fighting system is too clunky. It's mid."

"You just don't like fighting games!"

"And the archers are broken. Continuous shooting? Not possible."

"That's why the Spider-Man game is the best of *both* worlds," Martin argued, and beside him Murella licked her thumb and turned the page in a tattered copy of *Percy Jackson & Olympians: The Lightning Thief.*

And, to Kate's utter amusement, Ms. Marvel stood on the other side of the tabletop-tennis court, bopping a Ping-Pong ball on a paddle. Sometimes when saving the ball, her arm would stretch farther than it seemed it should, but the kids didn't notice. Guess the novelty wore off quickly for them. She was a petite superhero with warm brown skin and shoulder-length dark hair pushed behind her ears. She was in her usual uniform, a blue-and-red tunic featuring a lightning bolt layered over leggings, a scarf draped behind her. Ms. Marvel saw Kate on the other side of the fence and dropped the ball in surprise. "Oh! Hi, Kate!" she said in greeting, quickly hurrying over to her. "What brings you all the way to the park? Are you teaching a class, too?"

"Oh, erm, no actually, but you're doing a great job," she said, and Ms. Marvel's shoulders slouched.

"Ha."

Kate pointed her thumb back to the kids. "To be fair, they're *really* hard to impress."

"Tell me about it. How are you? I don't mean to sound alarmed, but you look . . ."

"Awful, I know," she deadpanned. She thought she'd feel more awake in her costume—a purple jacket she had tied around her waist because it was too *freaking hot* to wear a jacket, and a black sleeveless undershirt with black padded leggings—but she didn't *feel* any more awake. She decided it was time for her sunglasses, fished them out of her bag, and put them on. "Actually, I was just wondering if I could ask your kids a few things?"

Ms. Marvel cocked her head. "About . . . ?"

"Last night. I'm sure they told you about it?"

"Oh! Yes, I heard about Mr. Albright. It was horrible. They couldn't stop talking about how they met Misty Knight—*the* Misty Knight. I wish I could've been there, she's so cool. One of the best detectives the NYPD has ever had. Worked with Colleen Wing.

Roommates with Jean Grey, helped Daredevil deal with the Hand . . . She's *legendary*." Then she looked back at the kids and leaned into the fence to whisper to Kate, "I've got a feeling that Albright was murdered if Misty's on the case."

Kate's mouth twisted. "You probably aren't wrong."

"Really? I *knew* it! Are you working with her? Are you tag-teaming it like Clint and Natasha? Ooh! Did Misty take you under her wing? A grizzled, hardened detective and a young super hero, teaming up together to—"

"No, no." Kate waved her had dismissively. "Nothing like that." Then, as an aside, "I've already done that with Jessica Jones."

Ms. Marvel wilted a little. "Dang. Well"—she checked her watch—"might as well ask them now before our table-tennis tournament starts. Hey, kids!" she called, and the six of them looked over like rabbits in headlights. "Come here for a sec!"

They did, surprised to see Kate there.

"What's she doing here?" the boy with thick glasses—Martin—asked as they all came over.

"I wanna ask you all some questions, actually," Kate replied.

"About last night," Murella guessed.

Kate shrugged. "Kinda, yeah."

"You should've stuck around then," Rajiv said. "We told the cops and Ms. Knight everything already." The other kids agreed. "And it's not like we *saw* anything. We're useless."

Martin added, "Yeah, we're signed up for *tabletop tennis*."

Ms. Marvel made a face. "Hey now."

Kate bit in a smile. "It's a good thing, then, that I want to know about those Albright books. And I figured I might as well ask his *biggest* fans." Did she lay it on too hard? She might've laid it on too hard.

The kids all looked at each other. Skeptically. Then Murella held up a finger—"One sec"—and they all huddled together. Kate and Ms. Marvel exchanged a look before Ms. Marvel shrugged.

Irving muttered, "Maybe she can help us out."

Evelyn agreed. "Settle the auto-shoot once and for all."

Martin agreed, "Archers aren't *that* good."

Oh boy. Kate had a bad feeling about this, but she was already in too deep by the time the kids turned around, and Rajiv said, holding his chin high, "We'll help you—but we operate on equivalent exchange. You give us something, and we'll give you something in return."

Ms. Marvel looked appalled. *"Guys—!"*

At the same time, Kate said, folding her arms over her chest and cocking her hip, "What'll it be, then?" She arched an eyebrow.

Murella said, "Archers are overpowered in the *Fight Ready Go* Avengers game."

Irving added, "They're broken."

Evelyn rolled her eyes. "No they're *not*. I think that archers can fire continuously."

"They're not guns!" Martin cried.

"They're *talented*!"

As the children bickered, the two super heroes exchanged the same silent look before Kate sighed and popped her compound bow out of her bag, and nocked an arrow. Martin was arguing about whether Hulk's aggro attack could interrupt Hawkeye's shots, and Kate definitely had not gotten enough sleep for any of this.

She aimed for the Ping-Pong ball abandoned on the tabletop, and let it fly—and the headache flared, but she steeled herself so she wouldn't wince. The arrow bit into the table right at the base of the Ping-Pong ball, and popped it up. The kids spun around to watch as it sailed through the air, and Kate caught it with one hand.

They stared, openmouthed.

Then Martin adjusted his glasses and said, "Do it again."

Kate said, "I'm not a trick pony. So to answer your question, you should probably know a bit about the weapon first." She went to retrieve the arrow from the tabletop. Video games, TV shows, films—hardly any of them actually got it right. Those arrows were CGI, the physics all wrong. She bet these kids had never seen someone really shoot an arrow. The first time Kate did, it was magical. Well, partly because she'd been kidnapped by some goons that were after her dad and partly because she'd been saved by the greatest bowman in the world.

Not that she'd *ever* say that to Clint's face.

She nocked her arrow and elegantly pulled it back. Found her anchor point against her cheek. As easy as walking.

Nothing like her nightmare—nothing at all.

The kids watched.

"So, when you draw back your bow," she explained, "to aim you should make sure the fletching is flush with your—"

"What's a fletching?" asked Irving.

Evelyn answered, "The feather."

"Oh—why's it called fletching?"

Kate sighed and slackened her bow. "I don't know—"

Martin, nose in his phone, interrupted, "The internet says that fletching is related to the French word *flèche*, which means 'arrow,' derived from the root of Old Frankish fliukkijā."

Rajiv asked, "What the fliukkijā is Old Frankish?"

Kate resisted a groan. Maybe she should just debunk their assumptions about her field of expertise and move on. As the kids discussed Old Frankish— whatever that was—she tossed the Ping-Pong ball to Ms. Marvel and asked her throw it.

"How hard?" Ms. Marvel asked.

Kate inclined her head. "Give me a challenge."

A spark ignited in the young super hero's eyes, and she wound back her arm and threw it overhanded into the air. Kate quickly drew back her arrow and let it fly—

She winced away the sharp headache slicing through her brain like a dagger. It stole the breath out of her. Her ears were left ringing.

And yet, the two halves of the once-whole Ping-Pong ball fell onto the tabletop-tennis table.

The kids went instantly quiet.

"Oh fliukkijā," whispered Rajiv.

Martin quickly pocketed his phone and told Irving, "We might need to reassess our opinions."

Rajiv said, "Spider-Man still has better physics."

Evelyn scoffed and pointed at the two halves of the Ping-Pong ball. "*Clearly* you all underestimated archers. They're cool!"

Kate found her bearings again, shaking the ringing out of head. "And," she went on, trying to play it off, "we *can* shoot continuously. It's called speed shooting, though it usually depends on what kind of grip we have on the riser—erm, where we hold the bow. The Mediterranean draw makes speed shooting difficult, but we can use the Slavic draw, the Comanche draw, or the thumb draw to make pulling back the arrow less difficult, so you don't have to lace it through the bow—are we following?" she asked the kids, who all blinked up at her with big, vacant eyes. So she sighed and said, "Bottom line is, it can be done. It's not sustainable long-term, *but* in a pinch the speed of the shooting depends on the talent of the archer."

Evelyn took that to mean: "So all of you need to apologize to me. I was *right*. Archers are *not* OP! They're just really talented."

"Exactly," Kate replied with a grin. She liked Evelyn. "And some archers are better than others."

Rajiv said, "The Spider-Man game is still more fun . . ." for which he earned a glare from half his friends, nods of agreement from the other half.

But now it was Kate's turn. She set the compound

bow on the tabletop-tennis table and looked the kids squarely in the eyes. "Now I need y'all to answer some really important questions from me."

The kids gulped, but nodded, and finally Murella put a bookmark in *Percy Jackson* and said, "You've come to the right place. What do you want to know?"

CHAPTER TEN

LIGHTS, CAMERA, AUCTION

The kids didn't know *exactly* where a rare book would be, but they did have a very extensive knowledge of the Albright message boards, and rumors had it there was a rare edition of *The Immovable Castle Moves a Spell* to be sold at an auction that night in a warehouse in Chelsea, right on the water. It was going for a little over 7.8 million dollars. Kate *absolutely* didn't have that kind of money.

But she also hoped she didn't need to.

All she needed was a nice dress and a plan.

The dress she herself could provide—she had a spare evening gown in the back of her closet for emergency situations—so she and America met at her place in the Lower East Side. She ignored the guy standing watch, *still*, across the street, as Lucky slunk into the building ahead of her and they climbed to the second floor.

America flopped down on Kate's threadbare couch. "You were right. Someone's staking you out."

"Just another day in the office." Kate sighed, opening her closet to find the single evening dress she still owned—she'd pawned the rest for money. She took it out and unzipped the garment bag. It was a pretty silver mid-thigh dress, a few years out of fashion but she hoped no one would give her *too* much flak for that since she knew she looked phenomenal in it.

In her previous life, Kate's father had paraded her at enough black-tie affairs to make her sick of them forever. She used to wear the latest trends, fix her hair in the latest fashions, know how to pick the right statement piece to distract everyone from the things you didn't want them to see. Thanks to a childhood of drowning in Manhattanite social clubs, she knew this kind of crowd a little *too* well, and they wouldn't care about her lack of jewelry as they stared at her plunging neckline.

"Doesn't leave much room to hide your bow," America commented as Kate came out of her room and smoothed out the front of her dress. She'd pinned her hair into a messy bun, secured with a hair clip sharp enough to cut steel wire. An afternoon storm had rolled in, and rain drummed on the window.

"I'll stash it somewhere—I've been to this auction

house before. Years ago, with my dad," she added, a little bitterly. "I remember most of the layout."

America made a disapproving noise in her throat. "Are you *sure* you don't want me to go with you? I can cancel my date . . ."

Kate shot her a glare. "*No.* You won't cancel your date for me. Also? This should be easy, and it's not like I'm actually *stealing* anything."

"Then why go at all?"

Kate adjusted the silver straps and then took one more slow turn in the mirror. *Because something is wrong,* she thought, but it wasn't something she could say, not yet. "You know when you have a bad feeling? Right in the middle of your gut?"

"Your Spidey-Senses," America replied seriously.

She nodded. "They're a-tingling."

America understood the feeling. "Still, if anything goes south, you'll text me?"

"Cross my heart," Kate promised her best friend.

The rain didn't let up into the evening, and by the time Kate's Uber pulled up to the entrance of the warehouse, everything was waterlogged—including the pitiful-looking attendant who opened the car door for her with a bow. He was dressed in what she guessed was the theme of the auction house—a crimson suit cut short at the chest and pressed red trousers, and a name tag reading RODEO just underneath the auction house's name—

FAUST AUCTIONS

The doorman offered his hand and she took it, gracefully stepping onto the curb. He walked with her, an umbrella above them, to the entrance—an angular structure shaped like three slabs of stone erected as a doorway of sorts. Palms and other fronds populated the front plant bed, a waterfall gushing down from the roof of the warehouse into a koi pond that ran underneath the glass sidewalk and into the building.

It was a gorgeous place, and as the lights of the city popped on with dusk, so did the colorful landscaping lights across the sides of the warehouse proper, painting the gray exterior in reds and purples. Kate slipped into line behind a couple, the woman wearing one of the most expensive-looking necklaces that Kate had ever seen, and she immediately felt underdressed. She texted America.

I should've totally brought a shawl or something. I hope your night's going better.   KB

In reply, she got a picture of America with a cute South Asian woman with dark eyes, a bright orange pixie cut, and a nose septum ring the color of a Lisa Frank acid trip. Kate double-clicked the image to heart it.

Cute. Gross.   KB

She glanced among the people in line to see what the holdup was.

At the door, it looked like there was a man checking everyone in. Oh, *that* wasn't good. Of course there had to be an exclusive *list*, and it seemed like the man holding up the line wasn't on it.

The bouncer was shaking his head. "I'm sorry, sir, you can't come in unless you're on the list."

"My *grandfather* has a piece being auctioned here," the young man retorted. "How can I not be on the list?"

That made Kate's ears perk. She stepped out of line very slightly to get a better look at the young man in question. Broad shoulders. Curly dark hair. Leather gloves—she recognized those gloves.

Well, well, it looked like she had been right after all. Where there a book, Milo was bound to follow.

The bouncer was growing impatient. "I'm sorry, if you aren't on the list—"

"He's my guest," Kate said loudly, and *really* hoped her plan worked. Milo gave a start and glanced over his shoulder—and suddenly paled. She gave him a look, hoping he got the hint to play along, and rushed up to him, curling her arm around his. "I am *so* sorry, we arrived separately. I *should* be on the list," she went on, pointing to the data pad in the bouncer's meaty hand.

There were scars on the bouncer's hands, and calluses, too. He wasn't just any hired help, but actual security. She also figured that, because he was stationed here, he must've had a knee problem or something to limit his mobility, but his talent still made him indispensable. And all of that told her one very, very bad thing—whoever owned Faust Auctions wasn't messing around. And that meant security was going to be chokingly tight.

The bouncer asked, in a slightly Russian accent, "And you are?"

She smiled at him. "Susan Bishop, of Bishop Publishing," she said smoothly. Everyone always said how she and her sister looked so much alike.

The man skimmed down his list. "Apologies, but I don't see you, either."

Kate feigned shock. "*What?* I'm sorry—did you say you *don't* see me?"

"No, I don't."

"Well, that isn't my problem, now is it? That's your problem, and it seems you aren't very good at what you do if you can't even recognize *Milo Albright*, the grandson of the infamous author E. L. Albright! We were one of the first publishers to offer on his grandfather's novel, actually, though he went elsewhere," she added nobly, though it was all lies. She couldn't remember *who* published the Immovable Castle series, but it didn't look like Milo was moving to correct her about any of it. She hadn't paid attention to her father's legitimate business in years—and especially not since Susan took over as CEO. "It's quite a lovely story."

The man hesitated, looking down at his list of people, then back to the two of them. "I've . . . heard of you. . . ."

"Exactly. So, can we pass?"

"I might have to check with—"

Kate put a delicate hand on the top of his datapad and smiled up at him with her large doe eyes. "I can check for you, and at the same time mention how you are causing a rather embarrassing scene for both of us." Then she motioned to the line forming behind them, all guests waiting to come in out of the rain.

Quickly, the man clicked on something on his data-pad, either buying into the ruse or deciding that the trouble wasn't in his pay grade. "My apologies, Mr. Albright, Miss Bishop. Please, go ahead. Enjoy the evening."

"Thank you," Kate replied, and together, with her arm curled through Milo's, they went into the warehouse.

It was dark and cool, and Milo was stiff as a board beside her. She muttered out of the corner of her mouth, "Act *natural*."

"You just lied to get in here," he whispered.

"My sister won't care."

"Wait, you—you're related to *those* Bishops? *Really?*"

In the dark, she couldn't see his face, but she decided that he was being earnest, so she told him, "Sadly."

At the end of the hall, there was another man passing out auction numbers, and he let them into the main warehouse. The koi pond beneath them spread out across the entire glass floor, which was set with steel beams, like a checkerboard. Beneath it, hundreds of fish, orange and white and speckled, swam in crystalline blue water. The floor of the fish tank glowed aqua, a good ten, maybe fifteen feet deep. Whoever this auction house belonged to, they had *money*.

She'd seen wall-sized aquariums before, but not ones under the floor.

Milo muttered, "Thank you. But why are you here?"

"Probably the same reason you are," she replied, flicking her gaze across all the exits. Two emergency ones at the back, and then the front entrance. There was a stage to the left, lit up in slow-roaming purples and reds, and just beside it stood a door to what she remembered were private secured rooms where they stored the auction items. The book was back there. Though it looked like she would need a key card to access it.

"You want the book," he said. It wasn't a question.

"Sort of." She turned in front of him and played with his tie to make it look like they were being intimate while she clocked the rest of the warehouse. In the low light, she could swear he was blushing. "I actually want some answers." Then she wrapped his tie around her hand and gave a forceful tug. He made an uncomfortable grunt. "If you don't mind, Milo."

He swallowed. "What . . . kind of answers?"

"Of the book variety. I'm sure you understand." She searched his eyes, but he wasn't scared in the least. In fact, he looked a bit amused. Interesting.

"Kate, I'm not sure what you're—"

She tugged a little harder, causing him to gasp.

He winced. "Fine—*fine*."

"You said there are six books. How many are here?"

"Why would I—"

She tugged a little harder. "How many, Milo?" she repeated. A waiter passed, offering some expensive finger foods on a glistening glass tray.

"One—I think."

"You *think*?"

"Yes, I *think*. Unless the person auctioning it off bailed at the last minute, or a buyer already got to it. Or *Kingpin*."

"Why does Kingpin want the books so badly?" she asked, hoping Milo would tell her more than Misty had.

Milo looked away at the masses of rich people in their finest, showing off an opulence that most people in this city couldn't even dream of. The mood lights on the ceiling of the warehouse, twenty feet above them, threw his face into long shadows of pinks and reds.

She set her jaw. "I saved your *life*—you owe me, Milo."

"I realize," he replied dryly. She wrapped his tie around her hand one more time, until her clenched hand met his throat. "My grandfather used to be— Someone's coming over," he said, his eyes flicking to a person behind her. His face pinched.

"So? Tell me now."

"I promise, after the auction."

"After this *conversation*," she demanded.

He relented: "Okay."

She begrudgingly unwound her hand from his

tie and glanced over her shoulder at a couple coming toward them. The white man was tall, silvery-white hair cut short, a golden eyepatch across his left eye, and on his arm was a blond woman in an extravagant Dior dress and a kind smile. "Who are they?"

In reply, he shot her the exact same look she'd given him when they entered the auction—to play along—and took a champagne flute from a passing waiter to blend in. The glass was tinted red as well, the bubbles inside almost looking square behind the refracted crystal. "Gregory Maxwell," Milo said in greeting.

The man in question threw out his hands. "Milo, *my boy*! It's been ages. I am so sorry to hear about your grandfather," he added somberly. "You must be bereft."

The blond woman nodded, placing a gloved hand over her heart. The wedding ring on her fourth finger probably weighed more than a New York City cockroach. "I cried when I heard, Milo! He was such a wonderful man."

Milo smiled, but it was as hollow as the look in his eyes. "It was . . . quite a terrible night, yes."

What an understatement, Kate thought.

"Was he sick?" the wife asked. "You know, my book club last night said that perhaps he was *murdered*—"

"Cecelia," the man interrupted, chastising her. "We don't go spreading rumors."

She looked stricken. "Oh my, I'm sorry. That was very rude of me."

Kate wrapped her arm around Milo's again, because she noticed that he'd gradually started to go rigid the longer they talked with this Gregory Maxwell and his wife. "I'm sorry, I don't think we've met," she said, changing the subject. "I'm Susan Bishop."

The man gave a start. "Of *Bishop Publishing*? What do you know—I was just saying to my wife how we haven't seen your dad in quite some time!" Of course not, he was on the West Coast being involved in some sort of nefarious villainy to become immortal, or another exhaustive Ponzi scheme. "You know, I've been meaning to ask for a meeting with you to discuss your distribution model. How you've cut costs and managed to pull in a *staggering* profit since your father's departure is quite a feat. I'm sorry, however, for your marriage."

Kate's smile was strained. "That's quite all right, I should have listened to my sister. She didn't like him anyway. And you are Gregory Maxwell . . . ?"

"Of Pegasus Publishing! CEO, Publisher, Thinker of Thoughts—the works. It's so nice to finally meet a contemporary. I thought they were all in federal court for unwise hypothetical monopolies," the silver-haired man said, touching his bejeweled bolo tie, an emerald set in gold, probably worth more than an entire city block. Both the man and his wife dripped with opulence. "This is my wife, Cecelia."

"Pleasure," Kate replied, also shaking his wife's hand.

Milo said, "Gregory's publishing company specializes in children's literature."

"Yes, and isn't tonight such a *fun* occasion? There are literary collectors from all over the world here, and almost all of them are going to bid on Lot Sixty-Seven," he added with a sly wink. "I know that's why we're here! Though I think they're going to rob me of house and home with the price—it's quite lucky for the auctioneer, though, since art is far more valuable with the artist *dead* than alive. I will probably lose, but I can't help but try and bid for another piece for our private collection."

"I hear your collection's pretty extensive," Milo commented dryly. "Don't you have a first edition of *Alice Through the Looking Glass*?"

"I do!" Gregory laughed. "Though I probably wouldn't even need to bid tonight if we hadn't passed on your grandfather's books ages ago. We've been kicking ourselves ever since," he continued. "He would have made us millions."

"Because that's always what matters," Milo said with a tight, hollow smile.

"It's a business! It's important. And if you let us, we can do wonders to your late grandfather's brand," he added, taking a business card out of his inside jacket pocket, grinning like a shark. He handed it to Milo, who took it without a glance. "We could ensure your grandfather's legacy."

Milo pursed his mouth into a thin line, trying to school his expression as though he'd just tasted something rotten. "I'll give it a think."

"You do that, my boy."

Cecelia told her husband, "Sweetheart, I think I see Abbott with his husband. We should go say hello. We want to be on the guest list for his Christmas party. You know after the auction, you'll want to go home to go straight to bed—he's an early riser," she added coyly to Kate and Milo, as if it was a secret.

"Ah, yes, yes. It was nice seeing you Milo, and Susan," Gregory added with a nod, and turned to leave for another part of the warehouse. Kate expected to feel Milo unwind a little as they left, but he just seemed to grow more rigid with each step.

Until, suddenly, and—a bit peculiarly—he handed Kate his glass of untouched champagne and turned after the couple. "Gregory," he called, and took off the glove on his right hand and held it out. He said something quietly to the man, though Kate was too far away to hear, and with his back turned to her she couldn't read his lips.

Gregory glanced at Milo's outstretched hand a moment before he accepted it with a strong shake. "It won't be a problem," she read on his lips.

Then Milo put his leather glove back on and returned to Kate. She glanced back at Gregory Maxwell, who rubbed his temples a little painfully, a frown pinching his face. His wife whispered something to him, he shook his head with a smile, and they disappeared into the crowd. Milo took his champagne back from her and downed it in a single gulp.

She quirked an eyebrow. "That bad, huh?"

"Vultures, the lot of them," he grumbled darkly, putting the empty glass on another passing waiter's tray. The waiters shifted between people like shadows, and there were so many of them Kate had to figure that half of them were actually security detail, too. "Gregory Maxwell is one of the worst. He and his wife might *look* perfect, but rumors are they're separated."

"Give that man an Oscar," she replied commendingly. "At least we know that the book is Lot Sixty-Seven now."

"Now we just have to figure out how to get it," he agreed, flitting his eyes about the room and then up to the balcony that surrounded the main floor.

A few shadowy people leaned against the railing, the lights catching in their expensive watches and earrings. Kate figured that was the VIP section of the auction house, where the ultra-wealthy distanced themselves from the moderately wealthy. Couldn't have them *mingling*, after all.

Milo began to gravitate toward one of the tables, a glowing orb in the middle that pulsed a soft white, and gently tugged her along with him. They got to the table and staked out there, and Milo took another two flutes of champagne from a passing waiter and handed one to her.

"So, we were at the part where you told me why these books are important," Kate said, and he scrunched his nose as he remembered their deal.

"Right, right. Well, I doubt you'll believe me."

"Hit me with your best shot," she replied, pretending to nurse her drink. If anyone knew about those mysterious deaths surrounding the Albright books, she figured it'd be Milo.

He swirled the champagne around in his glass, watching bubbles rise to the top. His face pinched. "Have you ever heard of Project Shiver?"

"Am I supposed to?"

"No, but it would've been easier if you had," he said

matter-of-factly. "The collection we're after is a one-of-a-kind set my grandfather created to hide his research on Project Shiver. He used to work for S.H.I.E.L.D.," he added, a little quieter. People shifted and moved around them and Kate kept a keen lookout as they did. There was something predatory about this crowd. Something that made her skin crawl. "Back in the eighties, he worked with defectors from the Montauk and Stargate government projects on Shiver; they created a way to trick the amygdala—the part of the human brain responsible for identifying potential threats and, as a result, nightmares—into what they called a 'stop error.'"

Kate frowned. "Like a system crash on a computer?"

"Exactly," he replied. "In short, they found a way for a person's nightmares to, in fact, kill them, essentially scaring them to death in their sleep."

She felt a chill crawl across her skin, remembering her own nightmare last night. Those kinds of deaths could be ruled natural causes—like Misty said. "So, these books have a hidden formula to some sort of toxin that triggers encephalopathy and psychosis. Am I close?"

"No."

Huh. "*Not* psychosis, then?"

"Not a toxin," he replied, and that was surprising, given all the evidence she had so far experienced. "A written language."

"Well, *that* wasn't on my bingo card."

"That's what makes it so deadly. My grandfather and his team believed that we, as humans, could harness psychological warfare. You know how hypnotists use those hypnosis spirals to hypnotize people? It's close to a theory like that, but instead of a spiral, it's a shape, a visual language—and Project Shiver was born. They believed through visual cues—subliminal messaging—a person could be hypnotized against their will to do whatever the visual cue specified. They only tested and perfected one visual cue, however, before the research was shut down."

"The nightmare one," Kate guessed, "and the person hypnotized wouldn't be the wiser."

"Not at first, no. Not until the hallucinations begin, and by then it's just a matter of time before they die, or are driven to insanity."

"Oh. That . . . could make assassinations very easy."

He nodded. "It could have. My grandfather wanted to experiment on other sigils, other combinations— what else could they do? Did these sigils' power stop at nightmares, or could you harness them for other purposes, too?" He gave a shrug. "S.H.I.E.L.D. shut the project down, but before they could, my grandfather stole all work relating to Project Shiver and destroyed all backup copies—and fled. He needed somewhere to hide his research, and what better place to put such dangerous secrets than in a children's book?"

Kate muttered, "Clearly he underestimated a kid with an obsessive affinity for puzzles and a lot of free time."

Milo snorted. "He underestimated a lot of people. He created a fake language—the Unword—based on the visual cues from Project Shiver and left clues to the translation across the book series. He put his work into the six rare volumes written only in a language that someone who had read the books and figured out the code could understand. And then"—he gave a shrug—"he destroyed his original work and gave the books away—a few to his friends, another he sold to a second-hand shop, and he donated another. He only kept one of them, and I had it for safekeeping. He'd heard that Kingpin had acquired one of them, so I was on my way to deliver the book to him when . . ."

"Our bags got mixed up," Kate guessed.

Milo nodded. "Yeah. I didn't realize you had the book until I was already at the bookstore, and . . .

that's when I found him. In the back. I heard someone leaving and went after them, and apparently you after me, and the rest is history."

Kate leaned against the table. "That's . . . a lot to take in." And she still had questions, too, because if Milo was telling the truth, then why did Albright have the note on him that would've cursed his own grandson?

Unless he didn't trust his grandson. And if that was the case, Milo wasn't telling the truth.

"Try being his *grandson*," he replied, clinking his champagne glass with hers. "My grandfather and I never really saw eye to eye. And I sort of wish I could've talked with him one last time, you know?"

She could understand that better than he probably thought. "You couldn't have known you'd never see him again."

His Adam's apple bobbled as he struggled to swallow, pushing the emotions back down. "I suppose you're right."

She glanced around the auction room again. There was a twelve-piece orchestra playing in the far corner of the warehouse, which only made everyone want to talk louder over it. "Well, it certainly makes more sense now why I see so many familiar faces. Ties to the Maggia and Mister Negative. I think the woman in green over there is a representative of Doctor Doom. I'm sure there's someone for Kingpin here, too. It isn't about a *book* collection, but a weapon."

Milo sighed. "Why do super villains have such boring names?"

"Super villain rarely means super *creative*."

"If I were a super villain," he said, leaning over the table toward her, "I'd workshop my name for at least a week. Send it out to a control group. See if it strikes fear into the hearts of anyone."

"Would you now." She was amused by the idea.

"Absolutely. I'd choose something coy, maybe a bit of a pun."

"The best names are puns," she agreed, and finally—through the crowd, she spotted exactly who she wanted to see. A tall, gangly man slipped in through the door with the digital lock and quickly melded into the crowd. He would've looked like any other patron at the auction if it weren't for the bulky outline in his suit jacket—a pistol—and the flesh-colored earpiece. He also walked like someone who had training—on his heels, back straight, his fingers too still. "So, quick, tell me," she said, turning her attention back to Milo, "how were you planning on getting that book?"

He gave her a surprised look. "Oh, um, I wasn't. I was just going to see *who* got it and then . . . see if they would give it to me?"

"Seriously?"

"I'm not a super hero, Kate."

"Noted. So, I've got a better plan. Can you stay here?" she added, and before he could stop her, she slipped away from the table and disappeared into the crowd.

She was pretty good at slipping into crowds and disappearing herself. All she had to do was hold herself like everyone else—shoulders back, walk like she belonged, and soon enough everyone else believed it. Now she just needed to figure out a way to get that key card and slip into the back room beside the stage. The book should be easy to find after that—just look for Lot 67.

If she hadn't known what to look for, she wouldn't have noticed the door at all. It blended almost seamlessly into the metal wall, the only tell a square key-card reader. It was also, unsurprisingly, a part of the warehouse that guests stayed clear of, because it got a lot of traffic with waiters coming to and from the kitchens in the back.

Her fingers skimmed across the black belt at her waist. One of the reasons she chose this silvery dress wasn't just because it was the only evening dress she owned, but because, with a black belt at her waist, she could hide a dozen trick arrowheads inside. While she couldn't bring her *actual* weapons to the auction, the arrowheads were enough in a pinch. Putty arrowheads, sonic arrowheads, electric—she even had a net one. America joked that she should refrain from getting kicked in the stomach, but actually that was a real issue. She *really* didn't want to be electrocuted, sonicked, and puttied at the same time. That would be a *very* bad day.

So she had to be careful how she moved, what she did, *how* she did it.

And that included how she was going to get the key card from this security guy. Maybe she could distract him and—

"Kate?"

Oh, crap.

She winced and glanced toward the voice. To her absolute dread, it was the one person she absolutely did *not* want to see.

Misty Knight, in a stunning silver pantsuit the same color as her metallic arm, the color bright against her lovely dark skin. And she did *not* look amused. "I would say I'm surprised to see you here, but I'd be lying," she commented.

Kate tried to keep an eye on the security guy as he got farther and farther away. "I didn't know you liked auctions?"

"Hate them, you?"

"Hate them," she agreed.

Misty gave a sigh and leveled at Kate, "So, mind telling me why you're here, then?"

Kate had glanced away for a second—a *second*—and the man had artfully disappeared into the crowd. She gave a frustrated sigh and turned back to the undercover detective. "I'm sure you already know."

"Yes, which is why I can't for the life of me understand why you're *here*," Misty went on. "I thought I told you to stay out of this. It's dangerous."

"You did, and I know." Kate lowered her gaze. "But I can't."

"I could arrest you for impeding an investigation—"

"Will you? Because I'd like to get a head start that way if you are." Kate pointed her thumb behind her, and the undercover inspector just gave a long sigh. So Kate decided to give her a little something, at least. "Look, I'm not trying to get in your way, but I can't just ignore it, either. So, can we work together instead?"

"No," Misty replied quickly, "but only because there's a lot of paperwork involved. I'm here because the last call on E. L. Albright's phone was from the seller of the book at this auction."

"Are you here to meet with the seller?"

Misty checked her phone. "If I can."

"Let me guess . . ."

"The seller used a burner phone and therefore I can't track their identity? Absolutely."

Kate tilted her head to the side in thought. That couldn't be the only reason she was here—there were other ways to track down the seller at an action. "Something else happened, then."

"I heard you were a pretty decent PI."

"And an ex–Young Avenger. I hold my own," Kate replied.

The FBI agent stepped a little closer, her voice low as she said, "Two booksellers were admitted into the ICU with an unknown neurological disease earlier today."

"Two *booksellers*? Civilians?"

"Yeah. They both reported nightmares. Hallucinations. One of them woke up in the middle of the night and tried to stab his partner before being admitted."

That sounded an awful lot like the symptoms Milo described from Project Shiver. But why would two civilians have—

The note, she realized, horrified.

The same note that she saw, the one with the strange sigils. Did her nightmare last night have something to do with that? And if she had nightmares—what about the hallucinations? She thought about the strange bruise on her arm, the one that for a second had looked like an eye.

Oh god.

That meant—that meant *she* was infected, too.

"They fell ill this morning," Misty went on. "They're exhibiting similar signs as the other 'natural' deaths surrounding the case, but I can't shake the idea that there's something a little different about these. The other people exposed died very quickly after exposure. It's slower in these booksellers. If it's a toxin—"

"It's not," she told Misty. "It's hypnosis—I can't explain it. It has something to do with the Shiver Project in the eighties."

That was news to the agent. "*Shiver?* I thought that was shut down."

"It was, but Albright was part of it. There was a note on his body. I'm certain the booksellers read it, or at least looked at it."

"I'll have to see if the crime-scene division picked it up."

"Whatever you do, don't look at it. And if anyone did, get them admitted to the hospital immediately. It's important that anyone who is hypnotized doesn't go to sleep."

The FBI agent gave her a troubled look. "How do

you know all this, Kate? Weren't *you* in the back room, too?"

Suddenly she saw the guy surface from the crowd again, heading back toward the auction room. It was now or never. "I'm fine. I'll explain everything later, promise," she added, and quickly broke away from the agent and wove her way through the crowd.

She grabbed the gangly man by the wrist just as he swiped his key card against the lock and opened the door. "Darling-bear!" she cried, spinning him around.

The stranger gave her a baffled look. He had a crooked nose from a face that had been punched way too many times. "*Excuse* you?"

"Oh! I'm sorry!" She quickly let go of him, pretending to slur her words. "I thought you were someone else, ha!" The door began to swing shut, so she acted fast and planted her hands on his shoulders. "But you'll do." Then she shoved him backward through the doorway, and she went with him, planting a kiss on his mouth.

They stumbled through the door into the back room. The automatic lights clicked on above them. He quickly shoved her away. "The *hell*, lady?"

Kate wiped her mouth, lipstick smearing across her arm. "Anyone tell you you're a bad kisser?" she said, and slammed her forehead into his. He hit the ground like a lump of meat. "Ow ow ow," she hissed, rubbing her head. That did *nothing* for her headache. "What the hell, dude? Is your skull made of *metal*?"

In reply, he groaned on the ground.

There was no one else in the back room, sort of what she suspected, but there was a camera perched in the top corner behind her, right by the door. It probably would have worked, too, if she hadn't thrown a putty arrowhead toward it when they fell inside. Now it dripped with brackish goo that reminded her of . . .

The sludge from her nightmare, actually.

Huh.

She turned toward the rest of the room and planted her hands on her hips, looking at the tight aisles of metal shelves and boxes, all labeled and neatly organized just for her. "All right. I've got"—she checked the thin watch on her wrist—"twenty minutes until the auction starts. Let's boogie."

CHAPTER ELEVEN

SOLD TO THE GIRL WITH THE PEW_ PEW ARROWS

If Kate was a betting person, she'd bet someone would be by in the next three minutes once they figured out the camera was puttied, so she had to get this book— and get it fast.

She skimmed over the boxes, rows upon rows of them in neat and tidy shelves. She lifted the lids to a few of them, only to find Picasso paintings, a jewel she *thought* the British Royal Family stole last, and Kree daggers. Because of course there wasn't a cohesive theme to this auction, except for "what rich people can afford and probably shouldn't own." Then, at the third aisle, she opened the box to item number 67, and sitting on a stack of hay was a leather-bound novel that looked very similar to the one she had found in Milo's satchel. In relief, she snatched it out of the box and flipped to the title page: THE IMMOVABLE CASTLE MOVES A SPELL.

The second book in the series.

"Found you," she whispered. As she reached for the book, an eye formed on the back of her hand. It opened, blinked, and swirled its iris toward her. She choked back a scream as the doorknob to the storeroom rattled, and grabbed the book.

She barely had time to climb up on top of the shelves and perch there before an employee of the auction house slipped into the room, followed by two brutish men with gun holsters at their hips. They pointed at the putty on the camera and noted that someone was here.

Well, *duh.*

Kate quietly reached for the sonic arrowhead in her belt, which would suck if she used it—especially for the jewel in box 39—but it'd give her a chance to escape now that she had the book. She perched, silent as death, balanced on top of one of the shelves. Because the halogen lights hung level with the top of the shelves, as long as she didn't move she would be hidden in the darkness.

"Someone was here," the security guard said in alarm. "Tell the boss!"

His friend nodded and left the storeroom, quickly followed by the auction employee. Which was pretty rotten luck for the security guard below Kate. She shifted her weight, putting the book against her back, secured by her belt. The guard looked up—

And saw her perched on the shelves.

She loosened her aim and jumped down instead, slamming the side of her heeled shoe into his face. Suddenly her head flooded with pain. She landed with a stumble and caught the shelf in order to stay upright. It was like an ice pick through her skull again. Her breath caught. Like she—like she was having—

A panic attack.

This wasn't right. It wasn't normal for her.

The guard righted himself, then wiped a line of blood off his cheek from where her heel cut him, and licked it. "That all you got, girlie?"

She gritted her teeth and pushed herself off the wall. "What do *you* think?" she snarled, and threw a punch. Her head flared with pain again. He caught the punch, but didn't manage to block the knee to the stomach, or her next attack. Each movement sent another nail of pain into her skull. It made bile rise in her throat. She managed to grab his arm and twist him, using the momentum of her body to flip him onto his back. He hit the cement—*hard.*

By then her entire body was shaking.

On the ground, the guard groaned.

"Not the smoothest move, Bishop," she muttered to

herself, trying to shake her headache free. It made her vision swim. "Now how to get Milo out of here . . ."

She should have been more worried about who *else* was here to steal the book, because just as she opened the door to the main warehouse again, a familiar face stood in her way. He inclined his head, grinning, and tipped back his cowboy hat.

"Bishop," he purred.

She took a step back. "Oh, Monty . . ."

"Didn't Kingpin warn you to stay out of his business?"

"Technically he just told me not to break in to his towers again," she replied, trying to sound braver than she actually was. The room was beginning to spin.

Montana unhooked his lariat from his belt. "Well, then let me formally let you know, little miss, that—"

If he had something else to say, she didn't hear it before she took an electric arrowhead from her belt and shoved it against his stomach. He clenched up tightly, ramrod straight, and jerked with a howl. Then he tipped backward like a tree falling, and she hurried over him and into the warehouse again, sliding the door closed behind her, no one any the wiser. She quickly smoothed her hair out, breathing in, breathing out, trying to steady her nerves as she hurried back to the table where Milo was *supposed* to stay.

And he wasn't there.

Things were spiraling out of control very, *very* quickly. She took a gulp of air. Then another one.

Calm down, Kate, she told herself. *You're fine. You're—*

"*Kate Bishop!*" she heard Montana growl behind her. She spun around. The cowboy was tearing across the warehouse toward her, pushing aside patrons as he went. His spurs made sharp *clicks* on the glass floor.

"That is *mine*," Montana growled, swinging his lariat above his head. The golden threads in the rope glinted among the pinks and reds.

She couldn't fight him head-on without making her searing headache worse—and it was already so bad she felt like she wanted to vomit. But she put up her fists anyway, because like *hell* she wasn't going to go down swinging—

Suddenly Milo tackled him to the ground.

"RUN!" he cried.

So, against her better judgment, she did just that. She turned around and sprinted toward the exit, and as she did she pulled her phone out of her bra.

With shaking fingers, she typed a last-ditch message—

And sent it off to her best friend.

On the ground, Montana tried to pry Milo off of him, but Milo kept grabbing him, pulling him down, until Montana reared back his fist and slammed it into Milo's face. Milo let go. Montana grabbed his lariat and spun it once above his head.

Kate was almost at the emergency exit. The neon letters glowed—beckoned. She reached for the door—

The lariat fastened around her right leg. Montana pulled.

Kate felt the ground escape her, and she slammed into the glass floor. The koi below her scattered.

There was a beep on her belt. One, two—

"Oh no," she whispered.

A sonic arrowhead went off, sending a high-pitched squeal into the air. It was almost deafening—like standing too close to a motorcycle when it first revs up. Nearby people winced away, plugging their ears. It actually alleviated Kate's headache—just a smidge—because it was a different kind of pain.

At least, until she heard a crack beneath her stomach.

"Oh *no*," she whimpered.

Montana got to his feet and came closer, wrapping the end of his lariat around his hand. His spurs clicked against the glass. "You can't run very far from me, Kate B—"

She turned over onto her back, took the book out of her belt, and threw it into the air.

The nine-by-nine glass floor panel beneath them shattered.

They fell to the fish tank below. She began to claw her way back to the surface, but Montana grabbed her by her middle. Pulled her down. Her lungs shuddered, screaming for air.

Above them, Milo caught the book and brought it close to his chest.

The sonic arrow sank with Kate and Montana, still loud even under the surface. As it sank, it began to crack the glass panes around them, fractures rushing across the surfaces like tree limbs. People scattered, running away from the cracks.

Montana grabbed at her belt, having realized what was in it, and brought out his knife. She tried to slap him away, but he cut the belt off her, smiling widely, and took hold of one of the arrowheads.

"NO!" she screamed, her voice coming out in a rush of air bubbles. She bit his hand. He let go and slammed his hand into the side of her face. The arrowhead drifted away from them. Then a fish caught it in its mouth, thinking it was food, and started to swim away with it. The tip of the arrowhead blinked once—then twice—and then—

It exploded.

One moment she was fighting off a cowboy, and

the next she was scrambling to remember which way was up. The shock wave from the explosion threw her and Montana apart. It quaked across the aquarium, carving out a hole in the side of the warehouse, where evening rain swirled in with abandon.

And, of course, water rushed *out*.

Spewing into the harbor.

The current caught Montana first. He tried to grab hold of the glass floor above them, but he couldn't find purchase—much like Augustus Gloop caught in the chocolate pipe—and instead slammed his dagger into the bottom of the aquarium. The current carried his hat away.

Kate scrambled toward the surface and broke it, grabbing hold of the metal checkboard-like frame of the floor, cutting her fingers on the jagged glass. She coughed, sputtering.

"Kate Bishop!" Misty roared, emerging from the remaining crowd gathered on the panes of glass flooring that *weren't* broken. Misty reached out to her to pull her out of the water, clasping her hand tight. "You're going to get me *fired*!"

Kate felt the lasso around her foot pull taut. Montana must've lost his fight with the current. Her hand slipped out of Misty's as she cried, "Tell the FBI *it was meeee*!" before she was dragged under.

One moment Kate was being pulled across a quickly draining koi aquarium that probably would have *never* passed a building inspection, and the next she and her good friend Monty were being sucked out through the hole in the side of the warehouse and spat out fifteen feet toward the Hudson River below.

Suddenly Kate heard something shatter—so loud and piercing that it rattled her bones.

The next thing she knew she'd slipped through a star-shaped hole in reality, colors spinning around her like a kaleidoscope. She fell through a dimension of yellows and greens and reds, suddenly weightless. Her hair floated like she was submerged underwater, lobsters the size of people looking up to point at her, a falling waterlogged spectacle with a lasso tied around her ankle.

Another star-shaped portal opened beneath her, to city and grime and gum-speckled sidewalks.

Kate hit the cement *hard*.

The portal closed a second later, severing the rope. It dropped limply beside her. She groaned, coughing up water and bile, every bone in her body throbbing. She pushed herself over and rolled onto her back.

And there stood America Chavez, arms crossed, face pinched in anger, and she was the most beautiful sight Kate had ever seen in her entire life.

Transcript (cont'd)

[Katherine Elizabeth Bishop's Statement Regarding the Events at the New York Public Library Stephen A. Schwarzman Building on August 2]
Recorded by Misty Knight

KNIGHT: Ah yes, I remember that part. It took me a while to fish that man out of the Hudson River. I wondered how you escaped.

BISHOP: Always have a best friend who can kick interdimensional holes into the face of reality.

KNIGHT: Apparently. While we're on the topic of the auction, however, the owner of the warehouse in question would like to know where to send the bill?

BISHOP: [SILENCE]

KNIGHT: [SILENCE]

BISHOP: So after the warehouse, we went back to America's apartment. . . .

CHAPTER TWELVE

BACK IN A SPELL

Kate wanted to crawl under a rock and die.

She was tired, sore, and currently arguing with America. Which was kind of hard to do when you had a bag of frozen peas pressed against the side of your head.

"Seriously! I would've gone with you instead!" America cried, throwing her hands in the air as she paced back and forth in her living room. After their death-defying ordeal, Milo had met them outside the warehouse, the book in his jacket, and America portaled them back to her apartment in Washington Heights. Which might've been for the best, because if Montana was still around, Kate suspected that the guys casing her apartment belonged to Kingpin.

Milo currently had a bag of frozen diced carrots

pressed to his cheek, looking every bit as pitiful as Kate probably felt.

She sank lower into the lumpy couch. Lucky propped his head up on her knee, as if to say *There, there.* "I said I was sorry. . . . I wanted you to go on your date."

"And the date was great! I could've rescheduled!" America went on. "And then I got that *cryptic text* from you!"

Kate pointed out, "I don't think it was *that* cryptic. . . ."

In reply, America brought out her phone, pulled up the text messages, and recited, " 'SOS NEED A WAY OUT OF HELL.' "

She winced. " 'Here.' That was supposed to be 'here.' "

Milo pointed out, "To be fair, it was a bit hellish."

"Mmm-hm. So"—America looked between the two of them—"are either of you going to tell me what's going on? Like, what's *really* going on?"

Milo gave Kate a hesitant look, as if that wasn't the best idea, but if this nightmare hypnosis was going to keep messing with her head, then she would rather America *know* than not know. It might endanger her from whoever else was after the books, but it was the kind of calculated risk Kate knew she had to take. So, she took a deep breath, and decided to rip off the proverbial Band-Aid. "So, these books—"

Suddenly Milo interrupted, "She's doing it for me."

Both America and Kate gave him a baffled look.

He went on, unable to look at Kate, "My grandfather was eccentric and secretive, and he put highly valuable secrets to a deadly psychological study in exclusive collector's editions of his novels," he said, and held up the book from the auction: *The Immovable Castle Moves a Spell*. The binding looked identical to the first. "These novels were why my grandfather was murdered, I'm guessing, so I asked Kate to help me find them all and make sure no one can use the secrets in them."

America eyed the book cautiously. "Your grandfather hid them in *children's novels*?"

Milo smiled at that, but it was a bit too toothy. "Children's books are a bit more complex than many people give them credit for, and what better place to hide his legacy? My grandfather studied the effects of certain sigils, and how in certain sequential orders they could elicit neurological commands. Mainly, death by fear, which is induced by nightmares and, later, hallucinations."

"And that's why—" Kate's phone buzzed, interrupting her, and she looked at the text. The only person who'd text her at this hour was Clint—

But it wasn't.

America eyed her. "Who is it?"

"Misty," she mumbled, and sent a text back. "She apprehended Kingpin's guy from the Hudson."

"For the best," Milo said matter-of-factly. "I can't imagine what Kingpin would do if he got all six books." Then he cocked his head and added, "Murder, I guess."

"Or at *least* extortion," Kate replied.

America muttered a curse word under her breath and started pacing back and forth across her apartment, while Kate tried to keep her emotions level. She couldn't let them see her hands shaking, so she tried not to think about how those booksellers had come into contact with the letter around the same time she did. Neither America nor Milo knew she was infected, too—was that even the right word? Under the influence? Hypnotized? *Bespelled?*—and she'd rather keep it that way.

She didn't know how much time she had left. She and the booksellers had all been exposed at the same time . . . were they all closer to death than she thought?

Would she know when it happened? Would she just fall asleep and never wake up, devoured by that creature in her nightmare?

Lucky whined, as if to say, *Don't you dare go anywhere,* and she scrubbed him behind the ears.

"Well." America finally stopped pacing and put her hands on her hips—her favorite thinking pose. "You can't exactly go to every bookstore in the world to find these books, so if I were you, I'd trace back the books you already know about. If Misty's division opened a case because of mysterious deaths surrounding the book Kingpin already had, then perhaps those deaths can—"

Milo interrupted, "The hypnosis is untraceable. It will look like they died of natural causes. That's the allure."

"Yes, *but*." America held up a finger. "You said Kingpin can only find your grandfather's research through all *six* books. How are people dying of the hypnosis then if no one knows the sigils?"

Kate sat up a little straighter. "Unless it's someone who *already* knows the sigils."

"*Exactly!*"

"Well, my grandfather wouldn't use them," Milo said a little rigidly.

Then why did he write that note to you? Kate wanted to ask, but if she did then she'd let on that she'd seen the sigils and was hypnotized. No, she'd better keep that to herself for now.

"Maybe not," America agreed, "but if we can find out *who*—"

"It won't matter *who* if we can't reverse the effects," Milo interrupted. "And to do that we need all six novels."

"We can stop them from hypnotizing anyone else," America argued.

"And in the meantime? As Kingpin goes on a murder spree collecting all the books? Are they simply collateral damage?" he asked darkly. "It's the trolley problem—do we save five people in danger of being hit by a trolley by diverting it to just kill one person on the other tracks?"

America gave him a pointed look, and he held her gaze.

Then he tore his away first, dropping his frozen bag of carrots onto the coffee table, and pushed himself to his feet. "Where's the bathroom?"

Both America and Kate pointed in the direction of the hallway, and he left. When he'd closed the door, a rigid silence fell between the two of them. Milo had certainly turned sharp very, very quickly. Kate rubbed her face with her hands. She was waterlogged, smelled like a koi pond, and felt sore everywhere. All she wanted to do was sleep. But if she did . . .

America crossed her arms over her chest again. "I don't trust him, Kate," she whispered.

"He's gone through a lot. First his grandfather

died, then Kingpin tried to kill him, and now he's stuck cleaning up his grandfather's mess."

"I know, but . . ." She hesitated, and Kate could tell she wanted to say something more, but then she thought better of it and shook her head. "We should just be careful, yeah? I'll help you tomorrow on this wild-goose chase. I doubt all of the books are in the city, so you'll need me anyway."

Kate gave her a reassuring smile. "Wouldn't it be a stroke of luck if they were?"

"You're never that lucky. You're staying here tonight again, right?"

"Sadly, I think so."

"Good. You should take the couch tonight."

"Do I look *that* tired?"

"No offense, but yeah."

Kate scrubbed Lucky under the chin, trying not to think about what might happen if she *did* fall asleep. "I'll try and get some sleep."

"Please do. You're no good to anyone if you're exhausted. Good night, call me if you need anything, yeah?"

"Yeah—and thank you."

America winked. "I got you." Then she left for her bedroom and closed the door, and Kate sank down lower on the cushions again.

She felt helpless—and guilty for bringing America into this, *especially* since they knew so little about this strange research. She didn't want to bring her best friend into a dangerous situation—even if America ate dangerous situations for breakfast. She couldn't exactly punch a nightmare, and this hypnosis seemed tailor-made to get around America's every defense. If Kate couldn't even protect *herself*, how could she bring anyone else into it? Trouble seemed to follow Kate wherever she went. She couldn't simply find her sister a birthday present, could she? Just stop a *normal* robbery? No, she had to save a murderous edition of a book from a children's series that ended up being the key to basically ending the world as she knew it. This strange visual poison—this *spell*—didn't just affect her ability to sleep, either, but her ability to do everything else.

To save people, to save *herself*.

What kind of monster would create a spell like that?

What kind of monster would spread it?

When Milo returned from the bathroom, he grabbed the book and sank down onto the couch next to her and Lucky, who bared his teeth until Kate bopped him on the nose. "Sorry," she muttered. "I don't know what's up with him."

"They say dogs are a good judge of character," Milo replied, eyeing Lucky, "but maybe this one's broken."

Or maybe Lucky—and America—were onto something.

"The only thing Lucky can judge is a slice of pizza," she lied, and the dog harrumphed and plopped his head on her lap. "He loves a good pizza."

"Don't we all." Milo picked the book up off the coffee table and took the string bookmark out of it, the lot-number tag on the end. He tossed it onto the coffee table. "So, five more to go. At least we know where two are."

"For better or worse," she agreed, staring at the lot number. 67. She gave a start. "Wait. Sixty-Seven."

"What about it?"

"Your friend—well, not friend, but acquaintance. The guy with the gray hair and eyepatch? Didn't he say he was looking to bid on lot Sixty-Seven?"

Milo shrugged. "I bet almost everyone there was."

"Yes, but he said it was to *add* to his collection," she pointed out, and the same realization occurred to him, too.

"*Ooooh.*"

"Exactly." She grinned. "I think we know our next move."

CHAPTER THIRTEEN

GOOD TO THE LAST DROP

Gregory Maxwell's penthouse took up three entire floors in a very expensive high-rise on Park Avenue. It was exceptionally luxurious, with three good-looking doormen and a security guard posted at the front door. It would have been hard for Kate to sneak her way into this complex, but lucky for her, Milo had wilted and told her that there might have been a much easier way into Maxwell's house—

An invitation.

So, he took out the business card Gregory had given him and dialed the number. It was ten thirty at night, and Gregory had been baffled by Milo's call . . . until Milo showed his trump card.

"I would like to talk, after all. About your proposition."

And that was all it took for Gregory to invite Kate and Milo in. Hook, line, and sinker.

America had been a bit hard-pressed to let them leave, but Kate argued that the sooner they got all the books, the better. And besides, it was the perfect opportunity for America to do her own research into Milo while Kate had him distracted. So America made her promise to take Lucky instead, and she did. She felt a little steadier with the dog by her side, who was as good as backup as any. Besides, dogs couldn't read, so it wasn't like Lucky was in any danger from this strange spell.

Kate, Lucky, and Milo filed into the elevator, and it took them thirty-three stories up to Maxwell's penthouse.

The plan was simple: Milo would go in and distract Gregory while Kate snuck in with Lucky to hunt for Gregory's esteemed *collection*. (Kate hoped to find all three books neatly on a shelf. Wouldn't that be so nice?) It was an easy plan.

And best yet, it didn't involve any fighting.

Still, as the elevator ascended, she took her quiver out of the duffel bag she had slung over her shoulder, and her compound bow, and situated both. "Just in case," she told him with a flash of a smile.

The elevator let out onto the thirty-third floor— and that's when they encountered their first problem.

While they knew that Gregory had *three whole floors*, Milo hadn't realized the elevator let out directly *into* his penthouse. He stepped out alone, unsure of what to do.

Kate muttered, "Keep him talking. I got this," before the elevator doors closed again.

She pressed the button for the next floor up, and just as the elevator began to ascend, she jabbed the emergency stop button and pushed open the emergency exit in the ceiling. She lifted Lucky up first and then pulled herself up. She jimmied open the elevator doors to the next level with one of her arrows. It creaked open just enough for her to push Lucky through—"You *really* need to cut down on the pizza," she huffed—then wiggle through herself.

She found herself on the second level of Gregory's penthouse, full of oversized bedrooms and strange pieces of sculpted art. Plenty of the portraits on the walls looked to have been painted by the same man— Gregory himself, from the signature. They were the only pops of color in this depressingly white apartment.

There wasn't any personality in the entire space. The walls were white, the furniture was white, the rugs on top of ashwood floors. It was immaculate and creepy, as if the couch and the rug and the table existed because they *had* to. Or else the apartment would look much weirder.

Lucky kept close beside her as they crept down the hall to the circular stairwell. She perched at the top, quiet, as Milo followed Gregory into the main part of the apartment—probably the living room, if she had to guess the layout.

The first thing Kate noticed was that Gregory did not look well—at all. His skin looked sickly pale, almost gray, and he kept dabbing his forehead with a kerchief that matched his crimson silk pajamas.

"Ah, Milo, my boy! I'm sorry, you caught me at a terrible time. I'd dozed off on the couch and had the *worst* dream I'd ever had, so excuse my wardrobe. Come in, come in," he said to Milo. He'd replaced his gaudy golden eyepatch with a simple black one. "I must say, it was quite a surprise when you called. After that . . . *fiasco* at the auction, we were bereft of what to do! Apparently a man in a cowboy hat *stole* the Albright book. Cecelia and I were both so distraught we almost thought to burn our entire collection to the ground."

That seemed a bit excessive, but if Kate had learned anything, billionaires were just that—*excessive*.

At least the theft hadn't been attributed to her—yet. Probably because it was Montana that Misty Knight had dragged out of the Hudson River, long after Kate and Milo had left the scene.

Gregory and Milo sat down on the white couches,

where Gregory steepled his fingers, and slipped right into business. "So, you've come to talk about your grandfather's books. I must say, I was surprised this couldn't wait until the morning."

Milo lounged back on the couch, making himself right at home there far easier than Kate expected. He put an arm on the back of the couch. "Why wait when we can do business now?"

Gregory agreed enthusiastically. "Why wait indeed! I always said to my wife that your grandfather's books—"

"Speaking of which," Milo interrupted, and leaned forward conspiratorially, "where's your collection? I've heard so much about it. . . ."

"Have you now?" Gregory's eyes glittered. It was his one joy, it seemed, as he popped to his feet and led Milo over to closed mahogany doors on the far side of the living room . . . completely opposite from where Kate was. Completely out of reach. Of course it was. She muttered just that under her breath, and Lucky snorted in agreement. Maxwell went on. "I usually don't show my collection to anyone, but perhaps if it'll persuade you to sign Immovable Castle over to me . . ."

"It definitely wouldn't hurt," Milo replied with fake amiability.

Gregory clasped his hands together. "Excellent! Now, feast your eyes . . ."

Then he backed up into the double doors and threw them open behind him.

Kate's jaw dropped.

Like the rest of the apartment, the impersonal white bled into the room, over every built-in shelf and desk and chair, and *book*. A bad feeling began to swirl in Kate's stomach as Milo stepped into the study and turned in a full circle to get the scope of the . . . damage.

Because it *was* damage.

Every book, every collector's item, every precious journal and rare edition and uniquely bound copy of a lost text, had been painted over in white.

"My collector's copy of *The Trials of the Immovable Castle* is here somewhere," Gregory said, waving his hand toward the shelves and shelves of spines painted white, "though I can't really recall where it is. Perhaps over there by the window?" He frowned in thought. "Or over by the bust of Willy Shakes? Ah, they all look the same eventually," he said, and turned to Milo with hungry eyes. "Now, shall we, Milo my boy?"

"You definitely stretch the word *collection*, then," Milo said dryly, looking at the library. "Only *one* of my grandfather's books?"

In reply, Gregory wagged his finger and tsked, "You, my boy, should know it isn't about the *quantity* of books, but the *quality*."

Kate watched Milo's hands form into fists, and then relax again. "Of course," he replied, his voice vacant. "Living room?"

"Naturally. I wouldn't want to conduct business in here. It's so *impersonal*."

So they returned to the living room, but at least Kate knew where she'd be heading. She looked at Lucky and muttered, "Why can't any of this be easy?"

In reply, Lucky drooped.

It looked like there might be a hallway back the way she'd come to the other side of the penthouse—and hopefully another set of stairs that would get her closer to the study. She wasn't *against* using the air ducts, but she'd really prefer not to. So she and Lucky backtracked the way they came and turned down an adjacent white hallway. The hallways were all the same; the only difference was the portraits, but soon she realized that they were all of the same woman—

Gregory's wife. Wasn't Cecelia her name?

They seemed inseparable. Kate wondered why they had separated.

The other side of the second floor held much of the same as the first side—overly large bedrooms with white bedspreads, all so impractical, especially for an apartment for *two people*. It was like, even with all this space, they'd rather not populate it with . . . anything.

Her sister had been on a minimalist kick, too, a few years ago, but nothing to this extent. Living in such a clean, untouched apartment felt . . . hollow. As if it was never really meant to be lived in, but shown off and then sold to the highest bidder when the current occupants passed.

Thankfully, she found a set of stairs down to the first floor, and as luck would have it, the hallway led out to the living room right beside the study. Kate didn't realize it until she had already stepped into the living room, and quickly pulled herself—and Lucky—back with a yip.

Gregory looked around. "Oh, what was that sound?"

Milo thought quick—and knocked over his teacup. "Oh—drat! Sorry, sorry," he said, trying to salvage what he could. "I'm so clumsy when I'm nervous."

Gregory popped up to his feet and rushed toward the kitchen to get a towel, and Kate took that moment to slip around the corner of the hall and into the study. "Thank you," she mouthed to Milo, and gently closed the doors behind her and Lucky.

From the other side, she heard the billionaire return. "It's no problem! Everyone's a bit of a klutz sometimes. Why Cecelia . . ." He hesitated, and then decided to change the subject. "Now, Milo, my boy, as I've said before, Pegasus Publishing is the perfect home for Albright. We could be great together. Decadent collector's editions, exclusive box sets—we can make your late grandfather's legacy lucrative and legendary. . . ."

Kate slipped away from the mahogany doors as Gregory Maxwell waxed on and on. At least he liked hearing himself talk. "Keep him busy, Milo," she muttered, and fixed her attention to the painted-white books, "because I'm going to be a while."

She quickly set to work. The study was eerie, almost like a set piece. Made to be glanced at but not lived in. Kate tipped out one book, then the next. She was lucky that the entire *book* wasn't painted—just the edges that people could see. Which, unless it was the end of a row, was only the spine. It was still horrendous, but not as bad as she'd first thought.

Milo and the owner of Pegasus Publishing discussed acquiring the Immovable Castle novels, much to Milo's chagrin. He hadn't wanted to suggest the plan as they caught a cab to Park Avenue, but it was the only sure way to gain an audience with Maxwell, especially this late at night.

"As you can see," Gregory went on as Kate checked book after book as quickly and quietly as she could. Lucky sniffed around the room, growing more agitated by the moment. He'd whimper, and Kate would shush him each time. "Your grandfather's *current* publisher can't even keep up with demand—that wouldn't be a problem at my publisher."

To which Milo replied, "No, you just put out books without any marketing at all."

"It's better to have the book out there, available!" Gregory scoffed. "And the Immovable Castle series would never have that issue with marketing. If we re-release it, there will be midnight releases. There will be fanfare! Instead of some measly event in some nowhere shop in *Brooklyn*—" He sneered at the word, like he'd never set foot there in his entire life. "With Pegasus Publishing, we will give your family—may your late parents' souls rest in peace—actual *respect*."

"I'd rather you not bring up my parents," Milo replied icily.

Kate frowned. Milo . . . didn't have parents, either? That was a rather big part of his life to leave out. It was only him and his grandfather? And now just him? She and her sister night not have gotten along all the time, but Kate was still, always, infinitely glad she wasn't alone.

"Yes, of course . . ." Gregory hesitated a moment, as if he finally realized he had overstepped.

Kate skimmed through shelf after shelf. She

suspected the book looked like both the first one from Milo's satchel and the one from the auction. Leather-bound. Crinkly pages. Golden filigree on the front with the title of the novel.

Lucky paced back and forth near the door.

Kate glared at him. "Shh!" she whispered for the third time. The dog lowered his ears, but he still looked panicked.

Strange. Lucky never acted like this. Did he smell something?

"Just a few more seconds, boy," she whispered as she quietly dragged the ladder over to begin hunting on the final wall. One thing was for certain with Gregory Maxwell: He could fill silence easily. Milo barely had to say a word for him to go on long diatribes and tangents, only to circle back minutes later to answer the initial question. They talked about things that Kate had heard discussed before in her father's offices—distribution, publisher backing, marketing strategies, royalties. Gregory even offered to buy the books from the old publisher outright.

"They're not doing *anything* for you," the man insisted. "Why, if it weren't for your grandfather's reputation—"

Suddenly Lucky whined—loudly this time.

"What *is* that noise?" Gregory asked, and Kate heard the floor creak as he stood.

She doubled her effort, pulling books off the shelf just far enough to read the titles. No, no, definitely not, poor *Twilight*, no, no, William Shakespeare did not craft eloquent phallic jokes to be painted *white*—

The footsteps were at the door. Lucky hunkered down and bared his teeth.

Kate scanned the rest of the shelves, hoping she'd find a familiar spine—

There!

She reached up on her tiptoes, slipped a book out, and held in her hands *The Trials of the Immovable Castle.* "Bingo," she whispered.

Then the mahogany doors flew open wide.

CHAPTER FOURTEEN

BETTER THAN A GUILLOTINE

Gregory Maxwell frowned, looking around the empty library. "I swear I thought I heard someone in here!" He massaged his temples. "Forgive me. My head has been fuzzy all night."

Milo came up beside him, looking impossibly impressed. "No, no, I thought I heard something, too . . ." he admitted, flicking his gaze around the library, all the books, spines white, neatly in their places. Except for a single gap in the third row of the second shelf.

As Gregory started to turn toward it, Milo pulled his attention away with "Is that a first edition of *Pride and Prejudice*?" and pointed toward the opposite wall.

The collector brightened. "It *is*! I'm surprised you recognized it with it painted white!"

"It's hard to forget a spine like that."

Milo guided Gregory over to the shelf, asking about his favorite Austens, and Gregory was more than happy to tell him with large, flourishing hand waves. "You know good literature, my boy. Cecelia prefers the *Brontës*. Can you believe it?"

"What a mistake that is," Milo said in agreement. "Where is she, by the way?"

Gregory said, "Asleep, of course! It *is* late." Then, a bit conspiratorially, he added, "I know we've had nasty rumors floating around that we were *separated*, but we've recently gotten back together."

"Ah. I . . . had not heard, sadly."

"Sadly? Why sadly? It's perfect!"

Maybe if Kate had been paying a little more attention, she would've heard the nervous quiver at the edge of Milo's voice, but she was a little preoccupied, squeezed into the cupboard with Lucky, a hand clamped around his muzzle. Through the narrow gap in the cupboard doors, she watched as Gregory came toward the cupboard and poured himself a glass of bourbon from the decanter atop it. She held her breath, praying Lucky held his, too.

Gregory offered Milo a glass of bourbon. It smelled strong and rich. Milo made a face and set the drink down, deciding against drinking it. "Cecelia is my other half—do you have a love like that? It's quite refreshing. I daresay I'd die without her."

That . . . at least made Kate breathe a little easier. She thought something *nefarious* was going on here.

"I'm difficult, but that's why she loves me. I heard your grandfather was rather difficult, too," Gregory added.

Milo finally settled his gaze on the cupboard. Kate figured he'd puzzle out where she'd disappeared to, but now the trick was to get Gregory to *leave* long enough for Kate and Lucky to escape. They were so close. She had the book, all she needed to do was to get back to the freaking elevator before the doormen in the lobby suspected anything with the stopped elevator.

"He was peculiar, sure, but most creatives are," Milo replied.

"Yes, but I heard he went through four—no, five?— different artists until they could replicate that silly language of his to go along the top of his books. And then he never provided a key for anyone to figure it out!"

"Some children have."

"Resourceful little parasites, the lot of them."

"For someone who publishes children's novels, you certainly don't like them."

"Children? I love their spending power. A little

waterworks and they have their parents buying them the biggest, most expensive thing on the market. Then again, I wouldn't be caught dead *with* one!" And he laughed. "I'm sure your grandfather was the same."

Milo skimmed his fingers along the whited-out spines on the far shelves. "He actually loved kids. He loved their ingenuity. Besides, it's not the kids who ruin everything, but the adults."

Gregory stopped laughing and cleared his throat awkwardly. "Well . . . to each their own, I suppose—"

"But I certainly hate kids. Sticky, nosy, bratty—the worst," Milo added happily, and gave the publisher a catty, toothy smile. He almost sounded earnest.

Lucky gave a jerk, his claws scraping the inside of the cupboard door.

Kate held him tightly. "Stop, stop," she mouthed. Lucky had his head in the air, his nose twitching, like he smelled something off.

"Now I *did* hear that," Gregory said. "Is it coming from—over here, maybe?"

Holding her breath, Kate refused to move a muscle, clutching Lucky so tightly he couldn't squirm even if he wanted to, as Gregory Maxwell came closer. And closer. He stopped in front of the cupboard.

This was it, she was going to be found out.

Milo said, "Perhaps it was an animal?"

"Oh, I *hope* not," Gregory replied, and reached for the cupboard handle.

"I don't want to see it if it is. I have—um—I hate mice. I'm sure it's a mouse," Milo reassured him, and backed up toward the doorway to the living room.

Gregory paused. "You know, my neighbors *have* been complaining of something in the walls. It's probably a rat, really. You know how rats are in this city," he went on in disgust. "I'm surprised there isn't a super hero for rats. God knows there's one for everything else these days—two, sometimes!"

Kate rolled her eyes.

"But perhaps I should look, just in case. Turn away, Milo my boy, this might be dangerous!" Gregory announced, and squatted to open the cupboard.

This was it. They were done for—

Milo suddenly blurted, "Where do I sign?"

Gregory gave a start, and stood. "You mean it?"

"I think we could be a great team."

"Oh, absolutely! Let's go contact my rights people. Come, come, to my office!" he declared, and with a flourish he pointed toward the opposite end of the penthouse, up a wired spiral staircase, and into a lofty space with a rolling barn door and not nearly enough privacy. He welcomed Milo inside, but Kate listened to their footsteps fade out of the library, the door slide shut, and their voices cut off completely.

Then she and Lucky tumbled out of the cupboard and scrambled for the door. Lucky kept turning his head, distracted, but Kate managed to get him to concentrate long enough to return to the elevator and squeeze their way inside. She closed the ceiling hatch and pressed the emergency release button.

The elevator gave a jerk—and began to descend.

She waited on the bench outside the building until Milo came down about ten minutes later, looking as tired as she felt. Lucky didn't even growl at him as he plopped down beside her, and they stared, blankly, down the street.

After a minute Milo said, "I'm hungry." He glanced at Kate. "You?"

She nodded. "I know a good twenty-four-hour pizza place around the corner that allows dogs."

Lucky liked that idea, too.

CHAPTER FIFTEEN

BAD PIZZA

There was nothing like midnight pizza in the city that never slept. Greasy and gooey, it was exactly what Kate needed after cramming herself into a cupboard the size of a mouse hole and being hot-boxed by her favorite dog.

Bad Pizza was a small restaurant scrunched between a nail salon and a tourist shop, and because of its name, most tourists stayed away from it. The grease stains on the vinyl seats were permanent, the gum plastered on the checkered tables gray with dirt and time, and the small jukebox in the corner of the narrow restaurant murmured a soft pop song from the early 2000s on a loop. The pizza was delicious, however; by far the best in Midtown. The owners spoiled Lucky whenever they came into the shop, and gave him extra slices and the throwaway bits they usually reserved for the rats out in the back alley.

They ate their pizza in silence, because there really wasn't much to say. The heist had gone both great and poorly at the exact same time, and Kate wasn't quite sure how to process that. She was sure eventually she'd be able to tell Clint about it over drinks—

No, she could never do that.

After they'd finished eating, Milo finally asked, "Are you okay?"

She jerked her head up. "Hmm? Why?"

"Because this is the longest you've ever gone without talking since I met you."

"Wow, are you trying to say I don't shut up?"

He grinned. "Never. This place was an excellent choice, by the way. I'm usually not a fan of pizza, but I might make Bad Pizza an exception."

"That's a pretty good idea," she agreed. "When I was little, my sister and I weren't allowed to eat greasy pizza. It was always gluten-free, sprinkled with caviar, or . . . you know. *Expensive*." She tilted her head, recalling the first time she found this place. It'd been after one of her parents' fights. She'd been thirteen, maybe fourteen. Snuck out of the apartment. Took the service elevator down so the doorman didn't notice her slip out the side exit. She remembered walking for hours, and then finding this place, and her stomach felt like it was eating itself, she was so hungry.

She remembered that girl, fingers bandaged from the blisters of practicing archery, dreaming of the day she'd be as good as Hawkeye—when *she* could save people, instead of the other way around.

"Yours, too? My dad hated pizza, but whenever he was gone on business trips, my mom used to buy those frozen ones and stick them in the oven. She'd put extra cheese on them—whatever we had in the fridge at the time. Expensive cheeses on a five-dollar pizza—that was the kind of person she was. That was actually the last thing we ate together. I guess we're both part of the dead parents club," he said.

She bit the inside of her cheek, because her parents were a special circumstance.

Milo plucked two napkins from the dispenser on the table and wiped his gloves off. She thought it was odd that he hadn't taken them off, not even to eat pizza, but she didn't ask. After all, she was sitting in a cheap pizza joint in her super-hero costume, so she didn't have much room to talk. "My parents died when I was thirteen," he went on. "It was . . . a difficult time for my grandfather and me. We didn't see eye to eye for a long time after that. Not until recently."

They sat there quietly for a long moment.

"I understand—probably more than you think. My mom died when I was young," she said finally. Behind the counter, the cashier working the late shift had his earbuds in as he bopped around the kitchen, mopping. He was currently sashaying to ABBA, the song so loud she could hear it across the restaurant. "I always blamed my dad for her death. And myself. She came to my summer camp the day before she died, wanting me to go away with her and . . . I didn't. I should have. I don't know if my sister blames me or anything but . . . I blame myself enough for both of us. So I—I understand, if that's anything." She reached down and scrubbed Lucky behind the ears for a little comfort. "I miss her."

"I miss my parents, too," Milo agreed softly. He closed the book, his eyebrows furrowed in thought. "I can't remember the last thing I said to them, you know? Was I being bratty? Did I tell them I loved them? I don't know. They died in a house fire. I don't remember how it started—the entire night is a blur. My grandfather got out, though. Of course he did. He only ever thought of himself."

"I used to love the Immovable Castle series as a kid," she replied. "I used to imagine what it would be like to meet E. L. Albright—but I guess you shouldn't meet your heroes."

"They're not always super," he agreed.

Her mouth twitched into a half smile. "No, they're not."

She reached her hand across the table and set it on top of his. "I'm sorry. For everything—your parents, your grandfather . . . having to deal with the rest of this mess right now. It sucks."

He looked at her hand atop his. "Did you ever forgive your dad?"

"No," she replied without a moment of hesitation. She withdrew her hand. "I don't think I ever will."

"I feel the same about my grandfather," he admitted, and turned a critical eye to *The Trials of the Immovable Castle*. "And now *we* have to deal with his stupid mistake."

Kate sighed. "Why are they surfacing *now* of all times?"

"Beats me." He opened up the hardcover and pointed to the English words written at the top of each page—where, in the regular printing, there would be Unword instead. So the collector's edition was the exact opposite. "But at least it's a comfort to know that whoever is looking for the books needs all of them. To decode my grandfather's research, you need *both* the children's book and these books to know what the symbols look like and which are translatable—and which are sigils. They're hidden in the Unword language on these pages. So you see, it's rather foolproof."

"Seems like a lot of work. Why didn't he just, I don't know, *destroy* it?"

"He couldn't destroy something he'd spent his entire life working on."

"It also sounds like it destroyed his family, too."

"Exactly, so if he destroyed this research, it would all be for nothing." There was a thin line of anger in his voice. "My parents' *deaths* would be for nothing, or so he reasoned."

A cop car howled down the street, red and blue lights bouncing off the glass windows, toward the high rise. They both froze at the sound, but the cars whirled past them, toward Park Avenue.

Toward Gregory Maxwell's place?

No, they wouldn't send that many police to a robbery that had already happened, she thought.

No, the police were just heading in that direction. It could be for a completely different reason. She was just being paranoid, because their plan had gone off better than she'd anticipated. Now they had two books down, and four to go. At least they knew where two of them were—and she wasn't looking forward to figuring out how to steal them back from Kingpin.

Another two cop cars lit up the night as they whirled down Fifty-Seventh toward Park Avenue. Kate and Milo exchanged the same look.

"Time to go?" he asked.

"Time to go," she agreed, then fed Lucky her crust, and they dumped their plates in the trash can on the way out.

"Don't be a stranger now!" the cashier of Bad Pizza cried with a wave, and Kate returned it before they ducked out of the restaurant and turned left toward Broadway.

Milo stuck his hands in his pocket, falling into step with Kate on one side, Lucky on the other. "So, do you commit crimes often in the name of good?"

"I plead the Fifth there," she replied, recalling one too many times where she, uh, sort of did just that. It usually worked out in her favor. Besides, she wasn't always *lawfully* good—more chaotic neutral erring on the side of charity.

The eye on the back of her hand twisted to look at her, and she pressed her thumb against it—hard. Just to make sure the skin was still hers and the eye was just a hallucination. Her costume covered most of her body, so she hadn't gotten a chance to see if there were more. Though she was sure they were spreading.

"Is something wrong?" Milo asked, glancing at her expression. It must have been pinched—or at least pained. "Was it the pizza?"

"I'm fine," she replied quickly, letting go of her hand. "Just thinking."

"That can't be good."

She laughed. "Shut up."

The night was humid, the smell of trash mixed with the unmistakable scent of midnight food stops and car exhaust. Light from open windows and closed stores bounced across the recycled glass in the sidewalk cement, making it glitter like fallen stars. In the distance, towering over them like some benevolent overlord, was Stark Tower, its neon-red sign reflecting ominous red in the puddles on the street.

"It's nice," he said after a while, "to talk to someone who understands about the whole"—he waved his hand in an encompassing motion—"dead-parent thing. Most people just look at you like you're broken."

"Or that you're the thing they'll become eventually when *their* parents die, and they're just glad they aren't you yet," she added.

"Exactly."

Lucky trotted between them, sniffing at the ground as he went.

"My mom used to wear this really strong perfume," Milo went on. "After she died, sometimes I would just get a smell of it, like she'd just walked past."

"Isn't it weird how some things just linger?"

"Sometimes I thought that maybe she was a ghost, come back to haunt me."

"Yours is a ghost, mine's a vampire," she replied wryly, and he laughed, not realizing how bizarrely truthful she was being. "But when she was alive, she was a philanthropist. Her job took her everywhere, so she was gone a lot, but when she was home, she'd read to me and my sister, Susan." She found herself thinking more and more about those moments, these last few days. "She'd read us a chapter a night. I would always *beg* her for more. She died before we ever got to finish the last Immovable Castle book. I never picked it up after that."

He gave her a distraught look. "So you don't know how the story ends?"

She shrugged. "It was just . . . never the same after. I couldn't finish it without her, and she was . . . well, you know. Gone. Does it end right, at least?"

"That depends. How do you think stories should end?"

"Happily," she replied without a second thought. "I'm a bit of a romantic that way. I kind of have to be, to believe in the good of people day in and day out."

"Lest you become a villain like Kingpin," he replied cryptically. He kicked a piece of trash on the sidewalk, and it went skittering toward a pile of garbage bags heaped on the corner. "How do you think we'll get the books back from Kingpin, anyway?"

She shrugged. "I have no clue. Do you know where the other two might be?"

"I wish I did," he replied, and then something occurred to him. "How did you find out about the auction?"

"Funny story, actually . . ." She told him about the summer camp kids and how they were a *wealth* of Albright knowledge, from the forums they visited to their own private Wikipedia-like biography on a shared notes app. Milo was charmed by it.

Since it was past midnight, there weren't as many people on the streets, but still enough in Midtown for them to blend rather inconspicuously into the crowd as they made their way back toward Forty-Second Street and then took the subway up to Washington Heights. And bed, Kate supposed, though she wasn't quite sure how she was going to navigate that.

CHAPTER SIXTEEN

THE LATE, LATE SHOW

America was waiting up for them, lounging on the threadbare sofa, her feet kicked up on the coffee table, watching some late-night show on cable. They had Jennifer Walters on, talking about a very rare case of copyright infringement. The second Lucky trudged in through the door, America jumped to her feet and turned the TV off. "About time! What happened?"

Kate gave her a long, tired look as she held the door open for Milo, who shuffled into the apartment after her and plopped down on the sofa. He dug out the book from the duffel bag and held it up triumphantly. "We got the book."

America plucked it out of his hand and whistled as she looked at the spine. "Did he really paint everything white?"

"The *entire* apartment. It was the weirdest thing," Kate replied, and lounged back on the sofa. "But otherwise it worked out pretty well. Did you end up actually signing over your grandpa's books?" she asked Milo.

He rolled his eyes. "As *if*. I tore that contract up the second I made a break for it." Then he frowned, a troubling thought occurring to him. "But speaking of my grandfather, I guess I should . . . see about funeral arrangements in the morning. I don't even know how to go about it. When my parents died, he did all of that."

She and America exchanged a look, and then America gave in and said, "I can help you out with that. Kate can, too. We aren't really strangers to funerals."

"We've been to too many to count," Kate agreed.

"And you're still in this line of work?" Milo asked, baffled.

Kate shrugged. "You know what they say, doing the same thing over and over expecting different results."

"*Hoping* for different results," America corrected, and stood from her end of the sofa. She scrubbed Lucky behind the ears and gave a long stretch. "Okay, well, now that you're both home, *I'm* going to sleep. I have a date in the morning, because *someone* cut mine short tonight," she added with a pointed look at Kate.

"I really owe you one," Kate replied.

"You owe me a thousand. Good night," America added, and left for her bedroom.

Lucky jumped up into the warm spot America left behind, spun around on the cushions three times, and then plopped down with a tired grunt. Kate patted him on the rump. He was a good dog.

Milo gave a yawn—which made *her* yawn.

"Oh, don't do that," she complained.

"We should probably get to sleep, too. It's been . . . a hell of a day."

But Kate really didn't want to face her dreams quite yet. Especially when she was afraid she wouldn't wake up from them. And she was still two books away from any sort of cure. Not only did they have to *find* remaining novels, they also had to get two books that Kingpin stole, and she had no idea how they were going to do that. She'd barely survived Montana.

But instead of saying any of that, she lifted one of Milo's curls to look at the gash on his forehead from his run-in with Kingpin. "We should probably change your bandage."

"Would you kindly?"

"Sure." She stood and went to get the first-aid kit from the bathroom, then came back to sit down. "Tilt your head toward me." He did, and she opened up a packet of disinfectant. "You know, the more I think

about it, the less I can imagine inheriting something like you have—what was your grandfather going
to do, anyway, once someone gathered all the books
together?"

"He was quite adamant no one would."

"Why?"

"Because he was sure no one would ever find the
last one. He says he hid it too well."

"Oh. Well, do you know where it is? Sorry," she
added when she applied the disinfectant, and he
winced away with a hiss.

"It's fine, it's fine. And no. I do not. The only clue
I have is that it is somewhere where everyone can see it
and no one knows it's there."

"Well, that's a whole lot of nothing." She applied
the Band-Aid and sat back, thinking.

The ceiling fan spun in slow arcs. Even though it
was nighttime, the city was still muggy, and the wall
AC units in the apartment barely did anything to stave
off the heat, even at night.

"So Kingpin found one, then he got yours," she said,
counting on her fingers. "We have the auction one, and
Maxwell's . . . one is somewhere 'where everyone can
see it and no one knows it's there,' and the last . . ."

He shrugged. "It was the one he sold at a second-
hand store, that's all I know."

So the book could very easily be anywhere in the world by now—even destroyed. But if it was, then they had to confirm that, because it would be *very* bad for her.

They settled back into silence. Kate ran over all the details in her head once, twice, three times—the books, who she saw at the auction, who could *possibly* have them, and that last riddle of a book being somewhere everyone could see but no one knew it was there. It all seemed like the answer was *right there*, but her head was so foggy, she could barely keep more than one thought in it at once. She just wanted to go to sleep. Her eyelids felt so, *so* heavy. But she knew if she did . . .

"This must be one of the most far-fetched things you've had to deal with in a while, isn't it?" Milo asked wryly. "A children's-book series hiding a secret hypnotic message that can kill you in your nightmares."

Kate gave a shrug. "Not *that* far-fetched. Once, I fought *brainwashed frat bros* who liked to punch things. Then there was that time a group of vampires thought that America was a goddess. And then that other time I got transported onto an island outside of time where I had to fight all the best archers in the world—including Clint. Oh! And once, Madame Masque used *my own face* to—"

He threw his hands up. "Okay! Okay. I get your

point. It's not completely out there. And thank you," he added, lacing his fingers together, putting his elbows on his knees, "it means a lot that you're helping me."

She gave a one-shouldered shrug. "It's what I do. I mean, if Kingpin gets these novels and *does* manage to crack the code, who knows what he'll do. . . ." She trailed off, a thought occurring to her. If the people from Misty's original investigation died through hypnosis, then it meant someone else had to know about the research in order to kill them with it. It meant they already knew what was hidden in the books—so it also stood to reason they had worked with Albright at some point, if they knew how to use the research already. But then why were they going after the books in the first place?

Something wasn't adding up.

Milo cocked his head. "Is something wrong?"

She glanced at him, the newly cleaned gash on his head, his soft, dark ringlet curls, the way his eyes were a grassy sort of emerald green that discombobulated her a little bit, and she thought better of voicing her opinion. She didn't want to scare him, not tonight, knowing that someone else his grandfather worked with was likely entangled in this—not only that, but likely a murderer, too.

Tomorrow, she promised herself. She'd tell him both

about her new theory and that she was under the same hypnosis as the one that killed his grandfather. He'd freak out, and so would America, which was why she hadn't said anything yet. In her experience, emotions clouded judgment, and she didn't need anyone getting reckless.

She was already reckless enough for both of them.

"It's past midnight," she said instead. "You must be tired."

"I bet you are, too," he replied.

"We can take a few hours to rest. We're no good sleep-deprived."

"No, I suppose not," he admitted as he kicked off his shoes. They were nice loafers, scuffed from running around all evening. The white button-down had blood on the collar.

She asked, "Do you want some clothes to sleep?"

He feigned shock. "Are you telling me I *stink*?"

"No, I'm telling you you can't be comfortable in evening wear," she replied, and went back into the hall closet to scrounge up a shirt and some pajamas that would fit Milo from the donation box America kept from all her exes (and, let's face it, the people who just crashed here, like Kate). She returned as he was shrugging out of his three-piece suit, having a bit of trouble with the buttons on his waistcoat.

She motioned to him as she said, "Do you want me to . . . ?"

His shoulders sagged. "I fear my hands are still shaking pretty badly from . . . well, *everything*."

"That tends to happen," she replied. It *had* been a long day. Being tossed around and beaten up was just all in a day's work for her, but for a nerdy bookworm? She doubted he'd seen this much action since PE class. She stepped up to him and undid the vest as he had asked, then went ahead and helped him out of it. He moved like he was already sore, and winced when he turned a certain way.

"You probably pulled something. Frozen peas are the best for that," she advised.

"This, oddly enough, isn't my first rodeo," he replied matter-of-factly.

That surprised her. "You've been in worse situations?"

He started unbuttoning his white shirt. "I'm what you would call a contrarian most of the time, so I tended to be a magnet for fistfights at the private academy where I went to school."

"Oh, a *private academy*. Been there, got the school uniform."

He snorted. "My grandfather sent me away after my parents died. I was a bit too unruly for him, apparently.

Do you do this day in and day out? Break into auctions and steal private property?"

"Most days I'm not being actively drowned, so it's easier." She watched as he slid off his shirt and pulled the T-shirt over his head. She didn't realize that it had KISS ME I'M SUPER written across the chest until it was too late, and she bit back a laugh as he read it himself.

"Ah well, I guess we don't have to worry about that," he said dryly.

She snorted. "I doubt you have a problem getting kissed."

"You'd be surprised."

"Really? You *do* give off the aura of a heartbreaker," she decided, gathering up his jacket and waistcoat.

He tilted his head thoughtfully. "I'll take that as a compliment?"

"Good." Then she motioned to his gloves. "Do you sleep in those?"

As if he had forgotten he was wearing them, he glanced down at his hands, and then curled his fingers into fists and looked back to her with an embarrassed smile. "Ah. I forget I'm wearing them most of the time." He didn't make a move to remove them, though.

"You know, there's a joke about how only villains wear gloves . . . something-something Disney-cinema shorthand."

There was a glimmer in his green eyes, like a trea-
sure sparkling at the bottom of a well. He took a step
closer to her. Close enough for her to feel the heat
radiating from his body. A knot rose in her throat as he
murmured, "Do you think me a villain, Kate Bishop?
After all we went through?"

"It'd be a bit on the nose," she remarked. He reached
out and very gently slid his gloved fingers underneath
the trim of her shirt at her hip. Her heart jumped
against her rib cage. "I think . . ."

"Yes?" His voice dipped a little lower.

"You might be a bit of a villain yourself, if you put
your mind to it." He bent close to her, but never quite
close enough to close the gap between them as he studied her lips. Tried to decide whether or not he wanted
to, whether he could, so she decided for him. It was not
the time, and not the place, and Kate was never very
good at kissing people at appropriate times. So, she
cupped his face in her hands and closed the distance
for him. His lips were soft and dry, and he tensed the
moment they touched, a surprise in his throat like he
didn't think she would. Of course she would. There
were few things that got her out of her own head other
than the feel of someone else, bodies pressing together.
And she really, *really* needed to get out of her own head.

And as it turned out, so did he.

He raised his hand to her cheek and kissed her deeply, savoringly, as if she was a delicate dessert. And he might not have been a super hero, but dear god, he could *kiss*.

He kissed like he was well versed in exactly the kind of kissing she liked, the kind of kissing that she felt all the way down into her *toes*. His tongue slid softly across her lips, teasing her, tricking her into pressing against him deeper, because she wanted to explore a little more—

Transcript (cont'd)

[Katherine Elizabeth Bishop's Statement Regarding the Events at the New York Public Library Stephen A. Schwarzman Building on August 2]
Recorded by Misty Knight

KNIGHT: [AUDIBLY CLEARS THROAT]

BISHOP: Fine, fine. Lucky didn't let us do anything, anyway.

CHAPTER SEVENTEEN

FANCY KISSING YOU HERE

Very faintly, Kate noticed that something was growling.

No, wait—not something. *Lucky?*

The realization snapped her back to reality and she pulled away from Milo. "Oh gosh—oh gosh, I'm so sorry." Her lips were slightly swollen, his taste still on her tongue. "Wow, I did not— Let's forget that, okay?"

Milo was confused. "Forget about it? Why?"

"Because nothing happened," she quickly interrupted, turning on her heels and escaping into the bathroom as quickly as she could. "Lucky, come on!"

The dog tore himself away from his death glare at Milo, trotted into the bathroom after her, and lay down on the rug while she showered. She wanted to kick herself, because she was becoming far more entangled than she wanted to be in this gnarled mess of an adventure. If she could even call it that.

More than an adventure . . . it had felt like . . .

She wiped the mirror of steam and froze at her own reflection. "A nightmare," she muttered.

The bruise on her arm from yesterday was gone, replaced by eyes. Dozens upon dozens of eyes, crawling up her shooting arm, all the way up her shoulder to the side of her neck, across half of her torso. They blinked and stared at her, all the irises different colors and sizes, almost like they'd been painted on with a broad brush. And—worse—now that she saw all of them, she could *feel* them looking, shifting their gazes to her reflection, too.

A scream bubbled up in her throat, but she clamped her mouth shut and swallowed it back down.

You knew about this part, she told herself. First nightmares, then hallucinations.

If they were any indication of how much longer she had—not long. Maybe two days, by the way the eyes were spreading.

Still longer than the other people who died that Misty told me about, she thought, and began to wonder why that was. She wasn't a mutant or super-powered herself, so why were the eyes taking longer to infect *her*? The other booksellers as well. Perhaps it was that she hadn't slept all that much, so the hypnosis hadn't had time to kill her yet. It was the only thing that made sense.

She rubbed her face tiredly.

But how much longer could she stay awake?

She could last up to three days, she knew, before her brain started shutting down on itself, entering brief periods of microsleep—and she was certain once that happened, it would only quicken the hypnosis even *while* she stayed awake. So she had . . .

She had half a day—maybe a whole one if she was lucky.

One last day.

After she cut off the shower and changed into some more clothes she'd found in the closet donation box, she peeked out of the bathroom to make sure that Milo was asleep on the couch, put her hair up in a towel, and tiredly made her way to the chair she'd fallen asleep in last night. The window on the far wall let out to a fire escape and the noises of Washington Heights beyond, and the sprawling city of Manhattan, laid out like a field of lights.

She gingerly sat down and curled into a ball. Lucky put his head on the edge of the cushion and watched her, as if he could sense that something was off.

In the morning, she'd tackle this with renewed optimism, but tonight she let herself sink a bit into what she now knew was growing dread. What if this hypnosis permanently affected her talent? What if it was gone—forever?

She'd been shot at, almost drowned, thrown around so bodily that every single bone in her body ached . . .

No, *no*. Kate Bishop wasn't a quitter.

Resigned to keeping herself awake, she planted her hands on the side of the chair and forced herself to her feet.

She'd also spent *way* too long at *way* too many archery ranges to simply give up. Grabbing her bow and arrow from where she'd left them by the door, she slung them over her shoulder as she left the apartment and made her way to the rooftop, Lucky by her side.

The night was warm, the glow of Manhattan bright in the distance. Somewhere, a police siren howled. The city screeched on.

She closed her eyes and took a deep breath.

"Okay, Katie," she told herself, grabbing a soda can and placing it on the lip of the roof. Then she walked to the far side of the building—about thirty feet—and turned to face her target. She breathed out, gentle, calm.

Drew an arrow from her quiver. Nocked it. Pulled it back flush with her cheek. Her aim was true—her aim was always true—and then—

An ice pick of pain stabbed against her temple.

It made her loosen her grip on her arrow. It swirled through the air and bounced off the lip of the roof, inches from the can.

She cursed, and nocked another one.

"It's all in your head," she muttered to herself, and drew the string back. The pain flared in her head again, but she squinted through it, her eyes tearing up, aiming for the soda can—

She fired the arrow.

It went wide.

She winced. Her vision doubled. She tried to shake it, but she couldn't. It hurt. It hurt so badly she had to remember to breathe. All the while, her vision narrowed.

And narrowed.

"Oh, rats," she muttered, her eyes rolling into the back of her head, and she dropped like a piece of lead to the ground, and was out.

CHAPTER EIGHTEEN

THE NIGHTMARE FANTASTIC

Tall, dark trees towered around her, so high she could barely see the moon through the boughs. The path in the park was barely lit, the shadows longer than she ever remembered. There was a soft summer breeze that shifted through the leaves above her, whispering quiet things. It was late summer, early fall, as everything began to turn orange and vibrant.

It didn't take very long for Kate to realize exactly where she was.

When she was.

A lone street lamp flickered a little ways down the path, a single bench in its light. Her throat constricted.

Not here, she thought. *Not here.*

She took a hesitant step back, and then another, reaching for her bow—

But it wasn't there. Neither were her staves. Or the dagger she kept tucked into her boot. She looked down at herself—and she wasn't even in her costume, but her pajamas. Of *course* she'd dream this night in her pajamas. She waited for the night to come into focus like it did in her memories—the sharp cry for *help*.

The one that wouldn't be answered.

Not by the group of teens walking on the other side of the lawn. Not the homeless person sleeping on the bench about fifty feet away. Not the cops patrolling Central Park at night.

Not anyone.

Except, of course, for the fourteen-year-old girl in a private-school uniform, dark hair pulled back in a ponytail, weaponless and helpless, running *toward* the voice.

Even though everyone told her she couldn't do anything. She was just one girl.

She didn't even have any super powers.

There was a social psychological theory called the Bystander Effect. It stated that individuals were less likely to offer help to a victim when there were other people present, but of course there was more to the story that prompted the creation of the term. The theory originated when a young woman was murdered in an alley and no one came to save her—but there were layers to it. The media sensationalized a lone woman in distress, when in actuality, very few people saw the entire attack play out. People *did* try to help her, but the victim and her friends were queer, so there was plenty of reason to doubt the police and their reports of the incident.

Even if the theory *did* hold water—if, in dire circumstances, the whole of humanity would turn their back on someone in need—then Kate was the embodiment of its antithesis.

Always had been, always would be. If there was someone screaming *Help*, she was running toward the voice, and she believed she wouldn't be the only one. She'd always be surrounded by a ragtag group of weirdos who stick up for each other and the people who couldn't stick up for themselves.

The strange thing was, she hadn't dreamed about this night in years. It wasn't that it didn't stick like gum in the back of her memories—this night was one of the reasons she'd taken up martial arts, why she ditched most of her high school extracurriculars to focus on archery, why she wanted to help people so much.

Because she believed, deep in her heart, that there would always be more people running toward the sound of a scream than away.

"You seem troubled, Kate Bishop."

Startled, she spun around. She wasn't sure who she was expecting, but it definitely wasn't herself. And especially not herself from this very night all those years ago. She looked soft and unsuspecting, someone who *would* run toward someone screaming for help and think that she could. Because life had never given her a reason to think otherwise.

But then the girl who was definitely not Kate tilted her head to one side, as if in a question, and a thin line formed on her cheek. It opened into an eye. Another just below it, two more on her neck, half a dozen opening on her arms and hands and chest, all peering at Kate expectantly.

"You're not real," she muttered, taking a step back.

"I'm a nightmare, Kate. I'm just what makes you afraid. But then . . . what does that say about you?" the girl who was not Kate asked, grinning too wide and delighted. *"If I am what you fear?"*

Kate closed her eyes. "This isn't real. This isn't real. This isn't real—"

"You can't ignore me, Kate."

"I can," she bit back quickly—before a shriek bit through the park. Loud, shrill, laced with fear.

Her heart slammed into her throat.

"Help me!" the voice cried. *"HELP!"*

And even though it wasn't real—she knew it wasn't real—

Kate Bishop did what Kate Bishop did best: She ran toward trouble.

Through the brambles and thicket, like she had all those years ago, the branches scratching at her legs, catching in her hair. She ran, and she ran, and she ran, thinking that maybe if she ran far enough she could somehow find the person who called for help in her dreams, that she could finally save them.

What happened if she died in this nightmare? She wouldn't die in real life—*would she*?

This hypnosis absolutely blew.

Zero out of ten stars.

She needed a new amygdala. One that wouldn't use her younger self to heckle her.

Pushing her way through the trees, she figured she should have come across a road by now. A sidewalk. *Something.*

There was a sound to her left. She pivoted toward it. Pushed the dark branches aside, knowing exactly what she'd find—

Instead, her foot sank into something soft. And stuck fast. She pinwheeled her arms so she didn't fall and stared down at the sticky tar-like substance that her foot was now ankle-deep in. Cursing, she tried to pry her legs out of it, but the more she moved the faster she sank. Her heart hammered in her ears, high and anxious.

"You always run toward the things you shouldn't, Kate," Not-Her said. It perched on a tree limb above her, swinging its legs back and forth happily. *"I should know."*

"Don't you have some *other* face to wear?" Kate snapped. "It's not very imaginative of you to wear mine."

Not-Her blinked in surprise. Then it grinned, and the face it wore shifted into a tall and broad-shouldered young man with brown skin and warm sandstone eyes. The face of Elijah Bradley—Patriot, one of the Young Avengers years ago, a teammate and a man she once loved. "How about this?" the nightmare said in his warm baritone.

Kate averted her gaze. "Going through my Rolodex of ex-boyfriends? How original."

Its face shifted again—this time to a man with white hair and green eyes. Noh-Varr. Marvel Boy. Great kisser, better fighter. *Way* more emotionally available than Kate ever was, and another relationship that was hard-won and quickly lost. Because Kate was good at a lot of things, but love? Relationships? Relying on others?

Not so much.

It was hard to save people, to be a hero, when your weakness was everyone you loved.

"Makes me want to punch you more, sure," Kate replied cattily. She was now up to her waist in the sludge, and there was nothing to help pull her out of her predicament. It reminded her again of the putty arrows she used—and that was because it *was*. "And save your effort on Fuse—he started dating Noh-Varr, anyway."

Not-Noh-Varr grinned. *"They all left you for greener pastures."*

"Actually, I think I left them."

Then the creature's face shifted again, to that of a tall and slightly gangly young man with floppy dark hair and electric green eyes. *"And what about him? How much do you really know about him?"* Not-Milo hissed, the grin splitting his face wide. *"How much do you want me to tell you?"*

"I doubt you know anything I don't already," she deadpanned, deciding to lock the memory of *that* kiss in a box under the dust of her mind, never to be brought out or examined ever again.

"You're suspicious of him. You don't want to admit it."

She glared at the creature. "I'm not."

"You are. You're smarter than this. Where is the next book? you wonder. Why do you wonder when you already know?"

She . . . did?

"And you keep pushing the people away who could actually help you," it went on in Milo's voice. *"Maybe you know you're useless. Maybe you know everyone who gets close to you is a step closer to getting hurt. Like your mother . . ."*

Kate gritted her teeth. "Shut up."

"You're useless!" Not-Milo crowed from the tree limb it perched on. *"Might as well stop now before you get anyone else hurt. You're just a girl with a bow but—oh!—you don't even have that now."*

"I do—"

"You don't and you know you don't. You're just too scared to prove it to yourself." The creature leaned closer to the pit of miasma that swallowed her whole, its neck stretching absurdly long to stare down at her. *"You'll get someone killed, Kate."*

"I won't—"

"You will."

From the miasma around her, things began to float up to the surface. No, not *things*—people. Her friends, dead-eyed and pale, staring up at the sky. Friends who were still there, friends she'd already lost, faces she knew like the back of her hand. Clint, eyes wide and unfocused, staring beyond her. America, so close she could touch her if only she could free her hand, if only she could reach out, if only—

She struggled. Gritted her teeth and squirmed.

And through sheer force of will, she freed her hand and grabbed her best friend by the arm as the pit began to tug her under again, but Kate refused to let go. *This is a nightmare*, she told herself. Repeated the words like a mantra. *This is a nightmare.* And even so, she didn't let go. She held on tightly as it dragged them both down, far deep into the sludge. It crawled into her nose and ears and filled her mouth until she couldn't breathe and couldn't hear and couldn't see anything at all. She didn't know if she was still holding on to America, but she wouldn't let go. Not for anything.

Not ever.

Her lungs felt like they were on fire. Her heart hammered in her chest so loud, she was afraid it'd fracture her sternum. She wanted to breathe. She needed to breathe. But she couldn't.

She couldn't do anything.

She couldn't even move.

And it hurt—

It all hurt—

CHAPTER NINETEEN

FOURTH WALL

Kate sucked in a lungful of air as she came to. Her hair was sticking to her neck with sweat. She exhaled, and then inhaled again, filling her lungs, and her head spun with fresh air. Had—had she *actually* stopped breathing? Her fingers and toes were numb.

She *had*.

Lucky whimpered beside her and pawed at her shoulder. There was a slobbery bite mark on her arm, quickly prickling in a bruise. Kate rubbed Lucky behind the ears in relief. "Did you wake me up? Thank you. You're a good boy."

In reply, Lucky licked her cheek, tail wagging.

As her heart began to calm down, she slowly remembered where she was—the rooftop of America's apartment building. The last she remembered, she'd been trying to hit a can on the lip of the rooftop, and when she looked over, it was still there, reflecting bright in the moonlight. Gleaming at her failure.

"Perfect," she muttered, and checked her watch. She'd only been asleep for *thirty minutes*? No wonder even with all the adrenaline she still felt tired. Her eyes burned with sleep, and there was a tender spot on her head where she knew she'd banged it pretty good on the ground. She pressed her palm against an eye and rubbed at it sleepily.

That nightmare had almost killed her. If she was this bad—how were the booksellers? This situation had to be solved, and *today*.

And she just might solve it, because if her hunch was right, her nightmare had also given her a clue. Her subconscious was trying to tell her everything she needed—

She already knew where the fifth book was.

And, really, that only meant one thing: She knew where it'd been all along.

"All right," she whispered to her dog, almost resigned. "Let's go pay my sister a visit."

So, she pushed herself to her feet and made her way down to America's apartment, where she splashed some water on her face, changed back into her costume, and grabbed the spare set of America's keys in the Talavera vase on the kitchen counter. Milo was still on the couch, muttering in his sleep, and America's door was still closed. The apartment was quiet, and as she tiptoed around she tried to skip all the floorboards that she knew creaked the loudest. Kate scrawled a note and left it next to the vase on her way out.

The sky was still dark, the streets almost empty save for the curious few who prowled the city at night. Her bones were jumpy, her skin itchy everywhere the eyes blinked. She still hadn't been able to shake her nightmare, even as she concentrated on breathing in and breathing out. The night air wasn't doing her any favors—and suddenly all she wanted to do, standing on the dark street corner in the middle of Washington Heights, was to hear a friend's voice. She couldn't get their faces out of her head every time she closed her eyes—drowning, eyes vacant, the nightmare screaming how she was useless, how she couldn't help anyone—

And while she *knew* that was untrue, it didn't make her feel any less alone.

So, she took her phone out, Lucky's leash wrapped around her wrist as he sniffed at a fire hydrant, and phoned a friend.

It rang once, twice, three times—and just when she debated hanging up and trying again in the morning, the groggy voice of Clint answered, "If you're in jail, I'm not bailing you out."

She snorted a laugh. Just hearing his voice made her feel grounded almost immediately. "Well, you're in luck, I'm not in jail." She sat down on the curb. A lone taxi coasted by.

"Good. I don't have bail money anyway. God, what time is it?" And she heard him roll over. He groaned. "Katie, it's almost three in the morning."

"I'm surprised you aren't out partying."

"Partying was last night. Tonight was Tums and *Bridgerton*."

"Are you sure you're not a seventy-year-old spinster?"

"The latest season is fantastic, thanks for asking," he added wryly. "What's up, Katie-Kat?"

She pursed her lips and picked at a fray in the left leg of her costume. "I heard a great joke. Thought you'd want to hear it."

There was a beat of silence. Clint knew she hadn't called to tell him a joke, but he didn't push for the real reason, either. "All right, shoot."

"Why couldn't the pepper practice archery?"

"Uhhh . . ."

"Because he didn't habanero."

Clint barked a sleepy laugh. "That was *bad*, Katie."

"Not as bad as the time Orion lost an archery match. You know what happened?"

"What?"

She bit the inside of her cheek, because this one was worse. "He was given a constellation prize."

He groaned. "Okay, that's quite enough. I'm going to sleep again. Is that all right?"

"Yeah," she replied, feeling a little more herself. "Thanks, Clint."

"I'm always here to listen to your bad jokes."

"They're *good* jokes!"

"Mm-hmm. Good night, Katie-Kat."

"Good night," she replied, and sat there for a little while longer after he'd hung up, and tilted her head back and looked at the stars between the buildings. "Okay, Kate, you've got this," she told herself, and planted her hands on her knees, then stood from the curb.

The subway station was empty, with the exception of an older woman huddled up on one of the benches sleeping. Kate fished out a twenty and slipped it into the woman's coat as the train downtown hissed into the station, and she hopped aboard with her dog. It was slow going; the middle of the night always felt like it lasted a lifetime.

By the time she and Lucky trudged out of the

underground, the pinkish-oranges of daylight had begun to feather across the eastern edges of the city.

She found herself over on Park Avenue again, in a moment of déjà vu, until she came to a building that she could probably navigate in her sleep. When her sleep wasn't trying to kill her. The sleepy doorman to the building in question recognized her with a start.

"Miss Bishop! It's been a while," he said in greeting. He was an older gentleman who had worked as the doorman to the building for longer than Kate had been alive.

"Morning to you, too," she replied warmly. "It's a bit early, isn't it?"

"Never too early for your lovely face."

"Charmer." She laughed.

"Do you want me to ring your sister?"

"Oh no." She put a finger up to her lips and gave him a wink. "I want to surprise her." Then she dipped into the elevator and pressed the floor for the Bishop penthouse. The elevator groaned as it ascended, and Lucky sat impatiently, watching the numbers. He nosed into her hand, and she petted him. "I know, I don't really want to see her, either."

Not that it mattered what she wanted. If her hunch was correct . . .

The elevator doors opened and she stepped out into the pristine entryway of her sister's home. She dumped her satchel on the round table in the middle of the foyer. "Suze, don't call the cops, it's just me," she called.

At which her sister stepped into the doorway to the rest of the apartment, a pinched look on her face, her hair still in rollers, clutching a pink silk robe tightly across her chest. "Lennard buzzed me. He said you wanted to *surprise* me? At—what is it—six in the morning?"

"Probably more like five thirty," she replied.

Susan wrinkled her nose and dropped her disapproving gaze to the dog. She and Kate looked a lot alike, from their black hair to their blue eyes, but everything else about them couldn't be more opposite. While Susan had been the good child, the perfect one, Kate had . . . been a little harder to handle. They didn't like any of the same foods, the same music, the same *books*— with the exception of one in particular. One that their mother used to read to both of them at night.

"I thought I told you no pets, Kate."

She gasped, slamming her hand against her chest. "Lucky isn't a pet! Lucky is my best friend! And crime-fighting partner." She finger-gunned the dog, who flopped onto the marbled floor to play dead. "See? We're perfect together."

Her sister rolled her eyes in disgust, turned, and left for the kitchen. Which meant she wasn't going to kick Kate out. That was a start, at least.

Kate muttered to Lucky, "Stay, okay? I'll be right back."

Lucky whined, but didn't move from his flop on the ground.

"Good boy," she said, promising him a snack later, and followed her sister into the kitchen. Susan's apartment reminded her a little of Gregory Maxwell's—just without all the white. It was pristine and minimalist. There wasn't a lot to look at, outside of the gray walls and expensive art pieces. There were no stains on the carpet, no dishes in the sink, no clothes strewn over the furniture—it was a model house, not a home. Made for someone who saw life as merely passing through. Since their mom died, Susan hadn't really attached herself to anything, and after her ugly divorce . . . well, Kate couldn't blame her. Her sister had been through more than enough heartbreak, but she also knew her sister kept the things that meant the most to her. She was sentimental that way, but only ever admitted it in private.

Her sister loved perfection. She loved order. She

loved Excel spreadsheets and lists, so having such an impersonal apartment made more than a little bit of sense. Susan wasn't one to nest in places—she liked to be able to pick up and leave, untethered to anything.

The bishop-shaped salt and pepper shakers, however, were a bit much, even for Kate.

Susan asked, "Coffee? Tea? Why are you up this early?" Then, giving her a once-over, she said, "You look terrible."

"Ha, thanks. Coffee, please. And actually, I'm working on a—"

"Don't say crime-fighting thing."

"A case. For a guy I met. He's the grandson of E. L. Albright, actually."

Susan started the expensive-looking coffee machine and gave Kate her full attention. "The author?"

"Yeah. He wrote the Immovable Castle series? And he's looking for this rare edition of his grandfather's novels, and I think—and I might be wrong—but didn't Mom collect editions of that series for us? I don't remember a lot about it because I was so young, but . . . you have her collection, don't you?"

Susan sighed. "I *texted* you about that. I already donated almost all of it," she added, and pulled a donation receipt out of one of the kitchen drawers. She showed the yellow paper to Kate.

A cold feeling curled in her gut. "*All* of them?"

"You didn't tell me not to."

"But this one is different. It's not like the other books—it's leather-bound? Has weird writing in it?"

Susan slid a cup of coffee over to Kate and thought for a moment. "I can't remember. . . ."

"*Suze.*"

She rolled her eyes. "I *was* going to save it for Christmas, but never mind, I guess!" She threw her arms up and left the kitchen for her study. "And don't touch anything!" she added.

Relief welled in Kate's chest. "It'll be the best early Christmas present ever!"

"Stop *lying.*"

Kate rolled her eyes.

After a few minutes, as Kate sipped her coffee, her sister came back with a familiar-looking book. Both relief and dread warred in her chest as she took it and opened to the front page.

And there it was, the third book in the series. *The Immovable Castle Alone.*

"Though," Susan said, leaning against the counter, "that wasn't the book our mom read out of. If you look, all the pages are filled with these weird markings."

So they were, as Kate opened and flipped through it. Like the other exclusive editions.

"Do you know where Mom found it?" Kate asked.

Her sister shrugged. "I think she found it at a used bookstore? You remember the one, on West Sixty-Ninth? Pity it closed a few years ago. Couldn't compete with some of the bigger chain stores."

She skimmed through the book. There were some sigils that were different from the rest—bolded and backward. It was very peculiar, now that she got a closer look at it. Milo had been telling the truth; other editions did have different sigils.

"You know," Susan went on, "I've only seen a book like that one other time—Gregory Maxwell had it. His wife threw a New Year's party a few years ago, though I never got to meet him personally. It's a pity, what happened to him."

That drew Kate's attention from the book. She closed it. "What do you mean?" she asked, trying to keep her cool. Had word gotten out already that someone had stolen it?

"It's been all over the news since late last night," Susan replied, reaching for her phone, which was charging on the counter. She unplugged it and pulled up a news article to show her. Kate leaned over and skimmed the article with growing horror. "He jumped off his penthouse balcony. *Thirty-three* stories in the air. I feel really terrible for the guy."

Kate quickly took her sister's phone and read the article again—and again—a part of her hoping the name, the article, would change. But they never did. Though it was the subheading that truly caught her eye. "His wife was found, too?"

"Yes, in her bed—strangled."

Her eyes widened. Lucky—Lucky had been acting odd in that apartment the whole time, and it was because he'd *smelled* a dead body. Kate pressed her hand over her mouth, trying to keep her stomach from turning on her. If she'd been a bit more in it, if she hadn't been so sleep-deprived, maybe she would've realized. Maybe she would've done a search of the apartment. Maybe Gregory's wife could have still been *alive* when Kate and Milo made that house call—

"It's quite tragic, is what it is. Authorities are saying he killed his wife and then jumped. She seemed like such a lovely woman. Though I hated what he did with his books . . ." she mused, and plucked her phone and put it back on the charger. "Now, I would love company but it's still almost six in the morning and— Kate? Kate, where are you going?" she asked as Kate slipped off the barstool with the book, and then on second thought, grabbed the receipt, too.

"Sorry, I just thought of something," Kate said absently, and returned to the foyer, where Lucky had not moved a muscle. She pulled her bag over her shoulder, putting the book inside, and pressed the down button to call the elevator again. "Thanks for the coffee."

"Well, if this isn't just like you to come in, get what you want, and leave!" Susan accused.

The elevator doors opened and Lucky scrambled to his feet on the slippery marble and darted inside. Kate slipped in after him and told her sister, "Don't think I won't be back—remember your party's this weekend, Suze."

Susan scowled. "*Please* don't tell me you're coming."

"Who else is going to deliver your birthday present?"

"A courier if you really love me."

"Ha. I'll see you on Saturday."

Kate waved as she stepped into the elevator, and her sister called after her, "At least leave that mutt at home when you come!"

The elevator doors closed, and Lucky looked up at Kate with big, weepy eyes. She patted him on the nose. "Don't listen to her, you're a full-blooded pizza dog."

That seemed to cheer him up a bit. She wished that worked on *her*, but her mind was buzzing from what Susan had told her—Gregory Maxwell was *dead*. Walked himself off his own balcony.

She thought about how tired and pale

Gregory had looked, and the deaths from Misty's original investigation—deaths of people who *also* had an Albright book.

On her way out, she nodded at the doorman and pulled out her phone, tapping the most recent number. It rang twice before someone picked up.

"Hi, Ms. Knight?" It was six a.m. by then, and the city was noisy with morning, so she hoped it wasn't too early to be calling.

"Miss Bishop," the detective said, sounding a bit groggy. "To what do I owe the pleasure?"

"Gregory Maxwell and his wife died last night."

"I heard. It was reported as a suicide/homicide."

"Will there be an autopsy?"

That surprised the detective. "I think? It's pretty standard procedure."

"Then do you think you could use that FBI badge of yours to speed it along?" She quickly darted across the street before the Walk signal changed, and turned to go down into the subway.

Misty said, "You think it's related to the Albright case?"

To which Kate replied, "I hope not, but I have a bad hunch it is. He had one of the Albright novels."

"Noted. And—Kate?"

"Yes?"

"I know I can't *dissuade* you from getting involved in this case but . . . be careful. I haven't seen anything like this mess in a long time."

"I'll be fine," she replied, a bit tongue-in-cheek because it was too late, and she lost reception as she headed into the bowels of the subway system, bound for one of the last stalwart holds of humanity—the New York Public Library.

Not the fancy one with the lions, but the close one—the one over on Fifty-Eighth Street. She wasn't going to walk all the way down to the fancy one. It probably didn't have what she needed, anyway—it was a tourist trap more than anything else.

No, what she needed was a computer with an IP address that didn't point directly to her, and a little luck. Because if her subconscious was right about one thing—it might be right about another, too.

CHAPTER TWENTY

CHAPTER BY CHAPTER

As it turned out, E. L. Albright was the kind of character who left a paper trail wherever he went.

Kate figured that out pretty early on in her research. She also figured out that the New York City Public Library had an actual *wealth* of Albright books, mostly because he had donated his entire collection to them some odd years ago. The collection had been displayed in a wing in the Stephen A. Schwarzman building for a while, but it had been long removed, packed up into boxes, and put into storage.

She situated herself at the corner computer in the far side of the library, Lucky snoozing under the desk. It was easy enough to sneak into the library—she'd done it a hundred times before, and the librarians *never* closed the rooftop exit, and the security system was so old, as long as she didn't go out the front door she was perfectly undetectable inside. She'd picked up an energy drink and a pack of licorice from the convenience store a few blocks away and snacked on them while she scrolled through pages and pages of information.

Milo had said that Albright had changed his name after leaving S.H.I.E.L.D., so she didn't even try to look up who he had been beforehand—she was sure that info had been purged from the web. She also suspected that Milo's last name wasn't *Albright*, either. (Or Smith, but she already knew that.) But using what she knew of his history—where Albright lived, among other things—she eventually scrolled through enough digitized newspapers until she found an article about the mysterious deaths of a husband and wife in a tragic fire in the Hudson Valley.

"Penderghast-Chant?" she muttered, tearing off a bite of red licorice.

The article stated that Savannah and Edward Penderghast-Chant had died in the fire and were survived by their son (unnamed, but Kate knew it had to be Milo), but there was no mention at all of Albright. But what was more peculiar, however, was the cause of the fire:

The Penderghast-Chants themselves.

Some theories surmised that they had some sort of

drug in their system when they set the fire, because neighbors had noted that they had been acting strange for a few days: frantic, jumpy. One of the neighbors was even quoted as saying, "[Mrs. Penderghast-Chant] was usually so lovely and pleasant, but she just looked so exhausted, like she hadn't slept in a week."

And that, really, was all Kate needed to know exactly what had happened. Or at least get into the ballpark of the truth.

Somehow, she was sure that Milo's parents had been subjected to the hypnosis, and that had caused their insanity. Had they sleepwalked into setting the fires? Or had they stayed up so long they had gone mad with the fear of going to sleep? Either way, it couldn't have been a coincidence.

Just as Gregory murdering his wife and taking a quick jaunt off his balcony wasn't a coincidence.

Her PI senses were tingling, so she picked up her phone and speed-dialed Clint Barton.

After four rings, his grumpy voice answered, "Katie, if you're about to tell me another joke—"

"Can you call in a favor for me?"

There was a pause. "For what?"

"I need some information on something."

"What *kind* of information?"

"The kind that maybe rhymes with Y.I.E.L.D.?"

Clint yawned. "That's a heavy ask, you know."

"That's why I'm calling you."

"Obviously." He sighed. "Let me ask around. Who do you need looked into?"

She scanned through the article again. "It's not a *who*, it's a *what*. So the story goes, a researcher for . . . *Y.I.E.L.D.* . . . defected in the eighties, took his research with him, and left. It was called Project Shiver."

She heard him taking notes, probably on a bedside notepad. "Mm-kay. Anything else to go on?"

"I don't know," she added, squinting at the digitized article that recounted the tragedy. "Something just isn't adding up."

"Okay, I'll see what I can do."

"Thanks, Clint—"

"And, Katie?"

"Yes?"

"How do you improve your archery?"

She froze. Did he know about her degeneration? Had someone told him? "I—um—well—"

"With better *arrow* dynamics."

"Oh my god, Clint." She wanted to melt into the carpet and die.

"Get it? Because you use an arrow? Aero? Eh, *eh*?"

"Bye, Clint," she said, and hung up. Lucky gave a

whine, and she looked at him and said, "Don't say a *word*."

The dog looked away, having not witnessed anything at all.

She deleted her search history and coaxed Lucky out from under the desk. He didn't want to move, but after she poked him a little more, he finally got to his feet, and they left the library together before it opened and anyone could tell her that there were no dogs allowed—not that it had ever stopped her before.

It was eight a.m. by the time Kate returned to the apartment, the third book in tow. She set it down on the coffee table, along with America's apartment keys, and decided to go take a shower. Milo was still asleep on the couch, his hair ruffled from tossing and turning on the lumpy cushions all night, but America's door was cracked open.

Lucky trotted into the bedroom and hopped onto the bed, curled around three times, and went to sleep right at her feet. Kate bet he was tired—goodness knows *she* was, still, though she hoped a gigantic pot of coffee would wake her up.

As she turned back toward the kitchen, she heard

America mumble, "Don't just stand there and then *walk away*, you creep."

Kate's mouth twitched into a grin, and she turned back around and slipped into her best friend's bedroom. America rolled over in bed, hugging her pillow to her chest. Her hair was pulled back into a curly bun, her mascara smudged around her eyes. "Sorry," Kate said. "I didn't think you were awake."

"'Course I am." America sighed and sat up, rubbing her eyes. "Thanks for the note, by the way. Did you find what you were looking for?"

"Susan had one of the books," Kate replied, and sat down on the edge of the bed. America's room was bright and cozy, nothing like Susan's distilled life. Most of the walls were covered in photographs, or posters, or some sort of memory America wanted to hold on to. There were a few photos of her with her moms, smiling brightly, and a few with her adopted family, the Santanas, too. It seemed like all of Kate's friends were drawn to other foundlings, people lost in the current, clumping together as like called to like.

Family wasn't always born, sometimes it was found.

Sometimes, in Kate's case, she was lucky enough that they had found *her*.

America gave her a critical look. "Did you sleep at *all*?"

"I couldn't," Kate admitted, tearing her eyes away from one of the photos of when they were younger—with some of the other Young Avengers at the time. That felt like centuries ago, though it had only been a few years. Some of those faces were still around, some weren't, and others would never come back. "Do I look as bad as I feel?"

"Worse," her best friend replied. "You know, if you want my help, all you have to do is ask."

"You've helped me plenty already."

"I know." America pulled the pillow closer to her chest, studying Kate's face. "But I get the feeling you're keeping something from me."

"Your interdimensional-super-power-senses tingling?" Kate joked.

"No, just the best-friend ones."

Kate opened her mouth, but then thought better of her reply and closed it again. She looked away, feeling more than a little guilty for not telling America that she, too, was hypnotized. She didn't want to worry her yet, and worse, what if America fell under the spell, too, somehow, the closer they got to an answer? There were still too many loose ends: Albright's murderer free, the missing last book, *Milo* . . .

Instead of forcing her hand, America climbed out of bed, grabbed Kate's hand, and dragged her out of the bedroom and into the kitchen. "C'mon, let's make you some coffee."

"You *can* go back to sleep."

"I can't, actually. I have a coffee date in an hour."

Kate's eyes widened. "With the girl from yesterday?" Then she wiggled her eyebrow, and America rolled her eyes and shoved her away, then took out a bag of coffee.

"*Stop.*"

"It's exciting!"

They spoke in whispers so they wouldn't wake up Milo, who had taken the blanket from the back of the couch and wrapped it around himself in a burrito-like fashion. America started the coffeepot and rooted in the refrigerator for some leftover Thai from the night before last.

"Yours is still in there, too," she added, and Kate gratefully dug out her cold order of pad thai and grabbed a fork from the silverware drawer. They leaned against the counter and ate cold noodles as the coffee brewed. America said, picking out a bean sprout, "This kind of reminds me of our time in the Young Avengers. Sleepless mornings eating cold takeout."

Kate swirled the noodles around on her fork. "Everything felt simpler back then."

"If I ever see Loki again," America deadpanned, "it's still fight on sight." She took two coffee cups from the cupboard and set them down on the counter. "I need to get ready," she added. "Creamer's in the refrigerator." She closed her takeout, poured herself a cup, and licked her fingers as she retreated back to her bedroom.

Kate ate a few more mouthfuls of pad thai before she put their takeout back into the refrigerator and poured herself a cup of coffee.

On the couch, Milo turned over, muttering in his sleep.

What was he dreaming about? She hoped it was nice. She missed nice dreams. She missed dreaming at *all*. She'd trade her left kidney for a dream.

As she thought about dreaming, she overfilled her coffee cup and cursed the moment the hot liquid flowed over the counter.

"Aw, coffee, no," she mumbled, licked the spilled coffee off her hand, and cleaned the rest up with a paper towel. Then she took her coffee mug and left for America's bedroom again.

"So, where're you going for your hot date?" she asked.

America shrugged on her jean jacket, sewn-up

with homemade patches, and gave one last look in the mirror. "A cute new coffee shop with cats—she's a cat person, apparently."

"Oh, how *purr*-fect." Kate lounged back on the bed. "What's her name? Social Security number? Does she have a 401(k)?" She mock-gasped, pushing herself to sit up again. *"Health insurance?"*

"Stop it, it's just a date."

"We have to look to the future!"

"Not *that* far. She's nice, though." Then America gave her a pointed look. "How's you and Milo?"

She feigned innocence and sipped her coffee. "I don't know what you're talking about."

"Shut up, I saw you last night tongue-deep in my *living room*."

"Ugh, I was, wasn't I?" She scrunched her nose. "I make bad life decisions."

"I'm not saying *that*," America replied, and pulled her hair up into a high bun. "Does he kiss well at least?"

"Sadly, yes."

"Sadly?"

Kate sighed. "Yes."

"Why?"

She sank down on the edge of the bed and took another gulp of coffee. How come the caffeine wasn't even touching her tiredness yet? It felt wrong. "I shall never kiss him again. Work romances never work out." Then, a little quieter, "I think he's been lying to me, America."

That got her best friend's attention fully. She turned away from the mirror, narrowing her eyes at Kate. *"Lying?"*

Kate debated how much to say, because most of it was just suspicion, and she didn't like to accuse people before she knew the facts—call it her private-eye-senses. "Omitting some truths, I think. Nothing nefarious, at least not yet."

"Do you think he has ulterior motives for collecting these books, aside from what he's told us?"

"It *has* crossed my mind. . . ."

"Mm-hmm, and here's my question—and then I have to leave," she added, glancing at her watch. It was in the shape of a star, much like the marks on the outsides of her wrists. "Why would his grandfather go through all this trouble if the best person to trust with his secret was his grandson? Why hide it from even him?"

And America left her with that thought as she slammed her foot into the ground, dropped down into it, and was gone.

"Dramatic much?" Kate muttered, pushing herself up to her feet. She drained the rest of her cup and went back for seconds, decided to grab the entire pot, and took it to her chair in the living room to wait for Milo to wake up.

By the time she had finished her pot of coffee and changed into her clothes from two days ago—her purple T-shirt dress and bike shorts—Milo had finally woken up. The first thing he'd noticed was Susan's book on the counter. He'd taken it and sat back down on the couch, flipping through the pages. His hair stuck up in every direction, the curls gnarled from tossing and turning all night.

"Don't you know not to look through someone else's stuff?" she asked.

He gave her a look of disbelief. "How did you find it?"

"My mom collected editions of children's books my sister and I liked. I didn't realize she'd collected this, too, until last night," she said, motioning to the book. "It's the one your grandfather sold—my mom found it at a used bookstore. So, now that we have three, and we know Kingpin has two . . . we only have one left to find."

"The last book, ironically."

"Right, and since we have absolutely no idea where

to look for that one, let's concentrate on the other two." Then she took a deep breath and turned to Milo. "I have an idea about how we can get Kingpin's books."

He looked like he didn't believe her. "How . . . ?"

She wiggled her fingers in the air. "A little bit of Hawkeye magic. There's two of us, but which one is real?"

"Aren't you both the real Hawkeye?"

She smiled.

CHAPTER TWENTY-ONE

THE SMARTEST GUY
IN THE ROOM

Kate marched into Fisk Towers that afternoon and dumped a duffel bag down on the counter of the security desk. She flipped down her Aviator sunglasses and said, "Tell Kingpin I've got an offer he can't refuse."

The woman behind the desk didn't look all that amused at her Godfather impersonation. Huh, *she* thought it was spot-on. "And who are you?"

"Erm—" She faltered. *Seriously?* "I'm Kate? Kate Bishop?"

The woman didn't seem moved in the least. She blinked. "Do you have a meeting with Mr. Fisk?"

Kate opened her mouth. Closed it again. Frowned. "Do I . . . do I *need* one? I'm Kate Bishop," she repeated, and then quieter, "You know—*Hawkeye?* The better one?"

The woman gave her a disapproving look before she scooted away from the main computer and picked up a corded phone on the far end of the desk. A few moments later, she scooted her rolling chair back and pressed a button under her desk. "Mr. Fisk will see you on the thirteenth floor. Take the service elevator," she added, pointing to the right, toward a back area of the building, instead of the gilded chrome elevators on the left.

Kate hefted the bag onto her shoulder and went the way she was told. "Remind me to schedule a *meeting* next time," she muttered to herself, but her earpiece picked it up.

Milo said through it, "It sort of makes sense. Mob bosses have a lot to do in a day."

"Noted for when I take down the Hobgoblin," she replied. "How are you faring?"

"Good? Okay? I feel like an imposter in this security uniform," he added with a grump. "Are you sure this plan is going to work?"

"No, but it's worth a shot."

The plan itself was relatively simple: go to Kingpin and pretend to want to hand over the books in exchange for Susan's birthday gift. Which—*for the record*—Kate never found in her bag, so her only theory was that Kingpin still had it. Now she *really* wanted that birthday gift, especially since she owed her sister for the collector's edition of Albright's book, and she'd rather not deteriorate their relationship any further.

Besides, she'd spent *months* trying to find the perfect gift. She wasn't going to let a mob boss ruin that.

Meanwhile, Milo would infiltrate the building as one of Kingpin's security guards—which was embarrassingly easy to do (just knock out one of the guys on his lunch break; no one knew the difference)—and when she handed off the real books, he'd follow to where Kingpin kept his collection and swap them for some fake ones they'd made out of paper crafts and glue on America's kitchen table, which looked pretty solid from a distance, and they'd be home-free.

The service elevator was slow to come down. She rocked back and forth on her heels. Worse came to worst, she could sneak out of a thirteen-story building and *probably* land a grappling arrow on the rooftop across the street. There was a fifty-fifty chance at this point.

Suddenly something in the bag began to vibrate. Her phone? Who could be calling her *now*? She dug for it as the service elevator arrived, and she stepped inside. It was Clint.

"You have my info?" she answered in greeting, removing the earpiece so Milo couldn't overhear.

"Yeah—this Albright guy? His real name was Albert Savant, and . . . Katie?" Clint's voice was high and tight, and it set her on edge immediately. "Guy was a *nutjob*, thought he could control people through his made-up language. They laughed him out of S.H.I.E.L.D. Some fifteen years later, he called them saying that they'd better come see his masterpiece. Turns out, he had used that language of his on his own—"

"Son and his son's wife," Kate guessed, recalling the article she'd read at the library. The elevator ticked up slowly to the thirteenth floor.

But to her surprise, Clint said, "No, Katie. It's worse. He used it on his own *grandson*."

She thought she heard incorrectly. "Excuse me?"

"Milo something-Chant. I have the note here somewhere—"

"Penderghast-Chant."

"That's it! It should have killed the kid, but it *didn't*. S.H.I.E.L.D. heard that he'd started experimenting on this kid, teaching him about all the different Shiver research, so they tried to plan a rescue, but it went *horribly* wrong. Most of this stuff's redacted. I can't access it, but it's well documented that the parents set fire to the house themselves on purpose. The S.H.I.E.L.D. agents arrived with enough time to save the grandson, but not the parents. From the agents' testimonies, they had to—they had to *cut their son* out of their arms; they'd all been tied together with rope. It was horrific, every account I could find, *horrific*."

The elevator beeped on the thirteenth floor.

Oh, she'd screwed up. She'd screwed up *so* bad.

"The next day, the kid was sent to a school up in Maine for monitoring and he never had contact with his grandfather again—Kate? I think you should leave this to someone else. I've got a really bad feeling. At least wait until I'm back in town tomorrow—"

"Sorry, I gotta go," she said, and quickly hung up.

The doors opened as she dropped her phone into her costume. She pushed her rising panic down as she stepped out of the elevator onto a familiar hallway.

A tall cowboy stood there to meet her. He looked a bit worse for wear, his right arm in a cast and his left eye purpled.

She winced when she saw him. "Oof, Monty, my guy, I take it you landed in the Hudson wrong?"

He definitely wasn't amused. "Bishop," he rumbled, then turned on his heels and led her down to the same room where she'd found Milo in the first place.

She was beginning to feel like she'd been played.

Because standing on the right side of Kingpin was none other than Milo Penderghast-Chant, looking every bit as comfortable there as any other henchmen in this place. He gave her an unreadable look as she walked in.

Kingpin wore a different creamy-white suit today, a red kerchief tucked into his pocket. The chess game had moved ever so slightly, one of the bishops having checked the king. But it was a move the king could easily get out of.

Kingpin grinned, propping his elbows up on the mahogany desk, lacing his fingers together. "So, Katie. It's nice to see you again. Milo tells me that you two have been quite busy."

She glared at Milo. "Does he, now."

Montana grabbed Kate by the shoulder and forced her into a chair. Had Milo been with them since the beginning? Had the entire thing been a ruse? No, Milo must have gone to him again before the auction and made a deal, or perhaps while she'd been at the library this morning? Those were the only times they had been apart for any length of time in the last few days.

"Ooh, you look positively *betrayed*. Do you really think I wouldn't have Albright's grandson on my payroll?" Kingpin tsked. "Kids. Always thinking one step behind."

"I'm just here for my sister's gift," she forced out, because she didn't know what else to do other than stick to her plan. Which now, really, wasn't so much a plan as a last will. Maybe she could stay awake long enough to give the gift to Susan before her nightmares killed her.

"Ah, this?" Kingpin pulled open a drawer in his desk and extracted a small box. He put it between them on the desk. "I thought it was peculiar, so I kept it."

"It's rude of you to keep someone else's gift."

"For your sister? Susan? It says so on the tag," he added when she pursed her lips. "I wonder if your dad will be there. . . ."

"I doubt it. If you have issues with him, go to the West Coast and deal with them yourself."

Fisk threw his head back and laughed. He was in an infuriatingly good mood—she guessed anyone would be when they realized their plan had gone off without a hitch. "All you Bishops are pointed barbs. It's amusing. Montana, can you relieve Miss Bishop of her bag?" he added, waving to his henchman.

Montana begrudgingly did so with his one good hand and brought it over to his boss, who took it with greedy fingers and unzipped it.

He took out the three books. One of them had a painted-white spine. "Gregory Maxwell," he said, scowling. "Good riddance to that fool."

Kate bit the inside of her cheek, keeping herself

from saying anything that she would regret—which was about to be a hell of a lot. She watched Kingpin inspect every book, as if he thought that Kate would somehow dupe him. No, she wasn't the double-crosser. When he flipped through the last book, he pushed Kate's birthday present toward her.

"There you go, Katie. Job well done."

She reached for the gift and took it.

"I take it this didn't go as you planned?" Fisk asked.

"No, actually, it didn't. Milo was supposed to double-cross *you*, not me. Turns out I was the fool. Isn't that right, Mr. Penderghast-Chant?"

At his real name, a flash of alarm flickered across Milo's face—before he quickly schooled it. "It was only business, Kate."

"Always is." Then she stood.

Montana made a move to shove her back down, but Kingpin stopped him. "Let her go. Her pride's damaged enough."

"Besides," Kate added, "I'm sure your guy casing my apartment'll keep tabs on me, anyway."

To that, Kingpin smirked.

As she took her sister's gift and left, thinking about how she could have been such a fool, out of the corner of her eye she saw Milo turn to Kingpin, take off his right glove, and stick it out for Kingpin to shake.

"Thank you for your cooperation," Milo said to him. It was the exact same move she'd seen him do with Gregory Maxwell.

And she saw it then—the strange marks on his scarred palm. Ones that looked a little too familiar to her, duplicated almost exactly at the bottom of the letter that had been found with Albright in the bookstore.

Kingpin glanced down at the hand a moment before he shook it—

That was how Milo did it.

Montana grabbed her by her arm and pulled her out of the office down the hallway. In her earpiece she heard Milo, one last time, "Don't think that ill of me, Kate. I'm still on your side."

Yeah, well, it certainly didn't seem that way.

The cowboy shoved her into the service elevator, slammed the button for the first floor, and tipped his hat to her as the doors closed. She rode it down alone.

Transcript (cont'd)

[Katherine Elizabeth Bishop's Statement Regarding the Events at the New York Public Library Stephen A. Schwarzman Building on August 2] Recorded by Misty Knight

KNIGHT: You must be joking. You just gave him the books and left? But then how did—?

BISHOP: Give me a little more credit, would you? While Milo was off supposedly infiltrating Fisk Towers—which I guess now he and Kingpin were in, just sitting around laughing? Whatever, I got the last laugh—I was down at the Fedex store making friends with the employees who helped me scan all the books.

KNIGHT: You made copies of priceless pieces of psychological warfare?

BISHOP: I wasn't going to *use* them—what do you take me for? They're all destroyed now anyway. Tossed into some fire-and-brimstone dimension. I'm not *that* reckless.

KNIGHT: Oh? You could've fooled me.

CHAPTER TWENTY-TWO

BEST FRIEND MATERIAL

America massaged the bridge of her nose. "I told you not to trust him."

Kate sighed. "I know. I just want to expect the best of people."

"Which is one of the things I love most about you," her best friend replied. They sat across from each other in a crowded coffee shop in Midtown, well away from Fisk Towers. Kate had been humiliated plenty of times before, but none of those experiences really pissed her off quite like this one.

"He played me for a fool the entire time." She sighed.

Tourists lingered around the café, in shorts and I ♥ NY T-shirts, talking about celebrity sightings and the latest opening on Broadway, a musical rendition of the X-rated life of Deadpool as told through a Shakespearean lens. Apparently, it'd been a Tony favorite this year. The coffee shop was as good a place as any to hide after she left Fisk Towers. Her first thought had been to go back to her apartment to figure out what her next move should be, but then she did the one thing she should've done from the beginning: She called America, who showed up at the café not five minutes later, and Kate updated her on everything that happened—including what Clint had called her about.

"He was probably working for Kingpin when I met up with him at the auction, too." Kate sighed. "I swear, someday I'll have a better 'this guy is bad for me' meter, but that day is *not* today."

That, at least, America agreed with. She swiped through her tablet, looking at the scanned images of the books. "At least you thought ahead enough to scan these. You can let Misty handle it from here, right? And get some sleep yourself. Did you even *go* to sleep last night?"

Kate shifted uncomfortably. "For about thirty minutes. On the roof. By accident."

"*Kate—*"

"I can't sleep."

"You need to try."

She took a deep breath. "No, I mean . . . I *can't*."

And then, because she was all out of options and she was getting really and truly scared, she told America about the letter near Albright's body, and how she'd been infected with the spell since then. With each new revelation, her best friend just got angrier and angrier—until the ceramic cup she held cracked in her grip.

"So you're telling me that this entire time you've been *hypnotized*? And that caused the nightmare? And that if you sleep again you might *die*?"

Kate nodded. "That about sums it up, yeah."

America looked like she was about to yell at her, but then she simply shoved herself to her feet, took her cracked mug to the counter to pay for it, and brought a second cup of coffee back with her. "I told them to put as many shots of espresso in there as humanly possible. If you smell colors, that means it's working. We're going to keep you awake until we can find a cure. I'm not going to have you dying on me today."

Kate could almost cry. "I'm sorry I didn't tell you sooner."

America sat down again. "Why *didn't* you?"

"Because . . . I didn't realize how bad it was at first, I think? And then I just didn't want you to get too involved, because I didn't want the same thing to happen to you." She set her mouth into a thin line. "It's not just the nightmares. I see these—these *eyes* on my skin. They keep multiplying. I think it's some sort of subconscious timer for how long I have."

"And how long *do* you have?"

"One leg equivalent of time left?" she guessed.

"Seriously, Kate. . . ."

"I know, but that's not quite the worst part."

"There's something *else*?" America asked louder, and other people in the coffee shop turned to stare. She took in a deep breath, and said a bit quieter, more controlled, "What is it?"

"While I'm fighting I get—I get *scared*. And it feels like my head is about to explode. My heart slams in my chest and it's so, so hard to concentrate."

"And you went to that auction *alone*?" America's hands curled into fists. "I *knew* I should've called bull-crap on you earlier."

"I didn't know it'd be that bad," Kate replied truthfully. "So I guess fighting for me is off the menu until, you know, we can figure out a cure."

"Or else you'll . . ."

They were quiet for a long moment.

Then Kate smiled in that *worry-not* way of hers and waved off her own internal worry with a flap of her hand. "Die in my sleep? *Please.* I've weaseled my way out of worse."

Her friend didn't seem so sure as she looked back at the pages on the tablet and swiped through a few more. "I wish you had told me sooner. I feel awful having gone on dates while you—were *dying*?"

"I wasn't *dying*—"

"You know what I mean."

Kate winced. "I mean . . . you know now, at least?"

Her friend gave her an exhausted look. "Okay. So, we have to figure out how to save you, then. We know where all the physical books are except one, and with the copies you made, all we need is that last one, right?"

"Yeah."

"And no one knows where it is?"

She shook her head. "No, not even Milo."

"That'll give us some time, at least." America scrunched her nose, finally turned off the tablet, and handed it back to her. "If only we knew someone who was really, *really* into this Immovable Castle stuff. . . ."

"Yeah. . . ." Kate slumped down in her chair. In the far corner of the café, a family of five were arguing a little too loudly about whether or not to go to Central Park or pay for a tour of the Empire State Building. One was *free*, after all, but the other one was air-conditioned—and suddenly that gave Kate an idea. She sat up straight in her chair. "What time is it?"

Startled, America checked her watch. "Two thirty . . . ?"

"Good! They're still at the park, until three," she said, said, downing her coffee as she stood. "We gotta hurry, though."

"I know that look. You have an idea."

"And I'm taking your advice—we're going to ask some people for help."

The help in question were playing the last level of *Spider-Man: Dark Turn*, and Kate didn't know it had a *musical* number in it. Really, they put everything in video games these days. She wondered, briefly, what her video game would look like. Sitting around on couches, staring off into the ceiling, battling existential dread while waiting for someone to show up at her PI firm?

. . . Mostly.

Ms. Marvel was surprised to see Kate, and absolutely over the *moon* to see America. "Oh my god! America Chavez! It's *so* great to see you."

While the summer camp technically lasted until three, it was pretty clear that Ms. Marvel had given in to the kids and they all sat in the shade of a few trees on the outskirts of the field used for the camp hunkering over a portable gaming system. Ping-Pong had officially been abandoned at the tennis court.

America gave Ms. Marvel a high five. "Nice to see you, too. Working hard I see."

Ms. Marvel waved her hand at the kids. "It's the end of the day, and Martin accidentally hit Evelyn on the forehead with a Ping-Pong ball, so we decided to call it quits."

At the sound of her name, Evelyn looked up from the kid-huddle around the gaming screen. She had an angry red welt right in the middle of her forehead. She gasped when she saw America. "*Oh!* Another super hero!"

To which everyone else quickly looked up from the screen, too, and Rajiv paused the game. Kate introduced them all, and then told the kids, "I'm actually here because I think I need your help again."

Murella was on her third Percy Jackson book already, and bookmarked it quickly. "Did you find the auction?"

"I did, and it was such a big help. We were wondering if you could do it again?" Kate asked, and took out her tablet from her bag. "Long story short, I'd collected *three* of the books, but then a mobster stole them, though I managed to scan all of the pages before he did."

Martin asked, frowning, "Isn't that illegal?"

"Not when someone's trying to destroy the world," she replied gravely. "Now—I'm going to show you this on one condition: You tell me everything you see and know about it, okay? Things out of the ordinary, things that don't make sense—all of it."

The kids all exchanged the same hesitant look.

Ms. Marvel bounced on her heels. "This isn't dangerous, is it?" she muttered so only she and America could hear.

"Yeah," America added. "What if what happened to you . . ."

Kate shook her head. "I don't think it's that simple. If it was, then Albright would've hypnotized himself creating the book. And besides, none of these Unwords look exactly like the sigils I saw on the letter."

Ms. Marvel frowned. "Sigils . . . ?"

America looped her arm around Ms. Marvel's shoulder and led her away to explain as Kate offered the tablet to the kids.

"I know it sounds scary, but I really need your help. Why are you all giving me that look?" she added, because the kids looked . . . *excited*? No, that couldn't be right. This was dangerous. Scary even.

Murella took the tablet from Kate quickly and flipped through the scans. "The secret messages were *right*," she said to her friends, then turned away from Kate.

Kate didn't quite follow. "Secret messages . . . ?"

Rajiv said, "At the top of each book page, there's a message written in Unword. But the only way to translate it is context clues from the actual books, because Mr. Albright never ever gave us a *key*." No, because the key was in the rare one-of-a-kind books, Kate supposed. "So, we had to guess a lot of it, but if these books are a one-for-one, it should be simple! With the exception of the last book," he added, a glimmer in his eyes.

Irving nodded, leaning against the back of Rajiv's chair. "The last book was different. It doesn't have Unword written at the top, only a repeating text backward that reads, 'Hold a dream to a mirror to twist it around, and be wary of the nightmares that you found.' We always supposed it talked about the Blight and the eyes."

Evelyn nodded in agreement. "The Wizard managed to cure the Blight by confronting his mirror-self, the person he always wanted to be."

"But Maisey helped him realize that he was perfect the way he was," Rajiv pointed out.

Murella turned back around with the tablet, her eyebrows furrowed in vexation. She called everyone back around to her. "Rajiv is right, it *is* almost a perfect replica, except for these characters." She pointed to the ones that Kate had noticed earlier—the sigils that looked a little off, not quite the same family as the language around it. "They look different." Murella kept pointing them out as she flipped through the scanned pages. They were speckled across the manuscript almost randomly—

Kate shot her hand out suddenly, stopping the girl from swiping again. Her fingers began to shake.

She recognized one of the characters, but looking at it didn't *feel* like it had before. The character was also the wrong way—inverted.

Mirrored.

She asked Irving, "What did the sixth book's secret message say again?"

All of the kids replied, automatically, " 'Hold a dream to a mirror to twist it around, and be wary of the nightmares that you found.' "

"That's it," Kate muttered, and took the tablet back. She quickly flipped through the other pages, searching for another familiar character. There were a lot of strange ones, sporadically placed between the Unwords, so if she didn't know *what* to look for, the pages would all look like lines and lines of squiggles and strange characters. Albright put the entire hypnosis alphabet into these books, and she couldn't imagine what sort of disaster Project Shiver would have been if S.H.I.E.L.D. hadn't shut it down when it did. An entire alphabet to hypnotize people into doing anything the user wanted—it was downright terrifying.

On the second-to-last page, she found the second sigil she was looking for.

But not the third.

There had been three in the letter on Albright's body. Three characters that hypnotized her. The third one must have been in either the first book or the sixth—two of the books she *didn't* have. If she found it, and then wrote it down, and reversed it in the mirror— would that cure her?

In curiosity, she asked, "How do spells work in the Immovable Castle series?"

Ms. Marvel answered that one, coming back to the group after America had updated her on the issue. She looked worried for Kate now, her hands wringing together. "It's written spellcasting, so like, if you write it, it does one thing . . . and if you write it backward, it does another."

Backward. "So, if I held it up to a mirror . . ."

Ms. Marvel cocked her head. "Yeah, I think that happens in the third book, and it works."

Hope bloomed in her chest. *No way.* She knew how to save herself now—she could almost cry. In fact, she was so tired she might just cry anyway. "You guys are the best!" she said, and gathered into a tight hug all the kids who would let her—and even the ones who wouldn't. "I'll do something cool for you all—I promise!" she added, hugging Ms. Marvel, too. "Seriously, *my hero*."

Ms. Marvel hesitated. "Uh, you're welcome . . . ?"

"My hero—my *hero*!"

They said their goodbyes, and Kate quickly started toward the Upper East Side, America jogging to catch up. The sun was hot in the afternoon, hammering down on them like death rays, and it made the bags under Kate's eyes all the heavier on her way toward Fifth Avenue.

America looked worried for Kate. "Wanna update me on the plan, or . . . ?"

"I know somewhere we haven't looked yet."

That was news to America. "Where?"

"E. L. Albright's house—and thanks to a little early-morning research, I know exactly where it is."

America fell into step beside her. "All right. I'm coming with you."

Kate grinned at her. Under her costume, she could feel the eyes vibrating with excitement. "I doubt you'd let me go alone."

"You're my best friend," America said, slinging her arm around her neck. "We're ride-or-die."

"Even after I lied to you?"

"It'll take a bit to earn that trust back," America admitted, "but I don't think that's a conversation for *now*. Right now? We're going to kick some butt and be home before Lucky pees all over my apartment."

"I'm sure he hasn't even moved from your bed," Kate replied adamantly, pressing the crosswalk button to get to the other side of Fifth Avenue. "I doubt he even knows we're gone."

Meanwhile, in America's apartment in Washington Heights, Lucky the One-Eyed Pizza Dog, goodest dog in the entire world, was lying in a sunbeam in the living room, paws up, tongue out, having gotten into at least three chip bags that had been left on the counter, and one shoe.

He was enjoying his well-earned rest exactly how the goodest dog in the world should: naughtily.

CHAPTER TWENTY-THREE

THE HOUSE OF MANY WAYS

Albright's house stood like a looming brick castle on the corner of Eighty-Seventh and East End Avenue. It was in a small hug of residential houses that all looked equally grandiose, surrounded by brick walls topped with wrought-iron spikes, luxuriously old trees growing from courtyard gardens. Albright's house, however, was easy enough to pick out from all the flowers, letters from fans, teddy bears, and fan art on the front stoop. It was heartbreaking, a little, the way it always is when a person who has been such a pivotal part of someone's childhood dies.

It was also a little heartbreaking when that person turned out to be scum of the earth and his grandson turned out to be a villain in league with Kingpin, who could kiss far better than he should have, plot-wise, been allowed to.

"You sound like you're bitter," America commented as they rounded the outside of the house. Kate had been ranting ever since they'd come up out of the subway, venting her frustrations as she scrubbed at her arms. The eyes had been moving—twitching and roving—and she *hated* the feeling so much she wanted to peel the skin off her bones.

Albright's house was a gorgeous red-brick building with latticework in the eaves and beautiful bay windows with black detailing and shutters. It looked almost like a place you would find in the Immovable Castle series.

"I'm not bitter," Kate replied, very bitterly, resisting the urge to scratch her arms.

America gave her a look.

She rolled her eyes. "Okay, maybe I'm a *little* bitter."

"I keep telling you to keep your work and romance lives separate," America said, earning a playful shove from Kate.

"Shush, don't kiss-shame me."

"I'll kiss-shame you all I want if this Milo guy ends up having a villain name for himself. Like Doctor Penderghast or Shiver Boy or something."

Kate opened her mouth. Closed it again. Frowned. She said, "Okay, I might deserve it if he does." She glanced across the rooftop edges of the building as they rounded toward the side of it. "I'm sure there are security cameras around."

America muttered, "This has 'Two Former Young Avengers Trespassing on Private Property, News at Eleven' written all over it."

"At least you don't have bags under your eyes the size of Texas for the mug shot," Kate replied, massaging those exact bags.

"And you look beautiful even with them."

"Thank you for lying to me."

"What are friends for?"

Around the side, there were two more cameras pointed into the walled-off garden. Kate gave it a thought before she scooped her bow from over her shoulder and drew an arrow—no, make it two—from the quiver at her back. She nudged her chin toward the brick wall. "Can you hoist me over that?"

In reply, America laced her hands together, turned her back toward the wall, and squatted down. "Ready when you are, Hawkeye."

"Thank you, America." Kate backed up to the curb and then took a running start, planting her foot in America's hand. America hoisted her up over the wall and she spun backward in a flip, nocking her arrows. A slice of pain cut through her skull—she'd forgotten about it for a second—before she released both arrows. They swirled toward the security cameras on the eaves. She had anticipated her aim to be off, but not so off that the arrows embedded into the roof and sent twenty-one thousand volts across the rooftop and into the cameras. They sparked—and then the entire electrical system in the house went out.

Kate landed with a stumble and caught herself on the side of a dogwood tree.

"Wow, your aim is *really* off," America commented behind her.

Kate gave a start and spun around, confused. "How did you get in here so fast?"

America thumbed back to the star-shaped portal quickly closing behind her.

Kate frowned. "Huh."

"I could just portal us into the house."

"You could," she replied, "but I don't know what to expect in there. I'd rather approach it slowly than just—you know—drop into the middle of it all."

"You have a point."

"Sometimes. We might have twenty minutes," Kate added, looking at her watch.

"If the security system's lax, sure. But they'll probably check with the electrical company first. That's at *least* ten minutes on hold."

"Fair. Let's go quickly anyway?"

"Sounds good."

The garden was very green, full of flowers and the buzzing of insects. A fountain with a dejected-looking man atop it spewed water down across his very naked body and into the penny-laden basin at the bottom. Kate made a note of everything in the garden—the way it smelled, the way it felt too quiet, even as the city roared with cars and people and life, a pocket world unto itself.

"For the record," America murmured close to her ear, "I do *not* like this."

"For the record, neither do I," Kate replied. They started toward the door into the house. The gravel crunched under their feet. She nervously adjusted the string of her bow across her chest.

"Are you sure we'll find it here?" America asked, following her.

"Mostly sure. And if not here, then probably a clue as to where it is."

"Do you think Milo thought of this, too?"

Kate gave a tragic nod. "Most certainly."

Even in the evening light, the garden was well lit by lanterns posted at intervals, illuminating the soft pastels of the flowers, the bushes trimmed into stately squares. The gravel path led to the back entrance of the house and a pair of intricately carved oaken doors. It was hard to imagine the kind of wealth Albright had—the book series was *popular* but not *that* popular. She wondered what he'd done on the side, or was some of this wealth from his late son and daughter-in-law's life insurance? No, this stank of dark money. The kind that was old, and bloodied.

Kate reached out, took hold of the handle, and prayed it was locked—if it was locked then Milo was probably not here. But if it wasn't—

There was an eye on the backside of her hand. It swirled its red pupil toward her and grinned—she could *feel* it grin, the way the corner of the eye crinkled.

She shrieked and let go of the handle.

America quickly stepped forward. "What? What is it?"

"Eye," Kate replied tightly. She tugged her jacket lower over her hand, to her knuckle. "A new eye. It's fine—it just . . . It startled me." She didn't have much more time, so she grasped the door handle again and twisted it open.

The door opened easily.

She and America exchanged the same knowing look, and America pushed her jacket sleeves up to her elbows.

They went inside.

Every inch of the mansion was decorated in intricate wooden carvings, wooden trim, wooden statues peering from the corners of the walls. It was like Kate had walked into a book, and the words had been etched with a deft carving knife, translated into vines and crawling ivies and waves and shooting stars, all immovable in the deep oak wood. She turned in a full circle with a whistle.

"Is it just me, or does everything look like it's staring at us?" America muttered.

"It's an illusion," Kate replied, though she wasn't quite sure herself. *Were* the creatures carved into the wood stationary? Or had she just seen that fairy on another panel of wood on the other side of the foyer? And it felt like the dragon perched above the door was watching them. Kate absently scrubbed at her arms, the eyes squirming as if they didn't want to be perceived right now, either.

It was like wherever she and America moved in the foyer, the creatures shifted with them, like some intricate Roy Lichtenstein illusion.

At the other end of the foyer, America found the security keypad, and gave Kate a thumbs-up, indicating that it was still off.

They decided to quietly split up and start searching the house. America took the left-most door, which led into a bright red-and-white kitchen that looked absolutely *nothing* like the foyer, and Kate followed the foyer through the arch under the stairs toward the living area. Her footsteps echoed too loudly through the house. Her breath roared in her ears. The archway led into the front rooms. To the left was a living space full of—cubes. It was nothing but cubes. A cube sofa, cube lights, a cube TV. Everything was all right angles and perfect squares, some lines blending into each other so artfully that when Kate stepped into the room she didn't see the coffee table in front of her until she knocked her shin against it.

She hissed and hopped backward—only to collide into a floor lamp. She righted it before it fell, and quickly decided to leave that room before she ran into anything else. She came to a room with only a white piano, every wall a mirror. Her footsteps sounded weird in this room, until she looked down and saw herself staring back at her—a thousand faces of herself. The floor was a mirror, too, and so was the ceiling. She bounced around in every mirror, an impossible number of her turning to look at herself, until her stomach churned and she quickly left for the final room in the front—

A library.

CHAPTER TWENTY-FOUR

LOCK AND KEY

Quietly, she stepped into the last room. It was . . . oddly normal-looking, unlike the other ones. Like a normal library, filled floor to ceiling with books upon books. Unlike Gregory Maxwell's library, however, these books weren't painted over in white. There were so many books, spines out, colored in all different hues, titles encrusted in gold foil, accompanied by names of long-deceased authors. The ceiling was at least fifteen feet high, and the bookcases went all the way to the top, where a mural looked down at her. A mural that made her freeze in her footsteps and stare up at it with mounting dread.

It was an eye, wide and unblinking, looking down at her. And she could've sworn it saw her, too.

"Wow, I hate *that*," America muttered as she walked

in from the other doorway. She stared up at the eye, mouth open. "Is that what yours look like?"

Kate nodded. "But a lot smaller."

After a moment, she finally tore her gaze away to the podium in the middle of the room. On it was a box made of glass. She crept toward it, hope swelling in her chest, and peered inside. That hope then burst like a water balloon.

There wasn't a book inside. Of course there wasn't—it couldn't be *that* easy.

America stepped up to the glass box with her. She cocked her head and asked, "Is that a donation receipt?"

Kate squinted for a closer look. "I think it is. . . ."

"I can't read for who, though. Maybe Albright donated the book?" America asked.

That sparked a memory. "Oh! Milo mentioned something about his grandfather saying that the book was somewhere everyone can see it and no one knows it's there. So he donated it there?"

They both looked back at the receipt. America said, jokingly, "You know where I'd donate something? Goodwill. Everything gets lost in Goodwill."

"Ha, yeah, but they use a different-color slip—wait a minute. That looks a lot like the receipt I found. . . ." Kate trailed off as she pulled her bag over her shoulder, dug through it, past her sister's birthday gift, and took out a yellow piece of paper. She flattened it against the top of the display case. It was a bit faded, but more or less the same color as the receipt in the display.

"Those look alike," America muttered. "What's that from?"

"The New York Public Library. And where do you think there would be something that could be found by everyone but not seen?"

"A book lost in the stacks, for sure."

"For sure."

In the reflection in the glass, a third figure surfaced behind them.

"You arrived sooner than expected, Kate."

They spun toward the voice.

Milo leaned against the doorway, his arms crossed over his chest. He looked different, though, clad in inky black. The clothes he wore could be considered a costume, to Kate's absolute dread, his face the only skin showing. His long-sleeved jacket had a high collar, and it bled almost seamlessly into his leather gloves and black trousers and shined leather boots. There was a notebook clasped to the belt on his hip like a weapon, hidden by a cape draped over his shoulder, the underside glimmering like a night sky.

America shot Kate an *I told you so* look, and Kate knew she was *never* going to live this down.

"Nice costume, Milo. Did Kingpin pay for it?"

"I told you I was on your side," he reminded her in reply. "I wasn't lying."

"No, you just handed over the books to *Kingpin*. The guy who beat you up, might I add."

He sighed. "He found me out. He was going to kill you if I didn't—"

"Cut the crap," she snapped.

"Fine, fine," Milo said, giving in with a shrug. "Don't believe me." Kate and America watched him walk over to a wing-back chair nestled in one of the corners of the room and sink down into it. America took point on one side of the room, Kate on the other, so he couldn't escape. "You know, we're *all* actually on the same side, here. You, me, Kingpin—we all just want the books collected together."

"But we"—Kate pointed to herself and America— "don't want to use the psychological warfare inside of them to kill people."

He gave her a distraught look. "And you think I *do*?"

To which she replied, so very certainly, "Haven't you already, Milo?"

He began to say something, but then decided against it and rubbed at his mouth.

"You killed Gregory Maxwell."

His eyebrows jerked up. "You really think it works

that fast? No. No, I daresay I didn't kill him. I wish he would've walked off that balcony, but he was pushed by one of Kingpin's men. Kingpin was *that* close behind us, Kate. He'll stop at *nothing* to get those books."

"And Maxwell's wife?" she asked. "Was she just *collateral*?"

Milo's face scrunched in anger. "You really think I'm a monster, don't you? Because—what—of what my grandfather did to me?"

"I wouldn't be surprised if you *had* killed him, too—"

"I was giving him one last chance!" he snapped, jabbing his finger toward the ground. "I went to that bookstore with my copy because he said . . ." He shook his head. "It doesn't matter. Even if I had, don't you think he got what he deserved?"

She set her jaw. "And your parents?"

His posture went rigid. A conflicted, pained look crossed his eyes before he turned them, sharp and cold, to Kate. "So, you know, then. And you'd *fault* me if I had murdered my grandfather? The man who tortured me, made me live my nightmares, only to find that they couldn't kill me?"

"That must have been terrible."

"Terrible," he echoed, and shook his head. "Do you know what *is* terrible? I was supposed to spend a summer with my grandfather the year I turned thirteen, and I was *so* looking forward to it. When my parents came to pick me up at the end of that summer, I happily showed them the language my grandfather painstakingly carved in my hand," he added, pressing his thumb into the center of his other hand, massaging it as if he was suddenly struck by a phantom pain. "I didn't realize what I'd done. Of course I didn't—I thought . . ." He hesitated. "Have you ever watched someone sleepwalk, Kate?"

She shook her head. "I can't say I have."

"They don't even know they're doing it most of the time," Milo pointed out. "My parents were sleepwalking in a nightmare. They dragged me from my bed and tied us together. Someone started the fire, but I'll never know who. They kept telling me they wouldn't let me go, that they loved me. They loved me so much." His eyelids fluttered, breaking from his reverie, and he looked back to her and offered a small smile. "They loved me so much that I had to be cut out of their arms when help arrived. Everything was burned. I was burned, too. My grandfather was beside himself. A *tragedy*, he called it. No, the tragedy is I can't decide if those S.H.I.E.L.D. agents found me thirty minutes too late or two minutes too early."

What a horrific story, and Kate couldn't help but feel sorry for him. The entire thing really was a tragedy, from Milo's grandfather's hubris to his parents to everything that led him here. But still. He chose his path. She shook her head, "I'm sorry, Milo, that that happened to you, but whatever you want to do with your grandfather's research—"

Milo barked a laugh and forced himself to his feet. "*Do?* Kate, I *am* my grandfather's research. I know the language, I know the spells. I'm not collecting those books to *save* anyone." His eyes darkened. "I told you I'm on your side. I'm collecting these books so that no one can stop me when I burn them to ashes. And I'll do whatever is necessary to accomplish that. What's a few people dead," he went on, "when the world's at stake?"

America widened her stance. "That's not how this works, Milo."

"Then how *does* it work?" he snarled.

Kate tried to reach for America. "Wait—"

Two things happened in that moment. One, America launched herself at Milo, but he had anticipated her movement already and whirled to the side. The second thing that happened was just as quick. He opened his book—the pages blank, every one of them—and scrawled something on it with the tip of his gloved finger. Ink swirled out into a sigil, one that Kate couldn't see, but she had a feeling it was bad.

"America! Close your eyes!" Kate screamed.

America spun around on her heels, reaching for him again. He flashed the page at her. She stumbled as he stepped out of her way again. She fell to her knees and quickly pulled her arms around herself. Her breath hitched.

Milo looked down at her almost pitifully. "I doubt you can stop me."

Kate ran over to America and knelt down, but the second she touched her, America began to scream. High, piercing shrieks. She grappled for air, like she was trying to grab hold of something, her legs kicking out. Kate told Milo, "Stop this! Fix her!"

"Oh, calm down," he replied, tearing the page out of his notebook and folding it up. "She won't die. She just feels like she's falling. Apparently, that's her biggest fear. Falling and falling, and never finding the ground."

Kate froze. "You—you know other sigils."

He looked bored. "Of course I do. I am my grandfather's protégé after all."

"Then *fix* her."

America closed her eyes, gritting her teeth. "It's not real, it's not real, it's not . . ."

Milo tore the page with the spell out of his book and dropped it to the ground. "I'm sorry, Kate, but thank you for telling me where the last book is, by the way. You were a real help." Then he turned down the hallway, his footsteps light against the hardwood. She heard the front door open as she scrambled to follow him, turning out into the hallway. He stepped over the flowers as he descended the steps, closed the door, and was gone into the evening.

Kate gritted her teeth, torn between going after him or—

America screamed again, on her back, clawing up at the ceiling. Her hands were shaking, tears in her eyes. "Kate!" she cried. "Kate—help!"

Kate couldn't just leave her best friend. Cursing, she turned back into the library, glancing around the room. *Think.* What could she do? Where could she—

Her gaze caught the folded piece of paper on the floor. If she looked at it, then she'd succumb to the spell, too. *Think, think*—what had those kids said about the language? It could be reversed with a mirror?

The mirror room!

She grabbed the piece of paper, clamped it down between her teeth, and grabbed her best friend under the arms. She pulled her as America kicked and screamed, each scream breaking Kate's heart a little more, into the mirror room, where thousands of Americas writhed in pain and thousands of Kates looked on in worry.

"America—America, I need you to open your eyes," she said gently, cupping her best friend's cheek. "Hey, Mac. C'mon. You're not really falling. I promise."

"It *feels* like I am." America, sucking a breath in between her teeth, cracked open her eyes. "I'm going to kill that guy," she ground out.

"I'll let you," Kate promised, and then held the piece of paper up. "I need you to look at the ceiling, okay?"

America nodded. Her eyebrows knit together, tears streaming down her cheeks. She kicked her feet out, then back in again, trying to get ahold of her body as the vertigo sent her falling again and again. Her eyes could never quite focus.

Kate lay down beside her, in the room that was full of mirrors, and took hold of her hand tightly. She pressed it to her chest.

With her free hand, she shakily opened the page and flipped it so it reflected on the ceiling.

"Look at the sigil," she said, squeezing America's hand tightly, hoping it worked, praying it did.

America squeezed back.

In the ceiling above them, the character on the page looked foreign. Then, slowly, America's face relaxed, and her breathing calmed. She blinked and looked around, and then closed her eyes again. "It worked."

"Thank god," Kate muttered.

They lay there for a moment longer, their hands clutched tightly together.

Then America said, without a hint of sarcasm in her voice, "It's official. You have the *worst* taste in men."

"Yeah," Kate replied, swallowing the taste of vomit.

She'd been so terrified she wouldn't be able to cure America. She didn't know what she would've done if she couldn't. But she had. And that also meant, once she found that last sigil, she could cure herself, too.

CHAPTER TWENTY-FIVE

AS SOMEONE ONCE SAID, MAXIMUM EFFORT

The New York Public Library's flagship branch, the Stephen A. Schwarzman building, was an institution of learning that offered free access to all. Except, of course, after closing hours. Which was why Kate and America found themselves on the rooftop of said building at nine that evening, trying to jack open one of the windows. It was a pleasant night, at least. The humidity had finally broken to a gentle breeze, and Midtown's skyline actually looked *soft* for once against the backdrop of the velvet-dark sky. Maybe it was the smog, or maybe it was the whopping three hours of sleep over the last several days, but Kate rather liked the view.

"You know, I figured someday I'd be breaking into

a public institution with you," America commented as she propped open the window and peeked her head inside.

"Really?"

"Well"—she retracted her head and glanced at their third wheel—"the dog was a surprise."

Kate patted Lucky on the head. "He needed to go for a walk; he'd been cramped up in that wittle apartment all day!"

"We *are* going to talk about replacing my running shoes, by the way," America reminded her with a sharp glare to the dog.

Lucky pushed back his ears and gave a small whimper.

He was fooling no one.

America scanned the rooftop again. "Do you think Milo is here already?" She was still pretty unsteady on her feet, but she'd been trying to disguise it from Kate. It hadn't worked.

"Most certainly, and he probably told Kingpin, too." She had been thinking about this for a while, but she felt sure of it now. "If things go really south really quickly, I need you to leave me and go get help."

America furrowed her eyebrows in confusion. "What? Kate, I'm not letting you do this *alone*—"

"But, America—"

"If you're worried about me, I bounce back like memory foam. You know I do."

Kate gave her a deadpan look. "I love you, and I know, but please do this for *me*. I'm already going to die if I don't find a cure tonight—and we don't know what all Milo is capable of. He could've used the nightmare sigil on you instead and not left the paper behind, but he didn't."

"Then I should beat him up until he realizes he *should* have—"

Kate held on to America's arm tighter and looked into her eyes. "You're my best friend."

"Which is why I can't leave you—"

"Please. I'm not saying anything bad *will* happen, but if it does . . . I really need to know I've still got my best friend with a backup plan."

America's face crumpled, because the fact of the matter was, Kate was right. They had no clear way of stopping Milo, and the worst thing he could do to them he'd already done to Kate—even if it was tangentially. And if Kingpin got involved . . . "This is a death sentence, Kate."

"C'mon, you know me," Kate scoffed, pulling her bow up higher over her shoulder. "I'm like a cockroach—hard to kill. That's why I'm the better Hawkeye."

She hoped she sounded confident, and not as scared as she was inside. She wouldn't wish the eyes on her skin on anyone—not Kingpin, not her own father. No one. She felt them staring at her, looking through her lies because they could *feel* that she was lying, that she was scared. Going at this alone would probably be one of the worst things she'd have to do, but she had to believe in herself, and she had to have America believe in *her*.

Which she did. Unconditionally.

Kate held up her pinkie. "Swear it? At the first sign of trouble, you're out?"

America hooked her pinkie through Kate's, and they kissed their thumbs. "Who should I get?"

"Shoot for the big guns. I want everyone to see how cool Kate Bishop is," Kate said with a playful wink, and then she grabbed Lucky and slipped in through the window and down into the rotunda on the third floor. America crawled through the window after her and dropped down behind them.

The rotunda was lavish: marbled floors and intricately carved wooden walls and stone archways, inset with beautiful murals of ye olden people reading, the ceiling above them splashed with deceptively happy cherubs across a blue sky. There were tall six-foot candelabras standing on either side of the entrances to the rotunda. The place was opulent in the way that only somewhere that smelled of tweed and Oxford commas could be.

And that suddenly made everything very, *very* creepy. Especially at night. The only lights were the bloody-red exit signs, glaring from either end of the hall. Kate hurried over to the information desk and plucked a brochure off the stand. She unfolded it to study.

"Okay, we're here in the McGraw Rotunda. Now, if I was a priceless bioweapon, where would I be?" she muttered, flipping through the rest of the brochure, at a loss as to where to begin—when she caught sight of an ad for one of the collections in the basement.

America pointed to it over her shoulder. "'A Storybook Love: Collections from Childhood Fantasy'—there first?"

Kate glanced down to the dog, as if he had an opinion. He sniffed his butt.

She looked back at America. "Right, worth a shot."

The last time Kate had gone *inside* this building was during a field trip in high school, so she remembered very little of it, though at night it all looked different, anyway. The shadows were longer, their footsteps louder. The sound in this place seemed to echo on and on, as though she had just walked into an endless space.

They decided that the easiest way to get to the ground floor, based on the map, was down the stairwell on the left. It went all the way down. So that's the stairwell they took. Kate also vowed when this whole mess was through, and *if* she survived it, she'd visit this place in the daytime instead of just lounging out on the front steps, watching kids fall off the stone lions. She'd even promised to finally remember which lion was Patience and which one was Fortitude.

"And I'll actually come here and read or something," she went on, and America rolled her eyes.

"I don't know if they stock smutty romance novels in the esteemed Schwarzman building, Kate."

"What a shame. Some of the best fight scenes I've ever read."

Lucky was close on their heels as they reached the bottom, and then he suddenly stopped and drew his lips back in a growl.

Kate froze—and grabbed on to America's arm to stop her, too.

Suddenly there was a scream of irritation, and someone toppled something loud and large in what the map told her was the children's center.

Where they needed to be.

She cursed, because it had to be Milo.

Pulling her bow off her shoulder, she nocked an arrow and tiptoed down the length of the hallway to the children's center, America and Lucky close behind her. Inside, a young man dressed in black had laid absolute waste to a kiosk of library cards, and had pulled a stuffed animal who resembled—quite tragically—Winnie the Pooh out of its case in the collections and was shaking it in frustration.

Since she probably wasn't going to be able to shoot straight, she slackened her bowstring and stood in the doorway, much to America's confusion.

"And what did that poor teddy bear do to you?" she asked Milo just as he wound his fist back to punch it in the face again.

He whirled around to her in disbelief. His eyes were wide and wild, like someone at the end of his rope. Curious. For someone whose life didn't depend on finding that last book, he certainly was going through all the emotions as if it *did*. "*You?* How are you here so fast?" he snarled once he'd recovered, his hand going to the notebook on his hip. "You *and* your friend?"

"Oh, come on, man, you know my name. You slept on my couch!" America replied, throwing up her arms.

His face contorted. "I'm surprised you can walk."

"Better than falling," America replied. "That was a real Chad move, by the way, Milo."

Milo stared at her. Kate said instead, as his fingers leafed through the notebook on his hip, "I reversed your spell, so I wouldn't try another one on us. We know the trick."

"*Well*, it's a surprise you figured it out so quickly," he replied, and dropped his hand. He dropped the teddy bear behind him and turned to face them. "I wasn't trying to kill you."

America snorted. "And here I was hoping for an apology."

"I needed to slow you down. And it was better than inflicting a nightmare on you, wasn't it? That's what my grandfather would've done. Do you know how exhausting it is, every night for *years*, to keep running from the nightmare that's going to kill you in your sleep?"

"A little bit actually, yeah," Kate replied flatly. She stepped up to Milo, angry and tired. "And quite frankly, I don't see a difference between you and your grandfather right now."

A muscle in his jaw twitched. "Take that back."

"Hit too close to home?"

"I'm nothing like that *monster*."

"No, you're just a different font."

America interjected between them, her voice urgent, "Guys, I think someone's coming."

Neither Kate nor Milo heard her. Kate took another step toward him. They were so close now, she had half a mind to grab him by his stupid scruffy costumed collar and shake him.

"I am *nothing* like him!" Milo argued. He turned away from her and began to pace across the ruined collection, quicker this time. "He tried to *kill* me!"

Behind Kate, Lucky growled, as if he wanted her to pay attention, and America tried to interrupt again, "Hey, guys—"

Kate said, "So you killed him instead?"

"*No!* But I wish I would have."

She scowled. "I can't believe I kissed you."

"And you *liked* it," he volleyed back, jabbing a finger at her.

America cleared her throat again. "Anyone? Hello?—"

Kate scoffed. "I've kissed better."

"You're cute when you lie."

"*Excuse* me?" She rolled up her jacket sleeves and Milo took a step back, a bit alarmed. The eyes writhed but she was too angry to really care about them at this point. She said, "You better start running, because I'm about to kick your a—"

A deep and sly voice interrupted her from behind, "Well, well, it seems you brought some friends, Milo."

CHAPTER TWENTY-SIX

CHECKMATE

Oh, this was just getting worse and worse.

Fisk inclined his head, leaning against his cane like he was enjoying the most leisurely afternoon. He took up most of the doorway, and even then he seemed bigger than he was because of the way he carried himself. Like he owned the air he breathed. Behind him were a dozen of his men, their angry-looking assault rifles aimed at the three of them, like he was here to fight someone like Spider-Man or Daredevil.

Not Kate Bishop.

He waved his hand at his men, and they dropped their aim. "Really, you can't quite stay away, can you?"

"I could say the same for you," she replied, praying that Lucky didn't decide to try anything bite-y. She motioned for the dog to stay, and even though

Lucky had his ears back, teeth showing, he didn't budge.

Because he was the best freaking dog.

Who had, probably, tried to warn her about their visitor.

And, by the pissed look America was giving her, she'd also probably tried to warn Kate, too.

Kingpin gave a sigh and looked at Milo. "Have you found the book yet?"

Milo narrowed his eyes. "No. It's not here. It must be in another room."

"Useless, as I guessed." Kingpin made a motion for his men to split up and search for it. "Find it by any means necessary. I want this building searched, top to bottom. What's the title?"

Kate looked at Milo, imploring him to do *one noble thing* in his life. But apparently that wasn't in the cards. He said, without meeting her gaze, "*The Immovable Castle Dreams of Death*."

"What a ghoulish title—and parents let their children read such a book? Poor parenting," Kingpin muttered, and gave a command to his men. They went back up the stairs and distantly, the sounds of destruction—toppling books and shredding paper and chaos—flooded down from the upper floors. It sounded like heartbreak in a library.

"I should go help look as well," Milo muttered, and

started out of the children's center. He gave Kingpin a wide berth, his left hand slowly reaching for the notepad on his hip.

Kingpin raised his cane and blocked the rest of the doorway, stopping Milo from leaving. "Just a moment, my boy."

Milo's shoulders went rigid. His fingers touched the corner of his notebook, prying it open slowly, slowly, almost there— "Yes?"

"I thought we agreed, when you came on as one of my men, that my rules were clear: You only do what I say when I say it."

"I . . . wanted to get a head start." Milo lifted open the notepad, his index finger beginning to curve a spiral on the blank white page. "I knew Kate Bishop would try to stop me—"

Suddenly Kingpin slammed his cane into the side of Milo's left knee. Milo cried out as his leg crunched inward and he dropped to the ground.

"Milo!" Kate shouted, and jerked to help him, but America caught her fast by her arm. America shook her head—no. It was best to stay put.

"Hmm. You don't lie very well, do you, boy?" Fisk asked, grabbing the notebook at Milo's hip and tearing it off his belt. Milo writhed on the ground, holding his knee. Kingpin pocketed the notebook, pressed the end of his cane against Milo's forehead, and pinned him down against the floor. "You think I haven't read up on you? You think I don't know who I work with? I'm no *fool*, boy. If you'd have killed her like you were supposed to, she wouldn't be here."

Milo gritted out, "I don't kill people."

"That's your first mistake. Let this be a learning opportunity. To play chess, you have to remove pieces strategically." He leaned more of his weight on his cane, the tip pressing harder against Milo's forehead. Milo squirmed under the pain, tears in his eyes.

Kate couldn't watch any more. She tore out of America's grip. "Kingpin, stop it!" she snarled.

The mob boss turned a lazy look to her. "Oh, do be quiet, Kate, my dear. What have I told you about interfering in my business? I'm a very lenient man." He twisted his cane, and Milo whimpered. America shifted her weight, as if she was about to move. He tsked. "I wouldn't, Ms. America Chavez. You're fast, but I'm closer."

America gritted her teeth and stayed where she was.

Kingpin took out a kerchief from his suit pocket with his free hand and dabbed his forehead. There was a light sheen of sweat across his brow, his skin paler than Kate last remembered, and the more she looked at the mob boss, the more she noticed the little things—the circles under his eyes, the heavy breathing, the slight twitch of his arm (as though there was something on it, something crawling), and a thought occurred to her:

Milo had *hypnotized Kingpin!*

He looked much like how Gregory Maxwell had before he died. One doze, one catnap, and Kate suspected it would be all over for the mob boss.

He was already getting sloppy, after all.

Because while he had Milo under his cane, Kate and America in his sights, he forgot one very important piece in this game:

"You look tired, Fisk," she said.

The mobster drew his lips back in a snarl. "How *dare* you—"

During the confrontation, Lucky had snuck against the wall, close enough to Kingpin to do some damage. Kate gave a whistle, and Lucky launched himself at the mobster. He sank his teeth into Fisk's collarbone, just like he'd been taught to do. Kingpin gave a cry, dropping his cane, and with Milo out of trouble, Kate lunged forward and grabbed Milo by the arm.

She shouted back to America, *"GO!"*

Her best friend gave her an incredulous look. "Kate—"

"GO!" Then, quieter, "Like you promised."

America didn't have time to hesitate, the chaos quieting as Kingpin threw Lucky off of him and into a stack of books. The dog gave a yelp, but quickly got back to his feet and lunged for the mobster again.

"Please," Kate mouthed.

America took a step back, then another, and threw her foot into the air behind her, punching out a star-shaped hole in reality, and gave a whistle for Lucky to follow her. He hesitated, but decided to go, jumping into her arms as she slipped through the star-shaped hole like she'd never been there at all.

Kate pulled Milo to his feet, slinging his arm around her shoulder.

"*Damn it,*" Kingpin growled, pressing a hand on his shoulder to stanch the blood as it seeped onto his crisp white shirt. "You'll pay for that, Katie."

She held on to Milo's arm tightly, dragging him out of the children's center. As she went, she grabbed whatever she could to topple over behind them to give them more time to escape. "We gotta go, we gotta go!"

"I can't run," he hissed, wincing every time he put weight on his left leg. "I think it's broken."

Which just meant she had to work overtime as they started up the steps. Kingpin shouted after them to stop, upturning bookshelf after bookshelf on his way after them. Milo staggered at her side as she pulled him up the stairwell, all the while telling her to let him go.

"Leave me, you can't get past his men," he said through gritted teeth. "I'll just slow you down—"

"Sorry, bro," she replied, heaving him up onto her shoulder again. Sweat prickled against her forehead. "But in my line of work, no one's left behind."

"I would've left you."

"And that's why *I'm* the hero." She heard Kingpin's men gathering on the first floor. Milo was right—she wouldn't be able to escape while dragging him along with her, but if she escaped now, then that left Kingpin to collect the book. Wherever it was. She tightened her grip on Milo's hand. "Can you be truthful for once?" she asked urgently.

"I don't know what—"

"Can you? Quickly!"

He gave her an unreadable look. Then he nodded. Once.

"Do you know where the book might be hidden, if not the children's center?"

He shook his head.

"Okay, good. And here's the big one: Did you hypnotize Kingpin? Like you did Gregory? There's something on your hand, right? Something written there that does it?"

He seemed surprised that she knew about it—of *course* she did. She wasn't called Hawkeye for nothing. "Technically, yes."

"Excellent."

A plan was quickly forming in her head. It was a bad one, but most of her plans these days weren't Nobel Prize–winning. They didn't need to be. They just needed to buy America (and Lucky) enough time to execute plan Get Help.

Kate and Milo got to the top of the stairs only to find themselves greeted by Montana himself. He broke out his lariat, and before either of them could dodge, roped them together and pulled it tight, squeezing Kate and Milo together. He shook his head as he curled up the rest of the rope. He pulled them into the middle of the esteemed Astor Hall on the first floor, a place built for banquets and opulent parties, every sound echoing over the marbled floor and stone arches like pebbles in a cave. There were more of Kingpin's men, with their weapons ready, on the balcony that led to the second floor. If there was a way out of this, Kate didn't see it.

Panic built in her chest. *This is it.*

Kingpin finally made his way up the steps, leisurely and—to be truthful—quite angrily. He took out a kerchief and patted his brow, and she had to wonder, briefly, what monsters he was afraid of.

He raised his hand to signal their death.

"You don't want to kill us yet, Fisk," she said as confidently as she could. Which, honestly? At this moment, she wasn't very confident. *Fake it till you make it, Bishop*, she told herself.

He snarled, "Oh, Katie, I think I do—"

"Then I'm sure you have someone who knows how to read the Unword?" she replied, and her words stayed his hand. For the moment. Her hands were shaking, so she balled them into fists, her fingernails leaving indentions in her palms. "Got someone on your payroll who's as big of a nerd as this guy right here?"

Milo muttered, "That feels like an insult. . . ."

Kingpin narrowed his eyes.

"Oh, I thought not," she went on. "Do you even know what kind of book you sent your knuckleheads to go look for? I bet you don't even know where it is. This place is huge, Kingpin. Looking for that book is like looking for a needle in a stack of other needles that look exactly the same. It'll take more than an evening to comb it, and by morning everyone will know something's up. And *you'll* be out of time."

Kingpin took a kerchief out of his suit pocket and dabbed his forehead again. "I have plenty of time."

"Are you sure?"

Fisk inclined his head, his face purposefully blank.

"I'm sure you noticed already," she said, leaning in toward him, her voice just loud enough so that he could hear but the men around them couldn't, "how tired you feel? How the eyes keep crawling up your skin but no one else can see them?"

It was a fraction of a second, but she saw it in his face—recognition.

"It's hypnosis," Kate went on. "It will kill you as soon as you fall asleep. And if you kill us, you're just signing your own death certificate."

He didn't seem all that convinced.

"Maybe if you hadn't killed Albright," she mused, "you'd be in a better position to bargain."

While Kingpin wasn't shocked to learn that she'd figured it out, Milo certainly looked surprised that she finally believed him. Of course she did—at the end of the day, Kate liked to see the best in everyone, no matter how much they screwed up. God knows she wasn't perfect, either.

"I'm sure you didn't mean to," she went on with a shrug. "You lost your temper when he wouldn't reveal the information you wanted about the books, or maybe you thought Milo would be easier to control. Which is funny now, considering everything. You can call our bluff, but you're just one snooze away from total oblivion, Mr. Fisk. Do you want to risk it?"

"But that begs the question, Katie: How did I get—what, *hypnotized*?"

Milo, for what he was worth, lifted his hand and waved. "When you shook my hand. I needed insurance you wouldn't kill me. Or Kate, at this point."

"Aw, you shouldn't have."

Kingpin's jaw clenched. He didn't like being bested. And definitely not by children half his age.

"Besides," Kate went on, because she had this really terrible track record of being unable to shut up when she really should've shut up, "don't you want to get it sooner rather than later? You aren't the only one looking for it, you know. When Osborn or Doctor Doom comes looking . . ."

Milo hummed. "Which one was the man in the green at the auction?"

"They were both there," Kate lied, because she didn't remember a single damn person at the auction. "And I believe if you murder *me*, you're going to have to tell Madame Masque the bad news. I'm afraid she called dibs on my head *years* ago. . . ."

Milo gave her a troubled look. "Is there anyone *not* trying to kill you?"

"At the moment?" She thought for a beat, and then said, "I think—"

"Enough!" Wilson Fisk bellowed, clearly having had time to debate his options. His nostrils flared as he looked from Kate to Milo, who was slowly sliding to the ground because of his injury, and then back to her. It was probably no more than a few seconds, but it felt like eternity, stretched so far that Kate began to wonder if she'd already died and this was hell.

But then Kingpin said, "Secure the doors and fortify the windows. We'll be staying awhile—their friend, Ms. Chavez, has gotten out. Let's see if she returns before Katie here finds that book. If she returns before you find the book, we'll kill you both," he told Kate and Milo. "How long do you have now?" He checked his watch. "An hour? Less?"

Kate inclined her head, even though she was terrified out of her wits. "Challenge accepted."

CHAPTER TWENTY-SEVEN

A ROSE BY ANY OTHER NAME

She'd never wanted to *not* be rescued more in her life.

If she couldn't find a way to get them out of this mess, she could already imagine the disappointed look Captain America would give her at her funeral.

Never mind she was just so . . . *tired.* It felt like every bone in her body just wanted to sleep forever. But the second she closed her eyes and quieted her mind, the eyes would swirl on her skin and stare at her and wait for the nightmares to come creeping back in. She couldn't take that again. Watching that horrible, horrible dream, her friends swallowed up, drowning in darkness, while she stood by helplessly to watch. She knew it was a dream—she *knew* it—but that didn't make the nightmare any less real.

And next time, she wasn't quite sure anyone would be there to wake her up before she drowned in it.

Milo stared at the room that was almost an entire football field long. The Rose Main Reading Room. Full of heavy tables in long rows, lights placed periodically on each one, it stretched dishearteningly long, and on both walls, running down the length of the room, were shelves full of books from all across the world. And just to add insult to injury, there was a *second* row of bookshelves behind the first on a small balcony, which also ran almost the entire length of the room.

Great chandeliers hung from the intricately carved ceiling, full of murals of vibrant blue skies and billowing rose-colored clouds, trimmed in plaster rosettes and medallions. Cupids pressed themselves into the inlays on each side of the mural, looking down at Kate and Milo with blank plaster eyes, about as empty as their well of hope.

When Kingpin had asked Kate what room the book was in, she'd blanked at all the room names, but Milo piped in with this one. Of *course* it had to be this one. The biggest one of them all.

She shoved herself to her feet. Kingpin had locked them inside, and told two men in ill-fitting suits to make sure they didn't come out. She imagined Montana was sitting in a chair just outside, picking his teeth with a pocketknife. And here she thought the worst part about this weekend was going to be her sister's birthday party.

This barely beat it.

Barely.

Milo sat in a chair at the first table, massaging the bridge of his nose. His leg was propped up on the chair next to him, though his knee had already swelled pretty badly. "You know, a part of me would have preferred death to this."

"You might still get your wish," Kate warned. She wasn't sure where to start—the left side of this gargantuan room or the right? "This is going to be impossible. Why did you choose *this* room?"

"I don't know—I remembered this is where they stuck most of the books, so we have the best chance of finding it here?"

"Well, joke's on us, I guess. I think I'll take the left," Kate decided. "Should I start at the beginning, or in the *As*? Oh, they're the same thing." She groaned, dropping her head back. "I'm so tired."

"You get used to it." He pulled at his gloves. "You know, it took a few days for me to figure out that you'd been hypnotized. I just can't figure out how."

She glanced over at him, confused. "Really?"

He held up his hands and wiggled his fingers. "I'm the only one who knows the hypnosis besides my grandfather, and you met him after he died."

"There was a letter," she replied simply. He sat up straight—almost instantly. "It was addressed to you."

He stared at her. "There—he—what did it say?"

"I couldn't read it. I thought you knew about it."

"No. No, I—everything was a blur. I just remembered seeing my grandfather dead, and going after the person who killed him. I didn't see . . ." He slumped back down in his chair, staring at his hands intently. "He asked me to come to his event, and bring my book. I hadn't seen him in years—not since S.H.I.E.L.D. took me away. He promised . . . he promised to show me the nightmare sigils. The original ones."

She'd started skimming *B* when she paused and glanced back at him. "Why?"

He gave her a knowing look.

". . . *Oh,*" she mumbled. "But . . . you have the nightmare sigils then, too, right? On your hands? Can't you just reverse them on yourself? And, you know, *me,* if that's all right with you?"

"Yeah—about that." He took off the glove on his right hand and turned it palm up. Kate came back to the table where he sat and cautiously looked at it. "They won't hurt you. You can only be bespelled by one command at a time."

She scrunched her nose, looking at the sigils carved into his right palm, but half of the last sigil was marred by terrible burns.

"I can still cast the spell but this last sigil warped, so the outcome is a bit more . . . violent."

She gave a start, realizing. "That's why it worked so quickly with Gregory Maxwell—and now with Fisk—isn't it?"

"Yes, and it's unpredictable. I try not to use it if I can help it."

Kate chewed on her bottom lip. "Then the other deaths Misty talked about—the ones surrounding the books. Those were *you*, weren't they?"

He pursed his lips and looked away, putting his glove back on. "They were getting too close to finding the books."

"You killed them, Milo."

"I'm aware, Kate. They weren't good people."

"That's not for *us* to decide—"

"I know. I *know*, okay?" He interrupted, his voice hard. "You aren't like me, you don't understand. If I could keep people from enduring what I've gone through . . . it's easy for you. Fighting bad guys with a snarky quip and a smile."

She shook her head. "Because I *choose* to. You think my family's not a little messed up? You think I haven't gone through absolute hell to get here? Do you know what my nightmares are? That I stand, helpless, as my friends die. All of them, one by one. And the worst part?" She leaned closer to him, her chest tight at the memories, "I've *lived* that. I've seen friends die. That's why I choose to fight bad guys with a snarky quip and a smile, because I don't like the alternative."

Milo looked down at the desk. There were names carved into the mahogany, little sayings, dates. *I was here*, they wrote. He traced one of them, frowning. "Maybe I could've been more like you, if I'd found that letter from my grandfather instead. But I didn't, and I can't help but think he offered the cure ten years too late, anyway."

"Yeah, he does kind of suck for that."

"Just a little. At least the spell that we're under," he added, "is a lot more stable. We survive as long as we can escape our nightmares. And I have been running, Kate, for a very long time."

Kate scanned the bookshelves, knowing that she needed to find that last book, and then back at Milo, alone in his chair, a makeshift bandage wrapped around his leg, and she made a decision: She started skimming the bookshelves and said, "So tell me about them."

He gave her a strange look. "Excuse me?"

"Your nightmares. What are they like?"

He opened his mouth, closed it again, blinking furiously, because, she figured, no one had ever asked before, and it wasn't exactly like he could divulge his nightmares to anyone who'd *believe* him. After a moment, he said, "A lot of things. At first, it was normal childhood nightmares. Being late to class, or being picked on by bullies—there was one where I was trapped, constantly, by a pink-and-purple boa constrictor. Squeezing tighter and tighter until—" He swallowed. "My grandfather thought it was revolutionary that in my nightmares I could dream up ways to slither out of every scenario. If my bullies found me in class, I turned myself into a cloud. If I was trapped in a fire, I'd make it rain inside. It was a game at first. Over the summer I spent with him, I'd go to sleep and wake up the next morning, and he'd record how I escaped the nightmare. Again, and again. Then my parents arrived at the end of the summer and . . ." And Kate, sadly, knew the rest. Milo frowned, picking at the tips of his gloves. "After that, I dreamed of the fire. The faceless bodies of my parents chasing after me. Hugging me. Refusing to let go . . . I still dream about that most often, but in worse ways. Your nightmares get smarter as you do."

"Mine are smart-*asses*, honestly," she said with a sigh, grabbing one of the ladders to roll it over to the bookcases to check the upper shelves. "I keep sinking in the putty that Clint and I use for our putty arrows, and my friends all drown in it, and I almost drown, too. And then there's my fourteen-year-old nightmare self who keeps heckling me."

He snorted a laugh. "What?"

"Yeah, you don't have that?"

"No, sadly."

She sighed, exhausted, all the way down into her bones. Her fingers skimmed over the spines of old, tattered novels, but none of them were what she was looking for. She climbed down and started looking through the next section. "But you know the worst part about it all?"

He tilted his head and guessed, "The eyes?"

"The *eyes*! They're *awful*!" She threw up her hands. "And I can feel them when they move and I just—it's so gross. No one else can see them. I don't understand them at *all*."

"My grandfather thought the eyes had something to do with the language he—let's say *stole*, though I don't know from who."

"Demons from hell?" Kate joked, pulling the ladder

over to the next section, and she slowly started the climb again.

"I actually wouldn't put it past him."

She got to the top of the next bookshelf, and continued her search. "So, I hate to be that person, but if we don't find this book . . . do we have any plan Cs?"

"Plan C?"

"Plan A is finding the book, plan B is America rescuing us, and plan C is . . . ?"

"Oh. Well, I guess plan C would be not finding the book, Kingpin coming in and murdering us in cold blood only to dump our bodies in oil cans, fill them with cement, and throw us out into the middle of the Hudson River?"

She made a face and lowered herself on the ladder, and read through the next shelf. "I mean a *real* plan. They took my bow and arrows, and even if they didn't, I'm a waste at hand-to-hand right now with this . . ."— she motioned to her head—"*hypnosis*. Do you have that problem?"

He nodded, looking up at her as she grabbed the bookcase and pulled the ladder to the next section with her still on it. "It's why I can't just hypnotize our way out of here. Whenever I concentrate too much, I get so sick I vomit everywhere. After I hypnotized your friend? Immediately barfed in the bushes outside. *Immediately.*"

"That certainly puts a damper on things."

"Yeah, and besides, Kingpin took my notebook."

"Right, your notebook. I never asked what your villain name is, by the way. Writing Guy?"

"*Vigilante* name," he specified, "and no, not even close."

"Well, I hope your *vigilante* name has at least gone through numerous control groups."

"Says the girl who goes by 'Hawkeye.'"

"The *better* Hawkeye," she pointed out. "At least my gimmick is trick arrows. Yours is a *notebook.*"

"What's wrong with a notebook?"

"It's not very cool. I mean, America has a star-shaped dimension portal, Clint is four chaotic raccoons in a skinsuit, Squirrel Girl can talk to squirrels, Iron Man is rich, Captain America has a very nice ass . . ." She listed them off, counting them on her fingers, and then pulled out a book that looked a little like what they were looking for—*Aesop's Fables.* Nope. She slid it back and kept looking.

Milo held up his gloved hands and wiggled his fingers. "There's a supply of ink in my glove's fingertips. Does that count?"

"Oh." She blinked, recalling a few times he'd used them. "So, to use your hypnotism, all you need is a sheet of paper?"

He shrugged. "Any surface, really."

"Huh. And . . . what all can you bespell people to do?" *And have you used anything on me?* she added, quietly to herself, eyeing his gloves, suddenly quite glad she could only be bespelled one command at a time.

"Plenty of things," he replied reasonably. "I can make you feel like you're falling forever—"

"I'm aware of that one."

"I can make you think you're an animal. I can make you fall asleep, bid you to do something without you realizing that you're doing it . . . anything within reason, really," he added with a shrug. "My grandfather never stopped working on Shiver, so he learned all sorts of commands with me as his pet project. But like you, I can't do much of anything right now with this nightmare hypnosis in my head. So the best course of action would be . . . plan A: finding that book."

She rolled her eyes. Of *course* that was their best course of action, but the more she looked, the less she began to suspect it was in here at all. Wouldn't it be in the *A*s? Somewhere between Adler and Allen? Unless it was shelved improperly, and then it could be *anywhere*. . . .

If only they could leave this room—the Rose Reading Room was on the third floor, so if they could slip past the guards at the door, she and Milo could go through the window in the rotunda where she'd come in, but as it was, they were helpless to try to escape.

"Perhaps my grandfather didn't hide it here," Milo muttered, propping his head up on his hand, "which is a pity. I didn't think I'd die in a *library*."

She began to descend the ladder when a title caught her eye.

"Don't get me wrong, I have nothing against libraries. I rather love them . . . when I'm not about to be murdered and fed to sharks as chum."

"Uh-huh." She reached for the book. It was faded and dusty, having been forgotten in this library for . . . *years*. She drew it off the shelf.

"I just thought I'd die somewhere a bit more . . . *exciting*. It's a little too on-the-nose that the grandson of a famous children's-book novelist dies in a *library*—"

Kate slid down the ladder, book in hand, and dropped it in front of him.

He dusted off the title, his hands shaking.

THE IMMOVABLE CASTLE DREAMS OF DEATH.

He blinked at the title. "Huh."

Kate stared at the book. "What the—? It was just . . ."

"How did you—?"

"I just saw—"

"Huh," Milo said again.

Kate frowned. "Plot twist."

He quickly opened it and started skimming the pages, his fingers trembling as he searched.

"Do you remember what the third sigil in the letter looked like?" he asked, rubbing his hand.

"I do! I do, I'll recognize it anywhere—*there*," she added, stopping about a third of the way into the novel. She pointed to a strange-looking character that looked a little too large for the line. Her heart jumped into her throat. "That's it."

That's it.

Milo sank back in his chair, staring at it, though his gaze looked a thousand miles away.

Kate waited for him to write it, to break their spell, to do *something*, but he just sat there. "Milo?"

"Sorry. I—I'd given up trying to find it. I just . . . I was going to live with these nightmares. I thought it was my punishment for killing my parents. I deserve it. It was my fault. But, the cure is right here and . . ."

She put a hand on his shoulder. "You were a child."

He looked over to her, his eyes bright with unshed tears. "And that changes anything?"

"I think," she replied, choosing her words carefully, "it should. Punishment is useless if you aren't given the space to redeem yourself. Aren't you done with the tragedy? I think this is a good place to start your redemption arc."

He snorted, unable to keep a small smile from touching the edges of his mouth. "I wish you were more eloquent about it."

"I think I'm eloquent enough."

Milo took a deep breath. "Okay." Then he tore the page out and licked the tip of his gloved finger to get the ink going, and with a shaking hand he scrawled the first two sigils that had been burned into his palm for half his life, and then the new one. He handed the page to her. "You go first."

"Are you sure?"

"Please."

So, she took the paper and looked around for some sort of mirror or other reflective surface. She found it in the dome of the lamp, and she held up the page to read it—

The relief was almost immediate. The throbbing pain in the back of her skull melted away like fizzy rocks. She closed her eyes, tilted her head back, and relished—for a moment—the absolute silence in her skull.

The Kate Bishop in the brassy reflection of the lamp was smiling, and only a few moments later did she realize that she was, too.

The eyes had already begun to fade on her knuckles. She quickly pulled back her sleeve, and they vanished up her arms. As they left, they took with them her fears, and left her feeling a little hollower than before.

But more importantly—she felt like herself, because even though she was still bone-tired, the realization that she was back to *normal* gave her a shot of absolute ecstasy.

"How do you feel?" Milo asked hesitantly.

"Like a million bucks," she said with a grin.

"So it—it works?"

In reply, she turned the lamp to him. "It's time to let go, Milo. Don't live in the past."

He paused, but then he swallowed the lump in his throat and looked into the brass lamp. Something shifted in his gaze, and then his whole body unwound from the tense, rigid anxiety he'd held this entire time. He closed his eyes, and took a deep, deep breath.

Hesitantly, she reached over and patted him gently on the shoulder. Why was she always the one who got stuck consoling antiheroes? Deadpool, Wolverine, *Clint* . . .

All in a day's work, she guessed. She was just so happy to have that persistent headache gone—she could finally think clearly again. It was like stepping into an icy bath after a long run.

After a few minutes, Milo gathered himself back together and pushed himself to his feet. He tore the paper into tiny pieces. "All right," he said, and took a large breath. There was a new sharpness in his gaze. "I'm tired of playing by Kingpin's rules. I'm ready to play by mine."

"You okay?" Kate asked, studying him.

"Never better. Let's get out of here—"

He barely had time to look at her before she sent her fist into the side of his face. He stumbled sideways, catching himself on a table. "That was for bespelling my best friend."

"What the—*really*?"

"I couldn't before. You know, the whole nightmare pain thing."

He massaged the side of his face and mumbled, "I *guess* I deserved that. . . ."

"Fighting betwixt each other now, are we?" asked a voice with a peculiar Texan drawl from the doorway. Montana looped his lariat around his hand, his eyes flickering to the book that Milo quickly grabbed from the table. "So, Kingpin *was* right after all. I take it that's the book."

Milo quickly popped it open to write something on another page as Montana spun his rope into the air and flicked it out to lasso the book, but Kate caught it and wrapped it around her wrist.

She grinned. Because there was no pain, no hesitation. She *was*, in fact, back.

"You're dancing with me, partner," she told him.

Montana smirked. "I doubt you could handle me." He took his rope in both hands and jerked her forward, and she went stumbling.

It would've been an even fight, all things considered, if the last three days hadn't happened. But they had, and so Kate was very much not at the top of her game. And that was *not* a good way to go into a fistfight. Especially with someone rested up and *apparently* a black belt in bar brawls. She tried to score a hit, but Montana deflected every one of her punches, and as she stumbled passed him, he caught her by the ponytail—*low blow*—and jerked her backward.

She went stumbling back into a table so hard she knocked the brass lamp right off of it. She pushed herself off the table just in time to see Montana's fist half a second too late. It slammed the side of her face and she dropped like a rock.

Then Montana went for Milo, who at least had time to jot a sigil down over another page in *The Immovable Castle Dreams of Death* and show it to the cowboy.

The next moment, the henchman had him by the collar, slammed his face into the table, and he was out like a light, too.

CHAPTER TWENTY-EIGHT

SWEET CHILD, OF MINE

This time there was no nightmare.

The world looked like a fairy tale seen through rose-tinted glasses as she slowly came to and found herself in her childhood bedroom. It was just like she remembered it—the soft pastel walls, the fluffy comforter, the paper moon that hung in the corner as a night-light that threw stars across her ceiling while she slept. She was in her bed with her stuffed purple rabbit, which, in a few years, would be thrown away by a housekeeper on her father's orders. She clutched it tightly to her chest as she leaned against her mother's shoulder on one side, with her sister on the other, as they read . . .

It didn't really matter what they read.

It never mattered—it was never what made Kate love those moments, it was never the reason she snuggled into her pillow and listened to her mother's soft cadence, and her sister's smart questions of—

"Well, why is the rabbit always late if he has a watch with him?"

—she just enjoyed it.

This pocket of a memory, as fragile as a bubble, where for a moment her parents weren't screaming and she wasn't fighting with her sister and they were *here*.

Together.

And so Kate snuggled into her mom's shoulder, the smell of her perfume soft and heavy, the scent itself a memory of warm hugs and dancing across the living room to the radio and all the good moments that Kate bottled up inside her, and held tightly to. It was a scent that had gone out of production some years ago, so long ago that she'd almost forgotten what it smelled like: lavender and morning light.

Her sister kept a sweater of their mother's—soft and unwashed, the only thing they'd managed to hide from their dad when he sold all of her things after the funeral—and it still smelled like her. The last bit of her left, or so everyone thought.

If Kate wanted to look up into her mom's face, she might find a mouth full of hungry teeth. She might find blood on her lips. She might find a nightmare.

But Kate decided not to look at all, and let her mother read her and Suze to sleep.

Transcript (cont'd)

[Katherine Elizabeth Bishop's Statement Regarding the Events at the New York Public Library Stephen A. Schwarzman Building on August 2]
Recorded by Misty Knight

KNIGHT: So you basically decided that Milo was innocent in all of this?

BISHOP: Innocent? No. But I do think that the circumstances that surrounded his villain arc were *greatly* exaggerated. I mean, this was a kid who was experimented on and forced to *live* with his nightmares for years. Years!

KNIGHT: And he just . . . decided to turn over a new leaf? After you talked it out with him?

BISHOP: I am very persuasive, and he just wanted someone to listen to him who understood what he went through. I was sort of lucky—and very unlucky—that I did.

KNIGHT: Mm-hmm. [WRITES DOWN A FEW NOTES] That still leaves two glaring questions.

BISHOP: I'm about to *tell* you how we get out of this. But—wait—what's the second question?

KNIGHT: What hypnotism did Milo Penderghast-Chant cast on Montana?

BISHOP: Oh, just you wait.

CHAPTER TWENTY-NINE

HEART FULL OF DREAMS

And anyway, that was how Kate ended up upside down, a rope tied around her ankles, strung up from the chandelier of the New York Public Library Schwarzman building's Astor Hall.

The blood had already rushed so heartily to her head that when she finally *did* wake up, it was to an astounding headache. She tried to move, to get her bearings, but her hands were tied over her head with a zip tie, and there wasn't anything within her immediate vicinity she could use to un-cluster this cluster of a situation.

And the situation was *indeed* clustered.

Kingpin's men stood at various intervals in the lobby, way too many for her to count even *without* a pounding headache. But she didn't have nightmares, at least, and it'd been the first bit of sleep she'd had uninterrupted in *three days*. The smell of her mother's perfume lingered in her nose like a memory.

That was Kingpin's first mistake: letting her catch some shut-eye.

Beside her, Milo groaned. Somewhere between getting knocked out in the Rose Reading Room and here, he'd somehow gotten a black eye. A gash on his eyebrow bled up into his dark hair. "Wha . . . ?" He blinked blearily. "Are we dead?"

"If this is hell I'd like a refund," she replied. "The reception here absolutely *sucks*."

He made a pained noise. "I see you're back to your old jokey self."

"What a miracle a catnap can do."

"I feel *awful*."

"Probably because we're two heartbeats away from a brain aneurysm if we don't get out of this soon," she said, and he made an agreeable noise in his throat.

"Ah, you are both awake," said the rumbling voice of Kingpin as he came down the curving staircase. His cane clicked on each stone step as he descended slowly, his rings glinting in the light from the chandelier above them. How long had they been knocked out?

Kate chewed on the inside of her cheek. "Oh, he looks angry," she commented. "What did you *do*, Milo?"

"*Me?* Why do you think I did anything?"

"I was knocked out first."

"Trust me when I say I went right after you."

Kingpin's nostrils flared. In his right hand, he held *The Immovable Castle Dreams of Death*, and with his left he motioned for one of his men to hoist them higher into the air so they were eye level with him. And if anyone cut them loose, the fall would *hurt*.

A lot.

Kate squirmed, trying to test the zip ties holding her hostage. They were tight—there was no wiggling out of them. Where the heck was America? Hadn't she called in the cavalry yet? She hoped America hadn't run into any trouble.

"So I take it you both have found a cure for Project Shiver?" Kingpin asked, and slid a look to them. "Is it really that simple . . . that you both could find it?"

Kate rolled her eyes. "Give Milo some more credit."

"Please," Milo agreed.

"It was a lot harder than that, and who's to say we *did* find Project Shiver?"

"Because you're still alive, Katie," Kingpin said, grabbing her by the ear. She winced as he pulled her close. "No nightmares, I take it?"

"Besides you?" she ground out painfully.

"How original."

"At least it wasn't a 'your mom' joke."

"My mother is dead."

"See? It would've been a bad joke."

Kingpin let go of her and massaged the bridge of his nose. "Do you ever shut up?"

Kate and Milo—at the exact same time—replied, "No."

Wilson Fisk didn't deem that worthy of comment. Instead, he balled his hand into a fist and slammed it into Milo's stomach. He swung there like a punching bag, gasping for breath.

"HEY!" Kate squirmed, fighting against her binds. "He didn't do anything! *Hey!*"

"A bishop can never force a checkmate on a king. Isn't that something you should have learned by now?" Kingpin asked, grabbing Milo by his dark hair. Milo made an uncomfortable noise in his throat, but otherwise stayed silent, glaring at the mob boss with the kind of hatred that Kate didn't think Milo—much less anyone else—could feel.

Kingpin inspected him. "And who are you supposed to be? Her knight?"

"I'm just a pawn, dude. Don't think too much on the metaphor."

He let go of Milo's hair—and punched him again. This time in the face. Blood poured from his nose, and Kingpin took out a kerchief and cleaned it off his knuckles. He told Kate, "Either you tell me what you know, or I will kill him. I don't mind."

"I do," Milo replied hoarsely—and earned another punch to the face.

Kate said, "Okay! Okay—everything, I'll tell you everything."

"Good. I'd hate for him to die. Or"—Fisk grinned—"your sister."

Her eyes widened. "*. . . What?*"

"I asked Montana to go pay her a visit. Just in case. I'm not playing here, Katie. I realize you've never dealt with me before, but I assure you I'm not one to fool with."

She barked a laugh. "And you've never dealt with *me* before."

"You're just a child."

"I hate to disappoint you," she said, more than a little smugly. Smugger than she really *should* have been, considering she wasn't even all that sure. But half the lie was the presentation, so she grinned and said, "What—do you think I'd come here, *expecting* you to show up, and not have a plan? C'mon, I'm a little smarter than that, Wilson. No, like, a *lot* smarter than that."

He turned back to her with a curious expression. Milo echoed that exact same look.

She rolled her eyes. "I've done this super-hero

thing for a while now. I might not have super strength, or super smarts, or super healing, or super—I don't know—squirrel powers. But you know what I *do* got?"

Milo asked, "A super-big mouth?"

"Shush." She then puffed out her chest and added triumphantly, "I have some *super*-cool friends."

There was absolute silence.

Then Milo, still swinging from a punch to the face, deadpanned, "Wow, you really thought that was a moment, didn't you."

"I liked it," she replied, and told Kingpin, "You might want to check up on ya boy."

Kingpin took a step back and pointed to one of his men. "Call Montana."

The goon in question took out his phone and did just that. It rang and rang and rang. The color in his cheeks began to drain away. After a moment, he shook his head. "No answer, boss."

More than a little surprised, Kingpin returned his attention to the two of them hanging upside down.

Milo said, "I can't recall which character I hypnotized him with—the one for amnesia? Or the one that turns you, mentally, into a chicken? Jury's out, really."

Kate's smile only widened. "And you know what else, Fisk?" she went on.

"Let me guess," Kingpin droned, clearly annoyed

to have been outsmarted by a teenager, "you're the world's greatest archer."

"And in the top one percent of online players of *Chess Unlimited*."

Then she grabbed the tail of the zip tie with her teeth, tightened it as far as it could go, and with all her might slammed her tied hands against her middle. The zip tie broke with a snap. So what—she didn't have super strength or flight or whatever. She couldn't heal quickly and she couldn't hypnotize people with a word and she always had cuts and scrapes all over her face—but she *was* really good at one thing—

Well, *two* things.

One: She had some really great jokes, if she was being modest.

And two: She was the sharpest shooter in the world, and she'd tell that to Clint's face any day of the week.

So, Kate Bishop did what she always did best—

She pulled out her hair tie and quickly hooked her bobby pin into it. Then she aimed right at the light switch behind the welcome desk.

And fired.

The bobby pin zinged through the air and flipped the switch.

Bull's-eye.

The lights all flickered off—every one of them.

Except, of course, for the monstrous red exit signs that glowed in the far reaches of the building. The second Astor Hall crashed to black, chaos erupted, and Wilson Fisk flinched.

It was a blink-and-you-miss-it moment. He flinched like he'd seen something monstrous. He flinched as if he wanted to cover his face to protect himself.

He *flinched*.

Like the darkness was out to get him.

Kate grabbed Milo's shoulder and shoved him—hard. He went swinging into one of Kingpin's men, who swung around in retaliation, but Milo was already on his way back to Kate. He slammed into her with an *"Oof!"* and she went spiraling to the other side, where she grabbed a tall man by his middle—his belt to be exact—with one hand and patted down his waist with the other.

Gun, Taser, where was it, where was it—

"Hey, hey!" he cried, trying to swat her away.

"Aha! Sorry!" she cried, grabbing a pocketknife from what she hoped was his back pocket, and pushed away just as he turned at her with what felt like a punch. It whizzed past her face as she swung back toward Milo, and pulled herself up far enough to cut the rope holding her. It snapped—

She dropped like lead to the ground.

The guard Milo hit grabbed him by the shirt.

"Kate!" he cried as the man pulled back his fist, squinting in the low light.

She swung out her leg, slamming it into the man's shins. He flipped head over heels and landed with a *crunch* on his shoulder. She always forgot how hard it was to see when everything was awash in red.

"You okay?" she asked Milo, cutting him down, and caught him before he hit the ground. She slapped him on the back as she pulled him to his feet. "You're good, you're good."

"I think something is broken," he mumbled.

"Your pride doesn't count."

The foyer was in chaos. And she was quite sure everyone was about to get their bearings and come after her in three, two, one—

From the darkness Kingpin roared, "KILL KATE BISHOP!"

Oh, *that* wasn't good.

She pulled Milo's arm around her shoulder. He muttered, "We need to get that book from Kingpin."

"Yeah," she agreed. "We do."

"Do you have a plan?"

"I'm thinking. Do you?"

"Gimme some paper and I might."

The first henchman came at them in the red lights. She saw their outline just before he slammed a fist into her stomach. She doubled over, only to be yanked to the side by Milo, and steadied on her feet.

"Thanks," she wheezed.

"He's coming back!"

She turned and grabbed the man as he went to swing at her again and twisted his arm, using his own momentum to send him slamming onto his back.

God, it felt good to be able to fight again.

Milo bent down and patted the prone guy down— and came back with a pad of paper. "Bingo!" he cried. Then, distraught, "Duck!"

She did as a fist swung around where her head had been. "Tell me when I need to close my eyes!"

"Gimme a sec. . . ." He bent over in the low light and flipped past grocery lists and to-do lists to a blank page and scrawled a character on it.

Kate grabbed the next guy by the back of the jacket as he stumbled past and redirected him into a guy about to pile-drive Milo into the ground. They crashed together and went careening into a table set up with brochures and audio guides for tours.

"Okay—close your eyes!" Milo cried, and Kate did as she was told.

She waited.

For anything, really. Someone to punch her. Someone to swipe her legs out from under her. Someone to throw her clear across the room. Someone to *shoot* her—which was very odd no one had tried *that* yet.

Suddenly she heard a bunch of things hit the ground—like heavy sacks of potatoes.

"Okay, you can open them now."

She cracked open an eye. In the low red light, at least a dozen men who had been about to kick her and Milo's butts were on the ground, wiggling with their hands at their sides. She gave Milo a puzzled look, and he replied, "Oh, worms."

"Oooh." She nodded. "Don't do that to me."

Milo opened his mouth to reply, and instead pointed toward the stairwell. "I think he's getting away."

The man in question was taking the stairs up two at a time to the second floor.

"Crap," she hissed. Kingpin was getting away. She turned to Milo. "You got this?"

He motioned to the worm-men around him. "I mean . . . I guess?"

"Good, I'm going after the Kingpin boss guy— oh, wait, is that my *bow*?" she added, looking down at one of the men inching along on the ground. She grabbed her bow from him in disgust. "It *is*! And my arrows!" she added, jumping over the guy to wrench her quiver from another body. She fitted it over her shoulder and watched the other half-dozen men pour down the stairwell opposite them, reaching for their gun holsters.

No, she didn't think they would.

Pulling a grappling arrow out of her quiver, she nocked it to her belt and fired it through the balcony. The arrow tip stuck fast to the stone ceiling and pulled her up. She beat Fisk to the top of the stairs and met him on the second floor, where she nocked another arrow and drew it back.

She aimed it for his head. "Checkmate."

CHAPTER THIRTY

EMOTIONAL DAMAGE

"**L**ook," she said, because she was tired and she really didn't want to keep chasing Kingpin all night, "put down the book and I won't string you up by your toes. There's nowhere left for you to run."

Fisk snarled, "*Running?* No, I don't run."

"Okay, then you can just walk into my arrow if you want to. I'll make sure it doesn't hurt. This isn't the electrified-net arrow. At least, I don't *think* it is."

The top of his lip twitched. "Do you know *why* I'm feared, Kate Bishop?"

"Because you're a methodical businessman who climbed his way through the underbelly of New York City's crime syndicates backstabbing everyone you ever came across and somehow managed to avoid any extended prison time?" she asked, and cocked her head innocently. "Am I close?"

He looked annoyed as he shrugged out of his pristine white suit jacket. "Everyone I met always said that that young Hawkeye was a bit of a chatterbox. And you know what I told them?"

"That I probably have a lot of really fantastic things to say? That my jokes are amazing? That I am very talented at what I do, because I did in fact outsmart the Kingpin of Crime?"

"I told them," he said, and he rested his hand on one of the glass podiums that housed some of the current artwork on display—a vase with some very beautiful flower details peeling from it like paint, "that it was a good weakness to exploit."

The next she knew, Kingpin had grabbed the podium and, having already planted his feet, threw the vase at her. She ducked. It shattered behind her on a pillar.

Right. He was an Olympic-level weight lifter.

He could crush skulls like watermelons.

And she would have run then and there—really, she would have—if Fisk hadn't gotten to her first, grabbed her by her middle, and thrown her clear across the gallery. She slammed into the ground and skidded down the hall. Her vision spun. Above a closed door to her right read BERGER FORUM. To her left, the room for some Allens or something. Both closed. With electric locks.

So she couldn't even escape this hallway.

For a moment, she lay there afraid to move.

Everything hurt.

It hurt so, so much. It hurt so badly she didn't want to breathe because it'd just hurt more.

And yet somehow, through getting flung across a room, she'd still managed to keep hold of her bow. Not that she could feel her hand. Or her arm. Or her shoulder—oh no, *there* it was. She hissed in pain as she rolled over onto her back and stared up at the ceiling. This really was a nice library.

She was sad that she had to go and ruin it.

There were footsteps, faint at first—but running. Well, limping really. Then a blurry shape knelt down beside her. Her head was still ringing from the impact, and when she touched one of her ears, her fingers came away with blood. Huh. Guess things were pretty bad.

She squinted up at his face. "Hey, Milly-Miley-Lo-Lo," she croaked.

"Oh, thank *god* you're alive." Milo exhaled in relief and slowly helped her sit up.

She asked, "What's happening now?" but it sounded more like "Wazhappeningow?"

Milo looked toward Fisk. "We need to move."

"Is he doing a bad?"

"Worse!" he added, dragging her to her feet as something zapped just where she'd been standing, leaving a blackened scorch on the marble.

She glanced at it, then at Kingpin and the walking cane in his hands. "Oh. I forgot about the cane."

Milo made a disgruntled noise in his throat. "Let's go, let's go. There's a stairwell over there I came up; we can go down it and get away." He pulled her arm over his shoulder as he talked, adamant that they start hauling ass or get vaporized, too, with the disintegration cane. But even if they ran, they were going to die if she didn't do something, so—still aching, knowing she'd broken at least a rib, pretty sure she'd cracked her sternum—she reached into her quiver and pulled out the first arrow she felt. Didn't even see what it was before she nocked it. Drew it back to her natural anchor point.

Then released it.

The arrow spiraled through the air toward the rippling mass of muscle and terror—

And imbedded into his shoulder.

"Heck yes!" she cheered.

He ripped it out.

Milo said, grabbing her hand to run again, "Heck *no!*"

"I'm getting tired of nosy kids who can't mind their own damn business," Fisk growled, aiming his cane again, and Kate pushed Milo away from her as the six-foot-tall stone candelabra behind them vaporized into ash. "You think you're something, but you're just a B-level hero, Hawkeye."

Annoyed, she reached into the quiver and took two more arrows. "Why don't people think I'm cool? I'm *so* cool." She planted her feet on the ground and drew back the two arrows on her string. Then she raised her aim and shot at his head.

Probably would've pierced it, too . . . if Kingpin hadn't caught it.

"Come *on!*" she almost sobbed.

He snapped the arrow in half. "I'll grind you up, Kate Bishop, and put you in a box. I'll deliver you with a tiny red ribbon to your dear father's front door."

"I'd think as a dad you'd feel differently," Kate replied. "World's Worst Father? Maybe I'll ask your adopted daughter, Maya. Oh, wait, she tried to kill you."

"She'll come back."

"I doubt it. Also," she added, and held up two fingers, "there's a second arrow."

Kingpin gave her a peculiar look before the detonation arrow she'd shot into the wall beside him exploded, sending him through the wall into the Cullman Center, and through quite a few lovely couches and some marble furniture.

That explosion wouldn't keep Kingpin down for long.

A thought occurred to her. "Milo, *did* your grandfather make a pact with a demon? And was his name M—"

Milo's eyes widened as he stared through the hole in the wall. "Uh, Kate?"

A second later, something threw Kingpin back into the hall. He skidded across it and into the men's restroom, where his head hit the underside of a urinal.

Kate peeked around the hole in the wall into the Cullman Center.

A star-shaped portal closed behind a woman with curly brown hair pulled up into a bun, her hands on her hips, feet spread apart, glowering across the hall at the lump of muscle and flesh slowly getting to his feet like he was a bug on the bottom of her high-tops— and for the first time Kate figured that's what America Chavez looked like to everyone who she rescued.

Golden, ephemeral, and utterly beautiful.

Beside her, Misty Knight flexed her metal arm. "Kate," she said, "we're going to need to talk."

Kate could cry, she was so happy to see them. "I'll give you an exclusive interview—whatever you want!"

Sirens wailed in the distance.

"You hear that, Kingpin?" America called to the mob boss. "That's Misty Knight's cop friends coming to kick your b—" She froze. Her face went serious.

Kate turned to look at Fisk.

He'd managed to get back onto his feet and was pointing his cane at Milo. Kingpin grinned through his bloodied teeth. "I don't think anyone's coming for me, America Chavez."

America glowered.

He started toward Milo, who stood as still as a statue, paper-pale, and let Kingpin take him around the throat and shove the butt of his cane against his skull.

"Now I'm going to walk out of here, and you're going to do nothing. You're not as smart as you think you are, Katie," Kingpin went on, stepping back toward the side stairwell. Milo, pale and trembling, moved with him, shuffling his feet as he went. He dropped his notepad along the way.

Another few steps, and Kingpin disappeared down the stairwell, taking Milo with him.

America went to follow but Kate grabbed her shoulder to stop her. "I got this."

"But what about your—your hypno-thing?"

"Cured, and don't worry, I got this. I think Milo

just made it super easy for us," she added, grabbing his notebook from the ground. She faced it away from her as she tore the last page—scrawled in his glove-ink—and left down the main stairwell instead. There were two main exits out of the library, at least from what she recalled on the map: the front that led out onto Fifth Avenue, and the one on the ground floor that led out to Forty-Second Street.

She was *quite* sure he wouldn't go out the front—but she certainly would.

She just didn't anticipate how much everything would *hurt* at a full-on sprint out of the library, down the stairs, and around the side to Forty-Second Street. She didn't need to be close. She just needed a clear shot.

She *was* Hawkeye, after all.

Passing Patience the Lion, she took a wad of fresh gum from the base of the statue—*gross, gross, gross*—and stuck it to the back of the paper. She rounded the side of the building just as Kingpin pushed his way out onto the street, holding Milo still by the neck.

Kate reached into her quiver and took out a putty arrow.

She had one shot at this, or Milo was toast.

So, she nocked it. The fletching found its anchor

point. She aimed. Stilled her breath. Put her target into her sights and then—

She let the arrow fly.

It slammed into Wilson Fisk's cane. The putty exploded, sending his cane backward into the bulbous light pole behind him. Kingpin looked around, trying to find the archer—and then found her.

Kate nocked another arrow and patiently came down the sidewalk toward him. There was a person sitting at the bottom of the steps, enjoying a nice knish, but they quickly shuffled away and went to join a few late-night tourists who were gathering at the corner of Fifth Avenue. It must have been around midnight already, but the sharp, bright lights of Midtown brought everything into the day, even after the sun had gone down.

Kingpin gritted his teeth and pulled Milo closer. "Kate Bishop, you know I can crush him. You can't think to defeat me, I'm—"

"Can we not with the whole villain monologue? I get it," she said, and planted the piece of paper directly to her forehead with the gum, like a makeshift game of Heads Up. Kingpin knew what it was, and so he avoided her face entirely. Downturned his eyes. He didn't know you could only be bespelled by one hypnosis at a time, and that was exactly what she counted on. "You wanted Project Shiver, you wanted to make the world fear you, you wanted to sell it to the highest bidder, whatever. I get it, I figured it out. Bravo, me!"

Kingpin sneered, staring at the ground. "You're thinking too small."

"Oh, *world* domination, then?"

"A man would be a god with that kind of subliminal power, Katie."

She took out another arrow from her quiver and nocked it. "Don't call me Katie." She drew it back and aimed at an impossible target, and she was the only one in the world who could hit it. "My name's Hawkeye."

"A little girl with a bow."

"That you can't even look at," she taunted. "What's the matter, Fisk, can't meet my gaze?"

"I'm no fool, Katie."

"Tragic, really." Especially considering what was on the piece of paper.

Suddenly he twitched at the feeling of an arrow sliding by his cheek, and sneered, "You *missed*."

Kate pulled her aim tight. "I haven't even shot, actually."

Confusion knotted his brow. He glanced behind him, and sure enough, there was nothing there. No arrow, no place where an arrow should have been. His grip on Milo slackened just enough that Milo slipped out of Fisk's grip and stumbled away.

Though, strangely, Fisk barely noticed.

"What's wrong, Kingpin? Seeing things?" she taunted.

And by the looks of it, his hallucinations were more than just eyes on his skin or a whisper in his ear. What hunted someone who was usually the hunter? She'd love to know, but whatever Kingpin saw, making his eyes wide and his face fracture—ever so slightly, in the only way that Wilson Fisk knew how to look afraid—it must have been quite a nightmare indeed.

How *easy* it'd just be to drive an arrow straight through his skull. They'd never have to worry about Wilson Fisk again. He'd never ransack libraries. (Well, that was partially *her* fault.) He'd never bother anyone ever, *ever* again.

If this were a fantasy book, some epic with a magical sword and an evil skeleton king, death would be little more than the just end of a plot.

Death was just.

And Kate Bishop, despite all of her hang-ups, all of her failures and insecurities and nightmares, was not just.

She was kind. Not nice.

Kind.

And maybe that was a weakness, but it'd been her weakness since the beginning, since she first took up a bow and learned self-defense and remembered that night in Central Park years ago, when all she wanted to do was help.

Kate Bishop was kind.

And, most importantly, she didn't kill.

So, she raised her aim to him, as he snarled at some invisible opponent to get away from him, that he was invincible, that he'd never be tricked by stupid *illusions*, these *eyes*, why were there so many *eyes*—

"Bishop takes king," she whispered.

And released her arrow.

A net burst from the arrowhead and wrapped around Kingpin so tightly, he fell onto his side and stared off into the distance, as eyes, so many eyes, bubbled up across his skin. Ones that only he could see.

CHAPTER THIRTY-ONE

THE INTERVIEW

"**A**aaaaaand that's how I caught him," Kate finished, drumming her fingers on the metal table.

You'd think that if you saved the city—no, the *world*—from a maniacal crime boss bent on acquiring a weapon of psychological warfare to sell to the highest bidder, the FBI's Aberrant Crimes Division would be a little more lenient, and yet here Kate was in an interrogation room at the NYPD police station in Midtown. Being questioned by none other than Misty Knight.

Well, Kate *had* promised her an exclusive interview.

Misty hadn't even asked if she wanted a coffee or a cup of water or her single phone call. The FBI investigator kept reiterating that Kate hadn't been detained, she was just here for questioning—but it'd been a few hours and all Kate wanted to do was sleep.

Finally.

And, oh, it'd be blissful.

"Can I *please* go home now?" she added, leaning forward. "I know I'm so pleasant to hang out with, but I'd really love to catch a nap. For a year. Or two."

Misty shifted in her chair. She kept looking at something in her lap—a phone? Kate was too exhausted to even guess. It *had* to be a cell phone. She didn't think those were allowed in interrogation rooms. Then Misty glanced at the blacked-out window and, to Kate's surprise, ended the recording. She leaned forward and said, "You're in a lot of trouble, Miss Bishop."

"*Me?*" Kate gave a start. "What did *I* do?"

Misty replied without a pause, "Aiding and abetting a known criminal. There are four different undercover operations that have apparently been found out because of you. You put three of those undercover officers in the hospital, actually."

Kate narrowed her eyes, frowning. "I hope one of them wasn't Montana—you *did* pick up Monty, didn't you? I'd hate it if he was clucking like a chicken down Park Avenue. . . ."

Misty resisted the urge to roll her eyes. "You're just like the other Hawkeye."

"Should I take that as a compliment?"

"Take it any way you please. The fact is, the second I let you walk out that door, the deputy sheriff is going to arrest you on three counts of assaulting an officer and one count of aiding a known crime boss."

"I didn't *aid* him. . . ."

Misty gave her That Look, and Kate winced and shut up.

Her shoulders slumped even more. "And . . . Milo?"

"I suggest you only worry about yourself right now," Misty said, and stood, pushing her papers into a neat stack. Then she thought of something and asked, "What *was* on the piece of paper you stuck to your forehead?"

"Oh, that? Milo said he tried to draw a middle finger but it kind of looked like . . ."

"Ah. Well, that's unfortunate. I thought it might've been the cure to Kingpin's nightmare hypnosis. Wouldn't that have been a fun plot twist? His salvation right there, and he was too afraid to look at it."

Kate shrugged. "What can I say? Milo's not that smart."

To that, Misty nodded and gathered up her files. "Well," she said as the door opened and a grumpy-looking police officer stepped inside, "I can say Clint's stories about you didn't disappoint."

"Thanks, I guess—and, Misty? How are the book-sellers?"

"Thanks to Milo's cooperation, they're on the mend. And so is Kingpin," Misty added, and patted the officer on the shoulder. "Please don't cause a scene, and do exactly what this man says, all right Kate?"

And go to jail? Kate opened her mouth to rebut, but the police officer checked the handcuffs on her wrists and grabbed her arm, pulling her up from her chair. "W-wait! I didn't—this isn't—oh come *on!*" she pleaded, but the FBI investigator simply looked the other way as the police officer hauled Kate to her feet and led her toward the door.

For a split second, Kate wondered how much more trouble she could get into if she, you know, knocked this grunt out and hightailed it for the nearest air vent. That's how it worked in most movies, right? The air vents would lead her to some back room where she could make her escape and—

"I know that face. Don't you think about it," the grunt said, mouth hovering at her ear. Her heart jumped in her chest as she glanced—finally—at the man's face. Clint Barton quirked an eyebrow.

"Blue's not your color," she said in greeting, more relieved than she'd ever admit to seeing his smug face.

"You can't talk to an officer of the law like that," Clint replied matter-of-factly.

"Don't make me call you 'sir.'"

He made a face. "Gross."

"Exactly." Then she paused and said, "We need to get Milo."

"Who?"

"Milo—you know, Albright's grandson. Him!" she added quietly just as they passed the next interrogation room. Milo sat in a hard metal chair, his hands cuffed and placed on the table in front of him, as a squatty, broad-shouldered man screamed down at him. Milo was . . . behaving a lot better under pressure than she would have thought. He looked amused, frankly.

Clint commented, "Do we have to?"

She gave him a look. He made a disgruntled noise in his throat, then left her in the hall and shouldered open the door to the interrogation room.

"—AND WHO ELSE WILL PAY FOR THE LIBRARY COSTS? YOU AIDED AND ABETTED ONE OF THE WORST CRIMES IN—"

"Yo, Patrick just brought a dozen hot ones," Clint said, thumbing behind him.

The man paused mid-sentence, thought, and then jabbed a finger at Milo and said, "You're staying right there!" before he squeezed past Clint and down the hall. Kate angled her face away, but it didn't really do much good. The officer brushed past her so quickly she doubted he even noticed her.

A moment later, Clint had Milo by the back of his neck, leading him out of the interrogation room.

"Hey, let me go! I demand a phone call! I— Oh, Kate?" Milo hesitantly looked between Kate and the cop who had him by the neck. "Is this . . . ?"

In response, Clint muttered, "Roll with it, kid," and pushed them both forward, telling them to keep walking.

It was insultingly easy to escape the police station if the person who was undercover looked remotely like he knew what he was doing. Which Clint did. He was a bit *too* into it as he nodded to an officer coming in with a perp and said, "There're donuts in the conference room!"

"Aw man, there are *donuts*?" the returning cop lamented as they passed. "I've got paperwork to do first. . . ."

With the morning sun bright and glaring, Clint led Kate and Milo down the steps onto the sidewalk and hung a quick right. And there, parked on the next block, was a cherry-red 1972 Dodge Challenger. Kate never thought she'd be so happy to see it. The windows were rolled down, a golden retriever poking his head out of the back one, tongue hanging and tail wagging. Someone lounged in the passenger seat, feet kicked up on the dashboard. Brown curly hair, loud bomber jacket, legs for days—

America, Kate thought, somehow happier than she'd been about seeing Clint or the Challenger combined.

But of course, it could never be that easy.

"Hey! HEY! I'M NOT DONE QUESTIONING THEM!" the investigator who had been screaming at Milo cried from the entrance to the police station. With him, Misty stepped out of the doors and looked at the escaping convicts. "Agent *Knight*! They're escaping!"

To which the FBI investigator shrugged as she descended the steps from the police station. "I told you *I* was done questioning them. I didn't need them any longer."

Clint quickly uncuffed both Kate and Milo with a single smooth move. "Time's up, in the car!"

Since the windows were down, Kate just dove into the backseat where Lucky was sitting. Clint pulled the driver's seat forward to let Milo climb through to the back with her, and slid into the driver's side. Milo and Kate high-fived each other, mirroring the same eat-dirt grin.

America said, "I *could* have drove."

Clint kicked his car into drive. "Absolutely not." Then he looked pointedly at her feet. *"Ahem?"* She sighed and took them off the dash as the Challenger peeled out of the parking spot and down Broadway.

Kate forced herself to sit up, wincing at a pain that shot through her chest—right, her ribs. Probably bruised and not broken, but painful No-Touchy ribs nonetheless—and peeked out the back window, but . . . there were no pursuers.

She frowned.

Milo didn't like that expression. "Is something wrong . . . ?"

To which Kate turned back around, getting a faceful of tongue from Lucky, still too excited to see her, and asked Clint, "Why isn't anyone after us? And when did you get back in the city? Down, boy, just a second," she added, scrubbing the dog behind his ears.

"Questions, questions, questions," Clint singsonged as he took his Aviators from the visor and put them on, because the morning sun was glaring and there wasn't a single cloud in the bright New York sky. He also just looked cool wearing them.

America turned back to Kate and said, "It's nothing that impressive, I promise."

"Whoa, whoa now, don't steal my thunder," Clint replied. "As it just so happened, a buddy of mine owed me a favor. So, I had him cash it in."

Milo asked curiously, "Who, exactly?"

Kate glanced back one more time and squinted toward the police station only to see the very tall, very broad, very blond costumed super hero saunter into the station, looking like he'd stepped out of a 1920s UNCLE SAM WANTS YOU poster, and she slid down in her seat with a groan. "Oh nooooo . . . he's going to call me, isn't he? And give me his 'This Is Why We Don't Fraternize with Villains' speech again."

Milo said, "I'm not a *villain*, I'm a vigilante."

America turned around from the front seat. "What *is* your vigilante name, anyway? Paper? Quill? Hypno-geek?"

He inclined his head and said with his entire chest, *"Penchant."*

No one said a word.

So he went on, "You know, because my last name? Penderghast-Chant? And because I write my hypnosis? Anyone?"

America said, "That's . . ."

"Really great, Milo," Kate finished for her, giving her a *Don't you dare* look.

"Really?" he asked, hopeful. "Because you don't sound so sure. . . ."

"No! It's perfect, really—"

Clint blurted, "It sucks, kid."

You would have thought that Clint had told him that his favorite puppy had died. "It does?"

"Yeah."

Kate said, "It does *not*."

"It definitely does. *Penchant?*"

"Well—*Hawkeye* isn't any better," Milo argued. "What kind of super hero name is that, anyway?"

"It's a cool name!"

Clint agreed, "Best name, actually."

"And what the heck is a *Penchant*, anyway? I get it, your last name is Penderghast-Chant, but *really*? That's, like, going by your *actual* name."

America Chavez said, in complete deadpan, "Oh yes, because no one does that."

Kate winced. "You know what I mean."

"Do I, Kate? Do I really?"

"You could've gone by something else! Captain Great-Thighs is my favorite so far."

America turned around to glare at her. Kate shrugged.

Milo sighed. "*Fine*, I'll go back to the drawing

board." He reached out to try to pet Lucky, but the dog bared his teeth and Milo quickly retracted his hand.

Kate pointed at him, "*See?* You hurt his feelings, too. Lucky's the best part of Hawkeye."

Clint made a face. "Ugh. *Feelings?*"

"Ew, gross," America agreed as Clint put his blinker on to take them toward the Lower East Side and—finally, mercifully—bed.

CHAPTER THIRTY-TWO

PARTING IS SUCH SWEET SORROW

Clint pulled up to the curb of Kate's apartment in the Lower East Side and flipped down his Aviators. "Okay, kid, end of the line."

"Fine, fine, I'm starved. Anyone want takeout?" Kate asked as America got out, folded the passenger seat down, and helped Kate claw her way out of the back. "Pizza?"

"Pizza's agreeable," America replied, and reached to help Milo out, too, when Clint put his arm back to stop him from leaving.

"Not you, buddy," Clint said.

Milo wilted, crushed. "But . . ."

"You've got a few more questions to answer for some people."

Kate gave Clint a strange look. "Who? Misty already questioned him about Kingpin—"

"About other things. We have some more questions about the books, and the language . . . things that need to be recorded in case anything like this happens again in the future," he said, and looked back at Milo. "Is that capiche?"

Milo hesitated in the backseat, and Kate knew that look in his eyes—he was thinking about making a run for it—but then his shoulders dropped a little, and he nodded. "Yeah, I guess . . . I guess it wouldn't hurt."

"Don't worry, it's not going to be that scary," Clint said. "Lucky'll be with you."

"Oh, great . . ." Milo said, braving a look at the very dog who very much didn't like him.

Kate closed the door and leaned in through the window. "Remember, always look them in the eyes. Cap can smell fear."

Milo's eyes widened. "Cap—as in—as in *Captain America*?" He looked alarmed between Kate and Clint. "I'm going to be interrogated by *Captain America*?"

"I mean, maybe not," Clint replied with a shrug. "It might be Natasha. Or, I dunno, someone really pleasant." He paused. "Maybe I'll do it."

"Is it too late to get out of the car?"

"Absolutely." And to emphasize it, Clint locked the doors and flipped his Aviators back up.

"But—"

"Look at the time," he added, checking his imaginary watch as he put the car back into drive and started away from the curb. "I have to get you to the Tower, unpack, take a bubble bath, feed the *dog*—"

Lucky gave a woof in agreement from the backseat. Milo sank down beside him.

"Have fun, kids," Clint said, waving his hand out the window. "Don't go fraternizing with a villain again, Kate!"

She threw up her hands. "I wasn't— *Argh!* They're gone," she muttered as the Challenger belched a plume of black smoke and disappeared down the next street. She crossed her arms over her chest and frowned. "You don't *actually* think he's going to be interrogated by Cap, do you?"

In reply, America crossed herself and muttered a prayer.

CHAPTER THIRTY-THREE

ANCHOR POINTS

The last day of summer camp was hot and bright, and Kate was waiting on the green lawn with three extra shots of espresso in her coffee, Aviators on to disguise her gnarly black eye, as Ms. Marvel's Ping-Pong champions arrived.

And now, all five of Ms. Marvel's campers were coming over to her, sharing the same confused looks with each other. Ms. Marvel even looked a bit baffled by this turn of events.

She flipped down her Aviators. "Morning, kids."

Murella gave her a look. "What happened to your eye?"

"Did you catch the bad guy?" Irving added.

Evelyn agreed, adding, "Did you—did you do any rapid shooting?"

"Yes, and yes," Kate replied. "C'mon! It's your last day of camp! You have to be at least a *little* thrilled to see me?" she asked, and earned a bunch of eye rolls. Which, fair. "Look, I always keep my promises, okay? That's why I'm here. And I thought I'd show you today how I hit a moving target. You can call it an in-person *webi*nar."

On cue, the web-slinging super hero came swinging in from god knows where (how did he get *purchase* in Central Park?) and did one of those fancy flips in the air. But Kate was pretty fancy, too. She took an arrow from her quiver, nocked it, and without looking fired it at the flying man in a red-and-blue leotard.

He caught it in midair and landed a few feet away from them. Though Kate wasn't sure who was more excited, the kids or Ms. Marvel. "Hey, kids!" he greeted them, throwing up a hand to wave. "You must be the intrepid investigators I've heard so much about! Gotta say, Kate has told me some great things about you all."

Murella quirked an eyebrow. "That we suck at Ping-Pong? Or that we helped thwart a mobster boss from getting his hands on a weapon of mass warfare?"

"The second one," Spider-Man admitted hesitantly, rubbing the back of his neck.

Evelyn squinted at everyone's favorite neighborhood

web-head. Then she frowned and said, "I thought you'd be taller."

He gave a start and stood up a bit straighter. "Well, I—I was slouching a little bit."

Rajiv said, "No, you *are* really short. In the game, you're taller."

"And the costume looks kind of cheap. Are you the real deal?" Irving asked, highly suspect.

"I—uh—I . . . I think I am . . . ?"

Martin sighed. "See, this is why you should never meet your heroes." Irving nodded tragically.

Kate began to grin. She couldn't stop herself. It was cathartic, in a way, knowing that these kids roasted literally everyone they met. It wasn't just her. And she knew she was cool and super and really, *really* awesome. The kids did, too, even if they'd never admit it.

Ms. Marvel came up beside her, bouncing on her heels. "Oh my god, you actually got him to *come here*? How?"

"Oh, I just put one of his big bads away for at *least* a month, so he owed me," Kate replied, and enjoyed the beautiful morning, listening to Spider-Man get absolutely annihilated by a bunch of eight-year-olds.

CHAPTER THIRTY-FOUR

ALL'S WELL THAT ENDS WELL

Susan's party was about as fun as Kate figured it would be.

Which wasn't fun at *all*.

She'd showered and pulled her hair back into a ponytail, but she must've still looked like she'd been thrown through a window and laid out in oncoming traffic, because none of Susan's posh Manhattanite friends wanted to come within five feet of her. Which was just fine, since that meant she could camp out by the little sandwiches at the buffet table and hoard them all. America hadn't come with her after all, but not because she hadn't wanted to. There was apparently a *second* Roach Queen they had to deal with, seeking revenge for the death of her lover. Quite tragic, really.

Kate didn't envy that job.

Instead, she spent her afternoon keeping company with the tasty little sandwiches, at least until her sister slipped up beside her with a strained smile. "Katie, you look terrible this afternoon."

Kate popped another mini sandwich into her mouth. "Fell down the stairs."

"How many flights?"

". . . Three?"

"Are you sure?"

Kate hesitated. ". . . Yes?"

Susan rolled her eyes and snagged a sandwich for herself before they were all gone. "You don't have to look so stressed out, Dad's not going to be here. So you can rest easy."

"Huh, I wondered why this party actually felt— what's that feeling? *Fun?*" she asked, and her sister elbowed her in the side.

"Shush. And *you* don't want to be here, either, so stop eating my sandwiches and go droop over someone else's petit-fours."

"Oh, Suze, that's almost sweet of you," Kate said, putting a hand on her sister's shoulder. "I'm frightening your other guests, aren't I?"

Susan's smile never left her face. *"Immensely."*

"Okay, okay, then here." Kate pulled a small box out of her back pocket. It was tiny and white, the ribbon a bit smushed, but otherwise it looked quite presentable. "With love."

Her sister eyed her suspiciously, as she gently ate her sandwich, and accepted the gift. "What is this . . . ?"

"Exactly what it looks like. An elephant riding a moped."

"Ugh, why are you so weird?" Susan scowled as she opened the box. In it sat a simple, small vial of perfume. "Oh, this is . . . surprisingly thoughtful."

"Smell it."

"Kate."

She laughed, "No, it's not a joke—*really*."

So her sister did—albeit a little hesitantly—and her eyes widened. "You found Mom's perfume?"

"I went *everywhere* looking for it," Kate replied proudly. "It's one of the last ones, I'll have you know."

Susan wasn't the watery kind of person. She didn't cry all that often—if ever—so Kate didn't expect her to show any sort of emotion here, either, but she pulled Kate into a hug. "Thank you," Susan whispered, not loud enough for any of her friends to hear, but loud enough for Kate, and that was enough for her.

She returned the hug. "Always. Now, I *am* going to leave, though," she added, letting go of her sister before she grabbed another two petit-fours—with a sigh from Susan—and kissed her on the cheek. "Happy birthday, sis. C'mon, Lucky!" she added, and to Susan's horror, a one-eyed golden retriever came out from underneath the food table and trotted along at Kate's heels as they left the apartment.

When they got outside, Kate speed-dialed her best friend, so incredibly glad *that* ordeal was over with. "Yeah, I'm free already. You done with Roach Queen the Second yet? Oh? Cool. Meet you at the pool? Nah, Tony won't care."

And besides, Kate was on vacation.

After being thrown around, almost drowned, tossed down a hall, and almost killed *multiple* times, nothing quite beat lounging in Avengers Tower's private rooftop pool in the center of Midtown, the noise of cars and the clamor of people an afterthought hundreds of feet below them.

"Pass me the sunscreen," America said, and Kate did just that.

In the pool, Lucky floated on a giant inflatable dog bone. He deserved a respite just as much as the rest of them. "Aren't you the goodest boy ever?" Kate asked him, and Lucky turned over on his float, tongue out, living his best life. Kate snapped a photo and posted it to her social accounts.

"You spoil that dog," America commented, "and you're going to get in *so* much trouble if Tony or Cap or someone comes out and finds him. . . ."

"We'll cross that bridge when we get to it—speaking of *Avengers*, who do you think interrogated Milo?"

"No clue. He hasn't contacted you yet?"

Kate shook her head. "No. I mean, I'm not sure he *will*, but I hope he's okay—and I hope he didn't get himself into *more* trouble. Oh, hey, Jessica texted me back." Kate sat up and angled her phone so she could read the texts in the glare of the sun. "Aw, she can't come. She's having lunch with— Oh my god, seriously?"

"What?" America asked.

Kate showed America the text message and the photo, and America threw her head back with a cackle.

"Your worlds are coming together!"

"Seriously, they're probably both swapping dirt on me." She sighed, looking at the photo of Jessica Jones and Misty Knight before tossing her phone into her pool bag. "I didn't even know they were friends."

"The strangest people can be friends. I mean"—America peered over her sunglasses—"look at us."

Kate mocked a gasp. "I'll have you know, we're a *masterful* team."

"We are, aren't we."

"We are." Kate folded her arms behind her head and flipped down her Aviators, lounging back in the pool chair. "Thanks, by the way."

"For what?"

"For being my best friend."

"It's a tough job," America agreed, "but someone has to do it."

They laughed, and relaxed out by the pool. The sun was bright and it was strong, and *man*, was she sore. No broken ribs, thank god, but definitely a lot of bruises. She had to pick out a one-piece today because her chest and stomach were black-and-blue, never mind the cuts on her face, the black eye, the scrape on her shoulder . . .

She looked—and let's face it, *felt*—like a punching bag.

A few days' rest would do her good, though. A few days of just this. The pool. The sky. The sun. Her best friend beside her. Her favorite canine whining from his inflatable bone—

Wait, *whining*?

She felt a shadow come over her—the same way a cloud passed over the sun—slightly cooler, the backs of her eyelids a little less bright. She opened her eyes to look at the muscular, well-cut shadow disturbing her very peaceful, very relaxing, very well-earned rest, and slowly pushed down her Aviators.

"Uh," she said in greeting with an innocent smile, "I take it you didn't bring a swimsuit to join us, Mr. Captain America, sir?"

ACKNOWLEDGMENTS

Some old man once said, "You're gonna miss each and every shot you can't be bothered to take," and I'd like to think it was about more than just some fancy arrows. I was so lucky to be given the chance to write (the best) Hawkeye.

And I was so *incredibly* nervous.

I grew up in fandom. I cut my teeth on message boards and fanfiction archives long before AO3. It really is a wild thing to think that fifteen-year-old me was writing Marvel fic, and now fifteen years later I'm *still* writing Marvel fic. Except, you know, it's canon. This book is *canon*.

And friends: fiction is *strange*. The way you see characters might be a little different from how someone else sees them. You take from stories something different than the person beside you, because your life and your choices color in the lines of the stories you read—and also the ones you tell.

I wrote a fun and campy mystery about friendship, books, and the best dog in the world, and I hope you love it as much as I loved writing it.

The book could never have been possible without Megan Logan, John Morgan, Caitlin O'Connell, and the editor who saw it through with me till the very end, Emeli Juhlin. I also want to thank the team at Marvel Press and Marvel Entertainment for doing such an amazing job with every other aspect of this novel: Kurt Hartman, Emily Fisher, Scott Piehl, Rodger Weinfeld, Crystal McCoy, Holly Nagel-Riley, Kaia Hilson, Daniel Kaufman, Martin Karlow, Guy Cunningham, Jeremy West, Lauren Bisom, and Sven Larsen.

Also, a big shout-out to my favorite bookish people: Eric Smith, Mike Lasagna, Nicole Brinkley, Katherine Locke, Rachel Strolle, Taylor Simonds, Ashley Schumacher, Kaitlyn Sage Patterson, and Savannah Apperson. My sanity thanks you for sticking around.

And most importantly, to the fanfiction community who raised me: thank you for everything—the comments, the kudos, the flames, the friendship. Thank you for being somewhere I could go when the world around me felt like it was falling apart. Everyone needs a home like that, whether it's in person or digital. I wouldn't be here without you.

And to my readers: like Clint advised Kate—*Take the shot.*

You never know, it might be a bull's-eye.